Paul Burston was born in Yorkshire, raised in South Wales and now lives in London. A journalist and broadcaster, his work has appeared in *Time Out*, the *Sunday Times*, the *Mail on Sunday*, the *Guardian*, the *Independent* and the *Independent on Sunday* and on Channel Four. He is the author of *What Are You Looking At?* and the Marc Almond biography *Gutterheart* ....editor of *A Queer Romance*.

Also by Paul Burston

What Are You Looking At?
Gutterheart

as co-editor
A Queer Romance

Queens* Country

A tour around the
Gay Ghettos,
Queer Spots and Camp
Sights of Britain

PAUL BURSTON

An *Abacus* Book

First published in Great Britain by
Little, Brown and Company 1998
Published by Abacus 1999

A CIP catalogue record for this book
is available from the British Library.

ISBN 0 349 11178 2

Typeset in Goudy by M Rules
Printed and bound in Great Britain by
Clays Ltd, St Ives plc

Abacus
A Division of
Little, Brown and Company (UK)
Brettenham House
Lancaster Place
London WC2E 7EN

For Miguel,
with a big kiss.

Acknowledgements

A big thank you to my agent, Georgina Capel, for steering me in the right direction, and to Andrew Wille, my editor at Little, Brown, for his boundless enthusiasm and for patience beyond the call of duty.

For their encouragement and support, I am indebted as always to my parents, and also to Andrew Loxton, Carl Miller, Suzanne Moore, Tim Mowbray, Deborah Orr, Matthew Parris, Steve Pitron, Linda Rogers, Mark Simpson and Frances Williams.

A very special thank you to all the people who agreed to be interviewed, and who gave me the opportunity to pry into their lives. Some were happy to be identified in these pages. The others know who they are.

CONTENTS

Introduction

I WAS A TEENAGE BUNBURYIST

I used to be the kind of person who didn't travel well. And if there was one thing guaranteed to bring on an attack of car sickness, it was the thought of travelling anywhere in Britain. Unfortunately, such thoughts were fairly frequent when I was a child. Foreign holidays were a rare treat in our house. It's hardly the fault of my parents, but when I think of family holidays I think of interminable car journeys, each more gruelling than the last, all ending in some allegedly picturesque part of Britain. The destinations changed regularly. One year it would be North Wales, the next it would be Scotland. But the journey was always the same, with myself and my sister Debbie sat squabbling in the back seat, while my mother did her best to appease us with a tin of travel sweets. More often than not, her efforts would all be in vain, and we would end up amusing ourselves the only way we knew how – fighting over a copy of *Smash Hits*, pulling faces at the driver behind, or sighing dramatically and endlessly repeating the same tired question: 'How much further is it?'

I couldn't say exactly when, or exactly why, my attitude to travel changed, but I suspect that it had something to do with the onset of puberty. Certainly, from my early teens onwards, the prospect of travelling to a place I didn't know and where nobody knew the first thing about me was enough to bring me out in a hot flush – even if that place happened to be in boring old Britain. Suddenly, I was no longer prone to car sickness. Although I never fully appreciated it at the time, my excitement stemmed from the fact that being away from home provided an opportunity for reinvention, for passing myself off as somebody else. I suppose you could say that I was a teenage Bunburyist – long before I had even heard of *The Importance of Being Earnest*. I remember one particular holiday in Newquay, shortly after *Grease* opened in the local cinema, when I managed to convince everyone that my name was Danny and that my eyebrows really were this dark and hadn't been blackened with my sister's mascara. In a few more years, I would carry this talent for running away from myself to its logical conclusion by moving to London and becoming a gay man.

It is generally assumed that the moment a person comes out as gay they stop telling lies about themselves. In my experience, it is often the moment they start telling even bigger lies about themselves than they ever felt obliged to tell previously. The pressures imposed on gay men by straight society are many and various. But what about the pressures gay men impose on one another? The compulsion to look the same, act the same and think the same is particularly unfortunate, coming from a group of people who stand a chance of achieving equality under the law only if society as a whole embraces the notion of diversity. These days, adopting a gay identity and lifestyle demands just as much in the way of role-playing as being in the closet, and leaves only a little more space for manoeuvre. Instead of being required to pass successfully as straight by disapproving heterosexuals, one is required to pass successfully as gay by equally disapproving homosexuals. This, I think, is the reason why gay men's migration patterns are so extreme, why so many of us move so far away from home. It's much easier to be your own special creation when there's no one around who remembers you the way you used to be, and might expose you for the fraud you are. We leave our straight lives behind, not only because we're frightened of being victimized, but also because we're afraid of being found out.

In a sense, this book is an attempt to expose some of the lies told by and about gay men in Britain today. It is a book about the kinds of lives gay men lead and the kinds of places in which they lead them; about the injustices of living in a homophobic society and the absurdities of taking your sexuality too seriously. It isn't a book about lesbian and gay Britain, and for that I make no apologies. There is a whole book to be written about the experiences of lesbians in Britain; perhaps one day a lesbian will write it. Nor is this a book about the 'gay community', though of course you will already have your own idea of what is meant by that. The term 'gay community' is employed at all levels of public discussion of homosexual behaviour. Politicians condemn it, thank it, or court its votes. Police authorities issue warnings to it, consult with it, or make appeals for its co-operation. The mainstream media ridicules it, eavesdrops on it, or sometimes addresses it. The gay media attempts to represent its interests, while gay campaigners claim to speak on behalf of it. Its 'members' consider themselves at various times included in it, estranged from it, or well and truly past it. But what and where exactly is it? To be perfectly honest, I have never been entirely sure that it even exists, and writing this book hasn't persuaded me otherwise. If anything, it has had the opposite effect, confirming my suspicions that gay men living in Britain have too little in common with one another to ever be called 'a community'.

This isn't to say that there aren't some experiences we all share, or some political issues in which we all have a stake, whether we choose to recognize the fact or not. I have addressed some of them here, as and when it seemed appropriate to do so. But ultimately this is a book about people and places, not politics and campaigning. I have done my best to give voice to as wide a range of people as possible, though invariably this has been constrained by the conditions of writing. Arriving in a strange town, my first port of call tended to be the local gay pub – a place where, contrary to popular belief, drag queens don't rub shoulders with men in full leather, and you are highly unlikely to encounter a broad cross-section of gay people from all walks of life. Where possible I tried to make up for this by networking in advance. This way, I managed to track down a selection of gay men of various ages and backgrounds, many of whom weren't the least bit interested in their local gay scene but were more than happy to discuss the intimate details of their lives with a total stranger. The complete lack of inhibition shown by some gay men never ceases to amaze me.

If there was one thing that surprised me more than anything else, it was the discovery that gay men living in small communities tended to be far more open about their sexuality than I would have expected, and often led more integrated lives than those with access to the gay ghettos found in larger cities. Meeting them gave me far greater hope for the future than any number of Gay Pride marches, and was infinitely more enjoyable than ploughing through another essay by some cosseted gay academic claiming to speak on behalf of 'ordinary gay men' – whatever that means. In the course of my travels, I met very few gay men whom I would describe as 'ordinary'. Had my reason for writing this book been to persuade people that gay men are 'virtually normal', this might have been a cause for concern. Since this was never my intention, I am simply grateful that I wasn't forced to spend my entire time surrounded by people whose main preoccupation in life is to be just like everyone else.

Travelling around gay Britain, poking my nose into other people's business, was actually a lot more fun than I had anticipated. I hope this book conveys some sense of it.

1

SMALLTOWN BOYO

South Wales

Growing up gay is never easy. Growing up gay in South Wales is like being trapped down an abandoned mineshaft with a chorus of short fat men with hairy backs, pissed on foul-tasting beer and singing rugby songs.

You can tell a lot about a country by its national sport. Of all the sports designed for men to sublimate their homoerotic aggressions, rugby is one of the most violent. A game in which two teams of men rough each other up in the battle for possession of a funny-shaped ball, it's a bit like soccer, only with more fighting and less kissing. The Welsh take it very seriously – especially the menfolk. As a schoolboy, you're nothing if you're not on the school rugby team. As a man, you're nobody if you're not seen drinking at the local rugby club. It's hard to figure, but there are some, relatively large, towns in Wales without a single cinema or public swimming pool, but with a thriving rugby club. I know; I grew up in one. The rugby club has replaced the chapel as the single most important institution in Welsh public life. It is the institution around which many local communities revolve and upon which men are encouraged to build their entire sense of identity. In fact, it wouldn't be an exaggeration to say that rugby is to the Welsh what circumcision is to the Jews – a bloody rite of passage, signifying a boy's entry into manhood. It's also worth noting that rugby is a game in which you move forwards by passing the ball backwards.

The Welsh are not what you would call a progressive people. As a famous Welsh poet once observed, there is no future in Wales, and no present – 'just the past, and a people sick with inbreeding, worrying the carcass of an old song'. These days, this necrophilic urge takes the form of a campaign to resurrect the Welsh language. In some parts of North Wales, otherwise rational people who are perfectly happy to converse in English most of the time will suddenly start speaking in Welsh whenever a stranger enters their midst. Unfortunately for the Welsh nationalist movement, any attempt to reintroduce Welsh as the language of daily conversation is doomed to fail for two reasons. One, the people who teach Welsh are the least respected teachers at any school. Two, Welsh is one of the ugliest languages known to man, as anyone who lives in the HTV television region and has ever tuned in to a Welsh-language programme will surely testify.

Thankfully, this madness hasn't extended to the south. Not a lot of people know this, but the inhabitants of the South Wales valleys were actually the first to embrace Esperanto, only here it is more familiarly known as 'Wenglish'. A relatively easy language to master, Wenglish works on the principle of taking English words and arranging them according to a peculiarly Welsh logic. A typical example of this is the much-used phrase, 'I'll be there now in a minute.' In Wenglish, the object of a sentence can change at any point. So, for instance, someone might ask, 'Whose coat is that jacket?' Taken to its extreme (as it usually is in real valley communities like Maesteg and Abercynon), Wenglish can produce ways with syntax which are often quite dazzling. Consider the strange beauty of a story like, 'I lost my dog. I came home and there he was, gone.'

The only hint of nationalism you're ever likely to encounter in South Wales is on the roads. Several years ago, somebody with a pickaxe to grind decided that all road signs, place names, etc. should be printed in both English and Welsh. Given the often long-winded nature of the Welsh language, this has produced signs of far greater dimensions than those you'll find anywhere else in the United Kingdom. Needless to say, this has put enormous strains on the local steel industry. In days of old, there were more subtle and less damaging attempts to instil a sense of national pride. When I was a boy, there was an advert on TV for a bitter brewed and sold exclusively in Wales. It probably featured Windsor Davies; it definitely featured the slogan 'Never forget your Welsh.' I haven't, but it isn't for the lack of trying.

I have never really regarded Wales as my mother country. This is probably explained by the fact that I was born in Yorkshire. For reasons I'm sure they would sooner keep to themselves, my parents settled down in South Wales shortly after I was born. Although I am not one of those people who has ever entertained the fantasy of being adopted, I did grow up with a strange sense of dislocation. This wasn't helped by my mother's habit of reminding me at regular intervals throughout my childhood that, should I ever wish to play cricket for Yorkshire, my being born there meant that I would be perfectly entitled to do so. The fact that I had never shown the least aptitude for the game didn't seem to matter to her. A gay friend of mine recently suggested that 'playing cricket for Yorkshire' might have been my mother's euphemism for my being gay – as in, 'No, my boy isn't married yet. He plays cricket for Yorkshire.' Sadly, I don't think this was ever the case.

The town where I grew up avoiding rugby and never being picked for the cricket team is called Bridgend. I have always thought that place names which end with 'end' tend to foster a sense of doom. Compared to a name like Gravesend, I suppose Bridgend doesn't sound quite so bad, but you get the point. Bridgend is situated twenty miles west of Cardiff, on what is laughingly described as 'the heritage coast'. As children, my younger sister Debbie and I would go swimming at nearby Ogmore-by-Sea – the only pleasure beach in the world with its very own sewage works. Every summer, the kids would play a bizarre version of I Spy, in which the winner was the first to spot a floating turd. I never spotted any, though every time a wave washed over me I seemed to be surrounded by clumps of seaweed infested with used condoms and sanitary towels. Looking back, I've a suspicion that some kids deposited a few turds of their own in the water, just so they could win.

Assuming you lived to survive the steady tide of human waste and unmentionable disease, Bridgend was alleged to be a land of opportunity. The guidebooks describe it as a large market town. Aged twelve, I was assigned to write a geography project on this subject. I can't remember exactly what I wrote, but I'm sure there must have been some mention of shoe shops. Bridgend has more shoe shops per head of population than any place I know. There is a street in the heart of town which consists of nothing but, each one offering the exact same selection as all the others. Apart from its status as the shoe-fetishist capital of Europe, Bridgend is famous for two things. First and foremost, its rugby team. Second, the fact that Bonnie Tyler once opened her own nightclub there, imaginatively called the ValBon. As a teenager, neither of these things particularly appealed to me. Now that Bonnie is a bona fide gay icon, I suppose knowing that I had the opportunity to dance the night away in her name ought to count for something. It doesn't.

I first began to suspect that I might be gay around the age of thirteen. Other people seem to have suspected much earlier. The kids at school were calling me poof from the time I was six or seven. This may have had something to do with my poor performance at sports, or my somewhat better performance at other less 'masculine' pursuits like writing and drawing. Or it may simply have been an example of the extraordinary intuition children often possess. They are especially good at spotting when somebody is different from them. Aged six, they probably didn't know what a poof was any more than I did; what they knew was that I was different.

This difference became more pronounced at the age of eight, when my parents got divorced. In 1973, divorce was still a taboo subject – so much so that on hearing of my family situation a certain teacher at my school took it upon herself to advise the rest of the staff that I should be treated with extra sensitivity, what with me coming from a broken home and all. This resulted in my mother marching up to the school to put the teacher in question right on a few points. I was behind her all the way. Far from breaking up my home life, my parents' divorce was the best thing that could have happened to me. My relationship with my father is far better now that I am an adult than it ever was when I was a child. For the first eight years of my life, I was terrified of him. The day he walked out, it seemed to me as though things might finally be on the mend.

I had always formed close emotional attachments to my male friends. Even as a young child, I could be extraordinarily possessive.

This trend continued as I grew older, though I never regarded any of my friendships as in any way homosexual, and nothing remotely sexual ever took place. I was, however, becoming increasingly aware of my difference. And as much as I felt isolated and alienated a lot of the time, I also began to quite enjoy it. A large part of my childhood was spent building elaborate tree-houses and fantasizing about being an outlaw. Gay readings of Robin Hood and his band of merry men hadn't reached South Wales, but that hardly mattered. I wasn't interested in having a gang of my own. Instead, I adopted a series of unusual pets – grass snakes mostly, then a gecko and finally a wounded jackdaw I christened Oscar (after Oscar the Grouch from *Sesame Street*; Wilde came much later).

When I was ten, my mother got married again, to a sweet-natured Irish plumber named Windsor. My mother still remembers how Debbie was asked by her teacher to write about what she did at the weekend. In her schoolbook she wrote, 'Me and Paul stayed with Dad so Mum could marry Windsor.' We moved to a terraced house on a long street, close to the hospital where my mother worked a couple of nights a week as a staff nurse, caring for sick babies. Directly opposite our house was the local nurses' home and right next to it a territorial army base. You could say that I was being exposed to the kinds of role model essential to a young boy's healthy development. My mother certainly thought so, and encouraged me to join the TA. I lasted a week.

Shortly afterwards, my mother had another baby of her own, a girl named Jacqueline. It was around this time that I formed a series of relationships which got me out of my tree-houses and into the real world of girls, boys and pop music. Our neighbours were very strong on what you would call working-class community spirit. During the summer holidays, the woman who ran the local shop would organize a series of day trips designed to give parents a break from coping with children with nothing better to do than sit around complaining of how bored they were. Children of all ages would find themselves grouped together in the pursuit of fun, frolics or just a few hours' refuge from their parents. With the exception of one boy with whom I later became close friends, the boys didn't really interest me. It was the company of the older girls I craved. Through my friendships with them, I was introduced to the local community centre disco. It was 1977, the year of *Saturday Night Fever*, and between Saturday nights we'd spend hours at somebody's house, practising our dance routines for the coming weekend. I nagged my mother into buying me a pair of 'high-waister' flared trousers and platform shoes. I looked ridiculous, but felt fabulous. I didn't realize it at the time, but it was at the community centre disco that I was exposed to my first real-life homosexual. His name was Dean and he had bigger flares than me, silver spray in his hair and his own gang of girl supporters. We didn't exactly hit it off. I seem to remember telling him he looked like a big girl, but that was just another way of saying that he was a better dancer than me.

School life was a bore. I had always been conscientious about my schoolwork and took great satisfaction from earning good grades, but the social side of it was a nightmare. Because I was never very good at sports, I was fair game for all the school bullies Brynteg Comprehensive could throw at me – the games masters included. I'd had a couple of girlfriends by this point and was just beginning to fantasize about boys. Then Karen came into my life. Karen was a year or two older than the rest of my class. She had changed schools and was forced to go back a year. The other girls didn't really like her because she was different from everyone else. For one thing, she looked even older than she was. Plus, she had a boyfriend who was eighteen and rode a motorbike. And to top it all, she was a punk. Karen introduced me to many things. She gave me my first taste of alcohol – a disgusting concoction, mixed together from whatever happened to be lying around in her parents' drinks cabinet. She also turned me into a schoolboy punk by teaching me how to make chains out of paper clips and colour my hair with powder paint. Needless to say, I regarded her as a goddess.

Homosexuality was still a frightening concept to me. I remember watching *The Naked Civil Servant* with my stepfather one night. Afterwards, he told me that my mother was worried that I might 'turn out like that'. I laughed, but deep down I was far more worried than she was. The first time I remember my mother ever discussing homosexuality with me was in the middle of a conversation about a neighbour of ours, known to me only as Poor Old Mrs Jones (not her real surname). So far as I could tell, Mrs Jones was no poorer than half the people who lived on our street. Nor was she especially old. In fact, her only social disadvantage seemed to stem from the fact that her son, John, was gay – or, as my mother put it at the time, 'one of those'. Part of Mrs Jones's tragedy was that John hadn't done the decent thing and gone to live miles away from the neighbours, but was carrying on with his homosexual lifestyle right under his mother's nose, and with a man practically the same age as she was. Harold ran his own hairdressing business at the top of town and, if my memory serves me correctly, was a dead ringer for John Hurt in the final reel of *The Naked Civil Servant*. But that didn't really bother me. What did was that neither he nor his lover seemed to possess anything approaching a pair of buttocks. In my naïve thirteen-year-old way, I decided that this must be a direct consequence of them using their bottoms for things other than that for which they were designed.

'Bumming' was a favourite topic of conversation at school. During gym lessons and afterwards in the showers, the sporty boys would horse around, pretending to be 'poofs', rubbing their backsides together and shouting, 'Bum me.' I had a far clearer idea of what bumming involved than they did, which is probably why I never felt compelled to join in. I started developing crushes on the sorts of boys who wouldn't be seen dead with someone like me – the real hard-nuts who disrupted lessons and spent their lunch hours smoking behind the bike sheds. I was particularly impressed with the way they held their cigarettes between forefinger and thumb, screwed up their eyes each time they took a drag and then flicked the butt hard against the ground. Little did I know then that, one day, all homosexuals would be made this way.

These crushes continued well into my late teens, by which time I was your classic teenage freak – silly clothes, David Bowie posters on the wall and hair that changed colour on a weekly basis. This was my way of telling the world that I was a troubled teen, without having to spell out what the trouble was. I learned fairly quickly that the more outrageous I looked, the less likely people were to take it for granted that I was gay. Making a performance of my queerness actually became a way of disavowing it. Of course, I wasn't the first person to employ this tactic. Boy George was doing it very successfully every week on *Top of the Pops*. Like him, I wasn't short of female admirers. Straight teenage girls love a boy who looks a bit girly, and I took full advantage of their interest. Having a girlfriend allowed you to dress as outrageously as you liked. You could even wear eyeliner to school discos if you felt so inclined – which I did. So long as you appeared to be romantically involved with a member of the opposite sex, you were more or less accepted as one of the boys. Ironically, it was during my troubled-teen phase, when I looked the most 'poofy', that I had more straight male friends than at any other point in my life before or since.

Most troubled teens have one teacher who makes an enormous impression on them and with whom they develop some kind of special relationship. I had two. The first was Mrs Jones (her real name), who taught me religious education at A-level. Mrs Jones was unlike any other RE teacher you've ever met. She was on the short side, wore high-heeled shoes and low-cut tops, and had bleached blonde hair with black roots. To my mind, she was the closest thing to Debbie Harry that South Wales ever produced. She also had a unique approach to teaching religion. One afternoon, our class were having difficulty understanding the meaning of Jesus's outburst about a prophet not being respected in his own country. Mrs Jones provided an illuminating comparison: 'It's just like Shirley Bassey. Her name is dirt in Tiger Bay.'

But the teacher who made the greatest impression on me was Mr Archard, the rather eccentric head of English. Something of a hippie at heart, Mr Archard was also a bit of a living legend on account of his avowed atheism, and the persistent rumour that he once dared to read out a passage from *Lady Chatterley's Lover* during morning assembly. He was also given to making references to the fact that he and his wife had gay friends. One morning we were discussing *Sons and Lovers* when a girl named Alison remarked that she thought Paul Morel was 'a bit of a poof'. Mr Archard hit the roof, telling the class how he thought the attitudes towards gay people in our society were barbaric and recalling an incident in which he and a gay friend had been set upon by a gang of youths hurling stones. He finished by saying that he expected a bit better from people who were supposed to be intelligent. By the end of his speech, Alison was bright red. So was I. It was the first time I had heard anyone discuss the existence of gay people without making a joke about it or remarking on how disgusting they were.

My final year at school was in many ways the most enjoyable. I had a large circle of friends, a place at college to look forward to and a girl ten doors down the street who was a trainee hairdresser and would happily plaster my head in blue gunk whenever I wanted. The only trouble was, I was in love. I'd had crushes on boys before, but this was different. Billy Gregory was a gay teenager's wet dream. Absurdly handsome, he was also the first boy I ever knew who paid particular attention to his body. Billy was heavily into weight-training and would do ridiculous things like go running for miles and miles with a bin liner under his shirt so as to burn off excess body fat. He was also rumoured to have an exceptionally large penis, though this was a rumour largely put about by Billy himself. We became friends, of sorts. A mutual friend and I started working out together and would regularly bump into Billy at the town recreation centre. He never invited me to be his work-out partner, which was a shame, but I did get to see him naked on several occasions. He wasn't lying.

For a time, I convinced myself that Billy was gay. Sometimes I would catch him staring at me in class. Each time I caught his eye, he would blush. Then I would go home and write dreadful poems about sexual liberation, often derived from things I'd read in Angie Bowie's autobiography, *Free Spirit*. The lines 'You're a Chinese puzzle game' and 'You let taboo stand in our way' spring to mind with alarming clarity. I once showed one of my poems to a friend. He was too polite to comment. I never discussed my feelings about Billy with anyone – partly because I was ashamed of them and partly because I didn't want to risk him finding out. As things stood, I was able to enjoy what little time I spent in his company without fear of exposure or reprisal. On Friday nights a group of us would meet at a pub called the Three Horseshoes. The purpose of these outings was to get as drunk as possible. That and to boast about our sexual conquests. Each week, I would dress as outrageously as I dared. Sometimes, Billy would compliment me on my daring. Other times, he would just laugh nervously.

After leaving school, Billy stayed in Bridgend and became a fireman, and I went to London and became a drama student. I also came out to my college friends and joined a gym. By the end of my first year at college, I had a nice pair of disco tits I could flaunt on the dance floor at Heaven and Billy had a nice wife.

It wasn't until after I'd left home that I discovered that Bridgend was a seething hotbed of homosexuality. During my final year at school, I'd heard rumours about some of the older boys I recognized from the pubs – boys with highlights and muscles, and names like Aiden and Lance. But they were only ever rumours. Just because someone happened to look and sound like a gay porn star, it didn't make him an out-and-out homosexual – or, as my school chums preferred to put it, 'a fuckin' tog'. I actually knew quite a few boys who gave the impression of being 'togs'. So far as I was aware, none of them was fucking – not other boys, anyhow. For my own part, I left Wales with rather a lot of hair and no gay sexual experience, only to return six months later with barely any hair at all and a fairly intimate knowledge of what went where and what it felt like.

Naturally, I was in need of someone close to home to whom I could talk. This responsibility fell on my sister Debbie. Arriving home for the Easter holidays, I sat down with her in my bedroom and explained that I had something to tell her. Before I could go any further, she beat me to the punch line, assuring me that she didn't see it as a problem and that I could count on her support. Coming out to my sister proved to be enormously liberating in a number of ways. Not only did it mean I finally had someone in Bridgend I could confide in, it also provided me with a ready-made gay social life right on my parents' doorstep.

Clearly, Debbie knew me a lot better than I knew her. Either that, or she had changed a lot since I'd left home. Suddenly, it seemed that all of her closest friends were gay. There was Ross, who was renting a room further down our street, worked as a hairdresser and would later achieve a degree of local celebrity as a contestant on *Ready, Steady, Cook*. There was Andre, who lived a few miles outside town, had an older boyfriend named Edward and the best-looking wedge haircut since David Sylvian split from Japan. And there was Dean, the same Dean I had once, many years previously, called a big girl and who was now a dead ringer for the pretty, dark-haired one from Bananarama.

Ross was the dominant member of the group. Small and skinny, with bleach-blond hair and pale blue eyes rimmed with mascara, he had that toughened, brittle quality you often find in gay men at the camper end of the scale. Andre was like the puppy from the Andrex ad. Wide-eyed and always seeking attention, he was also hopelessly devoted to Edward (who was another hairdresser and was responsible for the upkeep of his boyfriend's hairdo) and to his mother (whom he informed of his homosexuality by slipping a note under the bathroom door while she was on the toilet – which shows a certain amount of initiative, you have to admit). Dean was the quiet one. Despite his outlandish appearance, he spoke very softly and could be painfully shy. This made him seem all the more effeminate in a town where the women aren't noted for such qualities. Dean also had a girlfriend, one he had been together with for many years and who appeared to accept the fact that her man liked to dress as a woman and have sex with other men.

All three embodied what gay activists of a certain generation call 'cultures of resistance'. That is to say, they wore their queerness like armour. Wandering around Bridgend town centre looking the way they did took some guts, but that was precisely what kept them going. On one occasion, I suggested crossing the street to avoid a gang of lads spilling noisily out of a pub. Ross wouldn't hear of it. At the time, I thought he must have harboured a death wish. It was only later that I realized he was doing what he needed to do in order to survive. Places like Bridgend impose enough limits on the kind of existence a gay man can lead, without him adding a few of his own. For me, crossing the street was simply a way of avoiding trouble until it was time to return to the relative safety of my gay life in London. For Ross and the others, it was an admission of defeat.

Together with my sister, we would meet for afternoon drinking sessions at a pub called the Wyndham. The conversation invariably revolved around three things – men, clothes and whatever plans the boys had made for that evening. Sometimes, if I was feeling particularly brave, I would venture out with them in the evenings. My sister shocked me with the news that the Three Horseshoes was having one of its regular gay nights and persuaded me to come and check it out. It wasn't exactly busy. There were us, a pasty-faced youth in snow-washed denims and a couple of girls with badly plucked eyebrows and purple curly perms. Purple curly perms are extremely popular in Bridgend. In fact, the only hairstyle more popular among women under the age of thirty is a strange hybrid of styles known locally as the 'Maesteg Frizz'. This consists of having 98 per cent of your hair set into a mass of curls, while the remaining 2 per cent is crimped into a fan arrangement which sticks straight up at the front of your head, thin enough to see through, but heavily lacquered so as to withstand the strongest of winds or the heaviest of showers. Obviously, for this style to be worn to maximum effect, the volume of the remaining hair is extremely important. Walk into any hair salon in the area and you will hear a woman explaining to her hairdresser, 'I want my 'air out yuh!'

Nights out on the town always made me nervous. It wasn't that I looked any more gay than anybody else. Unlike Dean, I didn't have to contend with people constantly coming up and asking me whether I was a boy or a girl. But the others had something going for them that I didn't. They may have looked a bit queer, but they had familiar faces. And they knew lots of people – girls especially. I knew next to nobody. In the year since I'd left, most of my peer group had moved on. Walking into a pub, I stood out on two counts. I looked as though I might be gay and I wasn't someone people recognized. It's hard to say which provoked the greatest degree of animosity. What I do know is that there were times when I felt as though I'd walked into that pub in *An American Werewolf In London*. I'm only surprised that nobody ever turned around and uttered the immortal words, 'We don't like strangers round 'ere.'

Saturday nights meant a train ride to Cardiff. Growing up in Bridgend, I had always regarded Cardiff as a rather special place. Cardiff was where my mother went if she wanted to do 'a proper shop'. Sometimes she would take me with her. For hours, we'd traipse around British Home Stores or C&A, looking for a nice winter coat that I would grow into. Assuming I didn't make too much of a fuss, my mother would treat me to a set lunch at the Chinese restaurant near the railway station, or a visit to one of the cafés where they sold frothy coffee. For years, my idea of Cardiff as a place of glamour and excitement was based solely on the fact that you could buy milky cups of coffee with froth on top. By the time I was old enough to shop for my own clothes, I was well acquainted with the city's second-hand clothes markets and trendy boutiques. I was also vaguely aware that some of the men who worked and shopped at them might possibly have been gay. When my older cousin Oliver moved to Cardiff to study art and began plucking his eyebrows, my fantasies of what went on in that city became almost too much to bear.

For Ross and the others, Cardiff was to Bridgend what Bridgend was to the straight lads who lived in the surrounding valley towns – somewhere bigger and brighter than the place they came from, and where they could behave as badly as they wanted and never worry about their mothers finding out. The Welsh are firm believers in the principle that you should never shit on your own doorstep – something they no doubt learned from the English, who have been shitting on them for centuries. Every Saturday, the valley boys would descend on Bridgend, looking for a fight. Simultaneously, the gay population of Bridgend would flee to Cardiff, looking for a few hours' gay abandon and maybe even love. Compared to Bridgend, Cardiff offered a wealth of opportunities. This probably explains why Edward was never very keen on Andre tagging along.

The train ride to Cardiff takes about twenty-five minutes, which is roughly the time it takes to drink two cans of lager and ensure that your hair is perfect. Arriving at Cardiff Central, we would make our way to a nearby pub called the King's Cross. Not strictly a gay venue, the King's Cross was the sort of place where everyone was equally welcome, so long as they didn't interfere with anyone else. There ought to have been a sign hanging above the door saying 'Bring Us Your Wounded'. They were all there – gay men, art students, straight girls with necklaces made of lovebites, dope heads, a smattering of lesbians, and goths. Lots of goths. South Wales has always had more than its fair share of goths. I blame the weather. After downing a few drinks at the King's Cross, we would move on to Cardiff's première gay nitespot, the Tunnel Club. The only strangers at the Tunnel were those people who didn't have big moustaches and a City and Guilds in fan-dancing. I was going through my Bronski Beat phase at the time – short hair, bleached jeans, white T-shirt and a commitment to every left-wing cause you cared to mention, as demonstrated by the hordes of badges adorning the sleeve of my bomber jacket. But this didn't seem to matter. On the gay scene, the arrival of an unfamiliar face is usually something to be celebrated – especially if that face happens to belong to someone under the age of twenty-five. I had a lot of drinks bought for me at the Tunnel – usually by people I had no intention of sleeping with.

The big song that year was a cheesy Euro disco number called 'I Love My Radio', sung by a woman rejoicing in the name of Taffy. Needless to say, the Cardiff clones loved it – so much so that it packed out the dance floor each time it was played, even if that meant four or five times in one night. Clubs like the Tunnel exist to remind us of why gay men are in danger of losing their reputation as cultural innovators, always on the cutting edge of the arts. Dancing to the same record five times a night doesn't leave much room for pondering the decline of abstract expressionism or the death of the novel. Gay hedonism is simply mindless repetition by another name. Hedonism operates on the assumption that if doing something once gives you a sense of pleasure, then doing the same thing over and over again will make you delirious. It's no accident that the concept of the twelve-inch disco remix was first developed in gay clubs. As anyone familiar with the subsequent evolution of gay disco can testify, innovation rarely comes into it.

I doubt whether Ross, Andre or Dean ever gave a thought to such matters. For them, repetition was the key to survival. Every Saturday they left Bridgend behind them for a few hours and danced the night away at the Tunnel. They didn't really care if the music was always the same, so long as it offered a change from the pace of their daily lives. Travelling home on the late train one night, I asked Dean how he coped with living in a town like Bridgend. He told me he didn't have any choice. He didn't have the money or the opportunity to get out. Some time afterwards, he and his girlfriend got married and had two children. The last I heard, they were divorced. Ross was living in Newport, had given up hairdressing and was training to be a nurse. Andre and Edward had split up. Edward had found some other boy's hair to devote his attention to and nobody seems to know what happened to Andre.

Coming out to my parents didn't go quite the way I planned. To be honest, I half expected them to tell me they'd known all along. In fact, I even considered sitting down and writing them a letter saying, 'Hey, you know how we always used to joke about me being a bit of a poof? Well, guess what? I am!' Then I thought better of it. Instead, I drafted a carefully worded letter to my mother, modelled on Michael Tolliver's 'Letter to Momma' in *Tales of the City*. I didn't hear anything for over a week. Then Windsor rang to tell me he had everything under control and that I should allow my mother a bit of time to get used to the idea. I told him I was surprised that she was surprised – after all, don't they say a mother always knows? Still, he sounded completely at ease with the subject, and I told him so. There was a pause, then he said, 'You remember Daisy, don't you? Well, I knew Daisy when she used to piss standing up with the rest of us.' I guess that was his way of saying, 'Some of my best friends are gay.' I soon learned that Daisy wasn't the only one. For a man who worked and socialized in what most people would take to be an extremely straight, even homophobic environment, Windsor seemed to come into contact with gay people all the time and in the unlikeliest of places. There was even a man in uniform he used to have the occasional drink with at the TA.

When I did finally speak to my mother, she said all the things mothers are supposed to say. She asked me if it was her fault. I told her I didn't regard my being gay as anybody's 'fault'; it was simply the way I was and I was happy with it. She said she was worried about some of the things she'd read in the papers and seen on television. I told her that gay men didn't all run around swinging handbags and molesting small children. She said she didn't mean that, she was thinking about all that dressing up in leather. At this point, I began to worry about the sorts of television programme my mother was watching.

Nowadays, my mother watches more gay television than anybody I know. Often, she'll phone me up and ask what I thought about a particular discussion on *Kilroy* or *The Time, The Place*, or a particular programme on BBC2 or Channel 4. She even watched *Gaytime TV*. Half-way into the first series, she rang to ask what I thought of it. I told her I thought it was rubbish. 'That's good,' she said. 'I thought it was just me being homophobic.' The only disagreement we've ever had about gay men on television was when she tuned in to Margi Clarke's *Good Sex Guide* one night to see me talking about how I enjoyed having my nipples sucked. Arriving for work the following evening, she was met by a contingent of middle-aged nurses asking, 'Wasn't that your boy on the telly last night?' Naturally, I apologized for my indiscretion.

In spite of the fact that I have the most understanding,

supportive parents anyone could wish for, I go home less and less. Bridgend has changed a lot in the last few years. As Windsor is especially fond of telling me, the town I grew up in now boasts one of the largest, most desirable housing estates in Europe. Apparently, there are people in Brackla who happily commute all the way to London to work, such are the attractions of living there. I have to say that I find this hard to believe. A sprawling network of modern red-brick houses and streets with names like Mount View and the Pines (and no view, no pines), Brackla has always struck me as the sort of place where young heterosexual couples with no imagination settle down and wait to grow into old heterosexual couples with no mortgage. Their children will be called Gary or Jason, Melanie or Kim, and will grow up to become car mechanics or shoe-shop assistants. Unless, of course, they're gay. If they're gay they'll either move away as soon as they're old enough to claim unemployment benefit or become another gay teenage suicide statistic.

I am constantly amazed that anyone gay survives in Bridgend – especially nowadays. Large-scale unemployment, an expanding population and Bonnie Tyler's decision to close the ValBon seem to have brought out the worst in people. Barely an evening goes by without someone being rushed to casualty to have a wine glass removed from their neck. Hence the local greeting – 'You're goin' home in an ambulance!'

Still, gay people do live there. My friend Frances tells me there is a small but thriving lesbian community, mostly consisting of the girls who were the toast of the school hockey team when she was at school, and who used to bully her mercilessly. Whether there is a corresponding community of gay men, made of the boys who used to bum about in the showers, I couldn't say, but I have never seen much evidence of it. I'm told that John and Harold have moved up in the world and are now living at the posh end of town, in a house that backs on to a family of evangelical Christians. Apparently, they get on with their new neighbours rather well, which is more than can be said for a lot of gay couples I know. Whether they are part of a local gay community is quite another matter. A community needs a focus, a place to call its own, or something its members feel they can each share in. At the very least, it requires a certain amount of social interaction. It may well be that Bridgend's lesbian population have created a sense of community through shared reminiscences about school hockey try-outs. For gay men to build a sense of community, it usually takes something a little more concrete. Like a pub.

The last time I spent Christmas in Bridgend, my sister Jacqueline persuaded me to join her and her friend Vicky for a pub crawl. Every pub we visited had bouncers on the door, though quite what their function was I haven't yet worked out. Inside, the scene was always the same – upturned bar stools and discarded pint glasses lying everywhere, and gangs of teenage lads with beer guts and straggly facial hair, tanked up on lager and spoiling for a fight. At the Wyndham, I walked into the toilet to find a man lying bleeding on the white-tiled floor while a bunch of lager monsters stood at the urinals waving their arms in the air and shouting, 'Nice one, mate!' Nobody seemed the least bit concerned that he might actually have been bleeding to death. I'm sure this isn't what Harry Secombe had in mind when he sang about keeping a welcome in the hillside.

Eventually, I managed to convince Jacqueline that I wasn't having a very nice time, and that we should go and join our parents at their favourite pub, the Victoria. The crowd at the Victoria were somewhat older, and a great deal less aggressive. To an outsider, the sight of a lot of middle-aged women dressed exactly like drag queens might have been cause for alarm, but when you've spent the first eighteen years of your life in South Wales, you learn to take these things in your stride. After a while, my mother sent me to the bar, telling me I might be in for a bit of a surprise. I was. The bar was run by a couple of men with very short hair and very big moustaches. One had a peculiar little ponytail, the kind you usually see only on small boys whose fathers dress them in matching football shirts, or on lesbians. Now, I could be wrong about this. It could well be the case that these two men who lived and worked together, dressed like clones and called everyone 'love' were in fact hot-blooded heterosexuals. But I somehow doubt it. Nervously, I ordered some drinks and enquired as to the whereabouts of the cigarette machine. Ponytail kindly escorted me to the machine and helped me find the right change. Returning to my seat, I found my mother in hysterics. 'I think he fancies you, Paul,' she said, loudly enough to attract the attention of anyone in a half-mile radius. Then, in case anyone had missed the point, she turned to the woman at the table opposite and shouted, 'I think he fancies our Paul.' Their Paul could have died.

Instead, he made a rapid escape. The night ended with Jacqueline and I dancing around Vicky's handbag at a tiny excuse for a nightclub called Shimmers. This is the sort of club where everything is done with mirrors, and people spend the night picking themselves up off the floor and realizing that, no, they aren't surrounded by lots and lots of other people, just lots and lots of reflections of themselves. This is especially confusing in a town where no two people look all that different. Just as we were getting ready to leave, a boy of about seventeen, half my size, with the body of an undernourished ten-year-old, came up and asked me for a light. I handed him my lighter and waited while he lit his cigarette and shuffled about a bit. 'Can I ask you a personal question?' he said finally. I told him it depended how personal. 'Are you a heterosexual?' he asked. I replied that, no, as a matter of fact, I wasn't. 'I thought not,' he said. Then, before I could congratulate him on his astonishing powers of perception, he spoke again. 'Don't worry,' he said, flicking his ash on the floor and staring me straight in the sternum. 'I'm not going to hit you.'

I think it was at this point that I decided to spend the rest of my life avoiding Bridgend whenever possible. Or, as they say in Wenglish, 'I saw I atto give it up as a bad job.'

2

THE VILLAGE PEOPLE

Manchester

Do you remember the gay old days? Do you remember when being gay meant bumping your uglies with members of the same sex – and very little else besides? Do you remember what life was like before the days of rainbow flags and gay gymnasiums, of cappuccino culture and gay shopping centres, of freedom rings and gay housing developments? In short, do you remember what it was like before we were all 'pink-pounded'?

I could never have imagined it, growing up in Bridgend all those years ago, but, these days, being gay has very little to do with being homosexual. Not that gay men today are any less preoccupied with sex – on the contrary, the commercial gay scene is probably more heavily sexualized now than at any other time in the last fifteen years. But ever since the first gay activist opened his wallet and said, 'Hey, look, there's a high disposable income in here! Why don't we call it the pink pound and see if we can't just shop our way to freedom?', gay men's sense of what it means to be gay has changed in ways few could have foreseen, and even fewer could begin to understand. More and more, gay identity is based not on what you do in bed (or in the darkened corner of a club), but on what brand of moisturizer you apply to your face in the morning, what clothes you wear, which gym you attend, what music you listen to, which bars, clubs and restaurants you hang out at, which holiday company you book with, what your favourite brand of vodka is, right down to the name printed on the elasticated waistband of your designer Y-fronts. In fact, it is perfectly possible to live the life of a gay man in the late 1990s without ever experiencing or even desiring gay sex – which probably explains why the most interesting men one meets on the gay scene these days usually turn out to be straight.

The reason is that this thing we call 'gay' is no longer a simple matter of sexual choice, or even a plain old-fashioned political construct, but a Lifestyle with a capital 'L', a word used to describe a particularly conspicuous kind of consumer, a niche market. For years, gay men have been the target of queer-bashers; nowadays, we're as likely to find ourselves the target of marketing consultants. And the worrying part is, we don't seem to mind one little bit. A few years ago, the Stonewall lobbying group made an appeal for funds through the pages of the gay press. The ad read: 'You've got the lifestyle, now get a life.' The tragedy is that a lot of gay men really can't tell the difference. For them, the lifestyle is the life. You have only to look at the way that most hallowed of gay events, Gay Pride, has been allowed to develop in recent years, to the point where it is now dominated by commercial sponsors whose interests lie not in the significance of the event itself, but in the unique marketing opportunity it offers. You have only to consider the impact of a conference like the one held in London in 1996, sponsored by *Marketing Week* and supported by the Pride Trust, during which delegates were advised on ways of targeting 'this highly lucrative market' without alienating their mainstream market. Should you feel so inclined, you could invest inordinate amounts of time and money in some market research of your own, to determine how the commodity fetishism of today's gay scene might shape the gay identity of the future. Or you could save yourself the bother and just go to Manchester and see for yourself.

No gay tour of Britain is complete without a visit to Manchester. This is the city, remember, that gave us such enduring gay favourites as Bet Lynch, the Smiths and Take That. These days, however, Manchester doesn't have to look to the past to affirm its queer credentials. Each year, usually around the middle of June, it hosts its own lesbian and gay arts festival, 'It's Queer Up North', dedicated to the very best in gay entertainment, plus a fair number of acts who really aren't all that talented but do have the distinct advantage of being lesbian or gay and residing in the north of England. Each August Bank Holiday it provides the setting for a very colourful, very noisy gay street party called Mardi Gras, named after the annual event that takes place under the somewhat sunnier skies of Sydney, Australia, and attracting something in the region of 100,000 revellers and as many pounds in profits to be divided among local AIDS charities. And for the remainder of the year it has the Gay Village – a thriving network of bars, clubs, shops, restaurants and other 'gay-friendly' businesses in and around Canal Street.

Whether the development of a commercial gay ghetto in the heart of Manchester is ultimately a good thing for the sanity and welfare of local lesbians and gay men is a matter of some dispute. What most people seem to agree on is that the Gay Village is a good thing for Manchester itself. After all, this is a city which has been through a period of industrial decline, is currently undergoing a process of urban regeneration and is keen to promote itself as the leisure capital of the North. It's hardly surprising, then, that along with other 'exotic' districts like Chinatown, the Gay Village is promoted as a local tourist attraction, part of a marketing exercise in which Manchester is presented as a progressive, cosmopolitan playground with a thriving service economy. Certainly, this seems to be the aim of the Greater Manchester Visitor and Convention Bureau, in whose literature the Village is described as 'a major factor in the city's unique sense of style', boasting 'some of the best eateries, drinkeries and danceries around'.

Personally, I would sooner jump in the canal than be caught dead in a bar advertised as a 'drinkery'. Still, the enthusiasm shown by the local authorities towards the Village and its inhabitants does have its compensations. Back in the mid-1980s, Manchester was presided over by one Chief Constable James Anderton, a particularly sensitive member of Her Majesty's constabulary whose response to AIDS was to accuse gay men of 'swirling in a cesspit of their own making', and who later became something of a laughing stock when his own daughter came out as a lesbian. A decade on, in 1997, Manchester City Council was proud to sponsor the Mardi Gras and declare its commitment to lesbian and gay rights, campaigning for an equal age of consent, a law to protect lesbians and gay men from discrimination, and the repeal of Clause 28. Clearly, the growth of a gay economy in the heart of Manchester has brought with it a certain amount of political leverage. Still, at the risk of sounding churlish, I have to say that the degree of local pride invested in the Gay Village does strike me as rather odd. I mean, for years Manchester has been promoting itself with the slogan: 'Shaping tomorrow's city, today'. Now tomorrow's city has arrived, and guess what, it isn't a city at all, but a village – and a village full of queers at that. Who'd have thought it?

I caught a train from London Euston to Manchester Piccadilly, arriving late one Saturday afternoon in February. It was raining. (It's always raining in Manchester in February – and for the best part of the remaining eleven months of the year, or so I'm told.) I had been to Manchester several times before, so I was confident that I knew my way around pretty well. What I hadn't counted on was the extraordinary rate at which the city is being redeveloped. Remember the opening title sequence for the last series of *Roseanne*, the one where her face mutates into something completely unrecognizable in a matter of seconds? Well, Manchester city centre is a lot like that. I hurried past the Britannia Hotel, where I once spent a happy few hours hanging out with Andy Bell and Vince Clarke of Erasure on the eve of one of their many British tours. (I remember thinking at the time that the Britannia Hotel was the ideal place to interview Erasure. It's just so tacky and overblown – in a charming, lovable sort of way.) I tottered past the Palace Theatre, then back towards Princess Street – which, rather fittingly, marks the borders of the Gay Village. Deciding to save the excitement of the Village for later, I made a detour via Portland Street and the bus station. And it was around this point that I got completely lost. Everything looked different somehow. Buildings I was certain I could remember seeing less than a year ago simply weren't there any more. Small shops had disappeared, to be replaced by much larger ones. It was all so disorienting. By the time I found myself heading back down Fairfield Street, in the general direction of the train station, I was prepared to admit defeat. I jumped into a cab and told the driver to take me to Chepstow House.

Chepstow House is the name given to a large block of flats in the city centre. This elegantly modern building contains about seventy flats in all, a third of them occupied by homosexuals. One such occupant is my friend Charles, who had kindly agreed to put me up for the weekend. What can I tell you about Charles? Well, I asked him much the same question and his reply was something along the lines of: 'Use my first name only, say I'm thirty-one and just say that I'm a lawyer – nothing too specific.' I asked if this was because he was worried about being identified as gay at work. 'Not at all,' he said, laughing. 'Manchester is a very small place. I don't want the queens knowing everything about me.' Here are a few things Charles doesn't mind people knowing. He was born and raised in Blackpool, attended university at Oxford and lived in London for a while, before settling in Manchester in 1988. He takes several holidays a year, is a keen member of a rowing club and works out at the Living Well Health Club – or, as he prefers to call it, the 'Living Hell Wealth Club'. You'll deduce from this that Charles enjoys what you might call 'a comfortable lifestyle'. He has a high disposable income and no family to support. In fact, he is exactly the kind of gay man the 'pink pound' advertisers are so keen to attract, precisely the sort of man you might expect to take full advantage of all that Village life has to offer.

We talked about the gay scene in Manchester. In the nine years since he first moved there, Charles had watched gay life in the city change beyond all recognition. Back in 1988, the emerging Gay Village was really just a handful of bars, huddled together for security and within easy cruising distance of one another. By 1997, the Village had grown into a fully fledged gay ghetto, rather like the Castro district of San Francisco (in fact, there is even a bar called Castro on Canal Street). Inevitably, this has divided gay opinion somewhat. Defenders of the Village stress its vital importance in providing the gay community with a safe space, a shelter from the violence and prohibitions of straight society. Critics claim that the main function of the Village isn't to keep straights out, but to keep gays in. A life in the ghetto is filled with opportunities, they say – particularly if you happen to be the one creaming off all those lovely pink pounds. I asked Charles where he stood on this issue. He said he could see both sides of the argument, which I suppose is an occupational hazard when you happen to be a practising lawyer.

For those who take the view that life in the ghetto is simply heaven and see absolutely nothing wrong in cutting themselves off from the rest of humanity, Manchester certainly has a lot to offer. The Village is the setting for what has been described as 'Europe's first gay shopping centre', the Phoenix Centre on Princess Street – though at the time of writing there was some dispute over the fact that two-thirds of the businesses operating from the centre were straight-owned. In fact, the only business which was entirely gay-owned and run was the video rental shop. The others – a tanning shop, a men's beauty clinic, a ceramics shop, a hairdresser's and a coffee shop – were all owned by known heterosexuals. Naturally, this prompted an indignant editorial in the national lesbian and gay freesheet, the *Pink Paper*, complaining that far from being 'a gay shopping centre', the Phoenix was simply 'a shopping centre in the gay district'. Despite this obviously very distressing setback, however, Manchester still provides the opportunity to live an almost exclusively gay existence – to eat in gay cafés and restaurants, socialize in gay bars and clubs, have your hair cut into a 'Funky Crop' at a predominantly gay barber shop, purchase underwear and sweatshirts at gay shops, work out at a gay gym, have your pulse checked by a gay doctor, even (and here's the really exciting bit) live in a custom-built gay home!

According to a recent article in the *Sunday Times*, designing and building homes for gay people has become one of the most lucrative construction markets in Britain (and one of the most demanding, I shouldn't wonder. An Englishman's home may be his castle, but an English queen's home is his fortress, boudoir and personal porn set all rag-rolled into one). Apparently, custom-built gay homes differ from straight homes in a number of respects. For one thing, they have fewer bedrooms, since most gay men don't plan on having children. Security is another key element, with the emphasis on sturdy front doors and reliable alarm systems. And of course it is a well-known fact that gays love nothing more than a bit of good-quality architecture. No poky little semis for us, thank you very much. Loft conversions are particularly popular, it seems, which only goes to confirm my suspicions that there isn't a gay man in the country who hasn't fantasized about living the life of an upmarket gay prostitute in downtown New York.

In Manchester, a construction company called Bellway Homes, one of the ten largest in the country, has been quick to capitalize on this growing trend. Full-page adverts have appeared in the gay press, inviting gay home-buyers to 'get closer to the action' and buy 'a stylish affordable new home near Manchester's famous Gay Village'. The ads even featured a grinning gay couple, dressed in carefully arranged casual wear, standing outside their lovely new home – which, the ad informed us, came complete with a fitted kitchen, gas central heating, alarm system and a turfed front garden. In the city centre itself, timed to coincide with the 1997 Mardi Gras, Bellway erected a forty-foot poster of 'Mr Gay UK 1997' to promote sales on ninety-three new apartments, situated next to the Bridgewater canal and costing an average of £100,000 each. The man on the poster was Sean McVeigh, a lift engineer from Wigan (aren't they always?). Mr McVeigh appeared dressed in nothing more than his 'Mr Gay UK' sash, a hard helmet and a strategically placed toolbox where his lunchbox would be. And to think that no one has thought of selling houses to heterosexuals with giant posters of page-three girls dressed in French maid's outfits. Still, there's gay men for you – always on the cutting edge.

Judging from what Charles had to say on the subject, it wasn't hard to see why Bellway are busy building gay homes in the heart of Manchester. The city centre doesn't have the infrastructure to support families with children. There are no schools in the area, for instance. Gay men are simply being encouraged to buy up properties where few heterosexuals are likely to consider settling down and starting a family. As for the properties themselves, I can't say that I have ever been inside one, but Charles certainly had and he wasn't overly impressed. 'I call them the Barratt boxes of the '90s,' he said. 'All these old warehouses are being snapped up and turned into so-called loft apartments. You have all these queens lining up to buy their very own loft apartment, and they're all exactly the same, just little rows of boxes. Even before you go inside, you know exactly how each flat will look – where the mezzanine bed will be, the exact shape and position of the windows, right down to which wall will be stripped down to show the bare brick.'

We ate dinner at Charles's flat – which, I hasten to add, doesn't have a mezzanine bed or a bare brick wall in sight. Afterwards, he offered to take me on a tour of the Village. As we walked the short distance to Canal Street, he explained how the Village really took off with the opening of a café-bar called Manto, and how all the bars which had opened subsequently had simply modelled themselves on its success, with a shared passion for plate-glass windows, polished surfaces and well-scrubbed, attractive bar staff. I suppose this was really only to be expected. Modern capitalism thrives on repeating tried and tested formulas, and despite our much-vaunted passion for personal expression, the vast majority of gay men are essentially conservative at heart (how else do you explain the continued existence of men who dress in matching outfits and are proud to call themselves 'clones'?). Put the two together and it's a foregone conclusion that gay capitalism should display all the imagination of a pig at a trough.

As you've probably gathered, I wasn't expecting to see the appeal of Canal Street – or, as the amended sign read, 'Anal Treet'. But I have to come clean and admit that I was pleasantly surprised. It really is quite extraordinary – a busy, buzzing row of bars and restaurants, packed with lively young things spilling out on to the pedestrianized walkway. I don't think there is a street quite like it anywhere else in Britain. Unlike, say, London's Old Compton Street, which has always struck me as a fairly jaded sort of place, filled with people waiting for their mobile phones to ring (well, the ad did say they were available twenty-four hours), there is an air of optimism and confidence about Canal Street which is quite infectious, demonstrated by the venues themselves, with their goldfish-bowl windows, and by the general willingness of the punters to pretend that they are in Paris, Rome or Barcelona, and not some cold, drizzly city in the north of England. Even on this grey February evening, the street was filled with boys in skimpy T-shirts, drinking bottled lager and shivering stoically. All very endearing, I'm sure you'll agree, but not quite endearing enough to persuade me to join them. Instead, we dived into the first bar that didn't have an enormous queue outside and ordered something to take the chill out of our bones.

The bar was called Via Fossa and I have to say that I liked it very much. Charles insisted on referring to it as 'Vile Fossils' (he has a way with words, does our Charles), but far from being 'vile' or 'fossilized', it struck me as a rather warm and cheery place – certainly compared to the chilly catwalks that pass for gay bars in London's Soho. It was nine p.m. when we arrived and the place was jam-packed. I was extremely pleased to note that we weren't the only people over the age of thirty. It's bad enough that so many gay men these days insist on acting like teenagers, without everyone looking like teenagers as well. And my, aren't Mancunians friendly? We'd only been in the place ten minutes and already we'd been approached by half a dozen smiling unfamiliar faces. First up was a young man with a Roman fringe and a Fred Perry T-shirt, who introduced himself as Terry and proceeded to ask me what part of London I was from, and what I thought of Manchester so far. Then along came two men and a woman, dressed for a night out on the town, slightly drunk but still capable of making stimulating conversation about which clubs were worth going to and which were overpriced, overrated and generally just over. Finally, I was approached by two lads, Richard and Mark, who gave new meaning to the term 'straight-acting', and wanted to know where I bought my silver combat trousers and whether I might be persuaded to part with them in exchange for a brand-new pair of Levi's and a rather fetching sweatshirt. I can't recall the last time I felt so popular in a gay bar in London, but I'm sure it was my round.

For the benefit of those readers unfamiliar with the social etiquette of the urban homosexual, I should point out that engaging complete strangers in conversation in gay bars is generally frowned upon. In fact, the only time when one is actively encouraged to even smile at other gay men is on Gay Pride day – and that's really done just for the cameras. Aside from this, you might get away with a smile at around three a.m. in a club, but only assuming that everyone is off their face on Ecstasy and smiling is completely involuntary anyway. At all other times, one is expected to look as surly as possible, and preferably stare at the floor whenever another gay man comes within a three-foot radius. If you happen to be standing in a designated backroom, or even a dimly lit toilet, then some physical (i.e. genital) contact may be permitted – but even then smiling is discouraged, lest it should put your new-found friend off his stroke and thereby detract from the uniquely horny and obviously very liberating exchange taking place between you. Observe these few simple rules and you'll avoid making a complete prat of yourself the next time you feel the need to be amongst your gay brethren. Of course, the question of whether or not you'll actually enjoy yourself is a different matter entirely.

You will begin to understand, then, the intense thrill I felt at being in a room full of people who clearly hadn't forgotten how to smile and who were capable of normal social interaction. In fact, I have to confess that I got a bit carried away with it all. I chatted. I laughed. I even bought a complete stranger a drink. Eventually, after much cheerful banter and feeling positively giddy with good-will, I staggered off down the stairs to find the loo. And it was there, sitting on the throne in the bowels of Via Fossa, that it suddenly hit me. Written on the door before me was a call to arms: 'Queers and Dykes Unite! Keep Canal Street Queer!' Of course, what this actually translated as was: 'Keep the Heterosexuals Out!' I remembered something Charles had said to me earlier, about the alleged infiltration of Canal Street by heterosexuals out for a good time, and the objections of certain sections of the gay populace to what they saw as nasty straights muscling in on their precious space. I also remembered thinking that Richard and Mark were too straight-acting for words. The simple reason for this, as I quickly confirmed when I returned to the bar, was that they were both completely, 100 per cent, straight. And what a crying shame it would have been had they been kept out that night. I mean, who else would have complimented me on my trousers?

Now, I know what you're going to say. And yes, you're probably right. Straight men in gay bars can sometimes present a problem. I can't pretend to know what went on at Via Fossa prior to my visit. For all I know, some butch little straight number may have wandered in one night, had a sudden homosexual panic and smacked some poor salivating queen in the face. Or maybe one of the few lesbians I spotted that night had been the object of unwanted male attentions and had complained of being sexually harassed. These things do happen. But if I may be so bold, might I suggest that the obvious solution to the problem is to impose a ban on those individuals concerned and not the entire heterosexual clientele. Imagine the uproar there would be if the tables were turned and straight pubs and clubs started displaying signs stating that gay people would be refused entry. You know what queers are like. Bar them from anywhere and pretty soon they'll be writing to their MPs and starting up a campaign group. Hell hath no fury like a faggot told that he isn't welcome to come along and play. Just look at the fuss those military Marys made when somebody took their guns away.

Besides, I've long been of the opinion that inviting heterosexuals to gay spaces is one of the best means there is of educating people and breaking down prejudices – ours as well as theirs. Cutting ourselves off from the rest of the world isn't just bad manners, it's an admission that we aren't worthy or capable of taking part in a constructive dialogue. Ultimately, it involves building more barriers, when really it is in our best interests to break them down. Remember, folks, there is a big straight world out there and it's not going to go away – no matter how many pink balloons we wave in the air, or how many drugs we take. Assuming that we are still interested in little things like equal rights and not just the really important issues like shopping, partying and fucking, then sooner or later we're going to have to deal with it. And think how much easier it will be if the people we're dealing with have some sense of where we're coming from.

Of course, there will always be those who argue that allowing heterosexuals into gay bars and clubs spoils the atmosphere. Well, yes – if by 'atmosphere' you mean a few dozen homosexuals standing around, scowling at one another or staring at the floor all night, before skulking into the toilets just before closing time in the hope of a quick grope. If that's your idea of an atmosphere worth preserving, then frankly I'd prefer it if you stayed well clear of the venues this particular homosexual likes to frequent and went somewhere better suited to your needs – like to the nearest therapist. Anyway, I've had my say. I'm not a regular at Via Fossa, so I don't suppose my thoughts on the future of the venue are particularly relevant. But assuming that the management do decide to introduce a 'no straights' door policy, I would like to take this opportunity to pass on the following piece of advice on how to impose it most successfully. Whatever you do, don't stand there asking people if they're gay. If they're not, and they want to get in, they'll say they are anyway. And you can definitely forget dress codes. Everyone is dressing gay these days – except for those pitifully sad poofs who insist on trying to pass as straight. No, there's only one way to be sure. Simply turn away anyone who walks up with a smile on their face. They're bound to be straight.

We left Via Fossa shortly before eleven p.m., exchanging conspiratorial smiles with a few suspiciously straight-looking punters on the way out. We popped along to Manto, which was pleasant enough but essentially no different from the place we had just left. I was keen to see a contrasting view of gay Manchester. Charles suggested a visit to Cruz 101. If any gay readers are planning a trip to Manchester and are worried about having their evening completely ruined by the presence of a few heterosexuals, I suggest they go to Cruz 101. It's so terminally unhip, there is very little danger of bumping into anyone who wasn't driven there by a desperate desire to dance to Kylie and find a bit of cock for the night. Kylie was playing as we arrived, followed by Whigfield, who was immediately succeeded by Gina G (who will, no doubt, be succeeded by some equally talented pop sensation in a skimpy bra top in due course). Sadly, we weren't able to give it 'ooh, aah, just a little bit more' on the dance floor, since we were interrogated for fifteen minutes at the door by a very stern-faced woman who had obviously missed her natural calling as the traffic warden from hell, being forced instead to eke out an existence squeezed into a little glass box at a gay nightclub, collecting money, issuing tickets and oozing resentment from every pore.

The problem was, I couldn't produce a keyring. Not the correct one, anyway. The correct keyring was one issued by the management featuring the Cruz 101 logo. The fact that I didn't possess such a keyring meant that I clearly hadn't been to the venue before, wasn't a fully paid-up member and was therefore deemed deeply suspicious. Precisely what I was suspected of I really couldn't say. My interrogator couldn't possibly have thought that I was straight, I was sure of that. Maybe it was because I'm a Londoner. I honestly don't know. But finally, once Charles had gone into criminal-defence mode and given me a glowing character reference, and I had handed over my £4 and promised faithfully to abide by the rules of the club (which presumably involved negotiating one's way around the dance floor in a clockwise direction only and giving way to oncoming traffic at the bar), my inquisitor relented and we were ushered through.

God, it was awful. I could see why they gave people such a hard time getting in – having gone to all that trouble to get your head inside the door, you were less inclined to turn heel and leave in a hurry. Even so, there is only so much a man can take. Any image I had of Manchester as a progressive, cosmopolitan metropolis evaporated the moment I entered the main bar and spied a selection of vests and moustaches that wouldn't have looked out of place in an old copy of *Zipper*. And as for the music! Gina G was about as progressive as it got. By the time Charles finally coaxed me out onto the dance floor, I was convinced that I was stuck in some kind of time warp and that the clones I had seen dancing at the Tunnel club in Cardiff ten years previously would reappear at any moment, waving their fans in the air. In the meantime, there was the dubious spectacle of half a dozen go-go boys in 'Mr Motivator' multicoloured Lycra one-pieces, jiggling around on their podiums, engulfed by billowing clouds of dry ice, which, although it left a nasty sting in one's throat and was probably likely to cause lung cancer, did at least have the highly beneficial effect of obscuring their mid-drifts – sorry, midriffs.

I was still recovering from the trauma two hours later as, somewhat worse for wear, we headed back to Charles's flat via Canal Street. A crowd was gathering outside Manto, waiting for the doors to reopen and the after-hours club known as the Breakfast Club to swing into action. As we passed by, Charles drew my attention to a converted warehouse overlooking the canal, explaining that this was one of the gay housing developments we'd discussed earlier. I looked up. Standing framed in one of the windows was a young man with perfectly gelled hair and a gym-honed body, dressed in nothing but a pair of white briefs. In my inebriated state, I tried to imagine what he could possibly be doing, standing practically naked in a window overlooking one of the liveliest gay streets in the world. Maybe he was hosting his own private underwear party and had come to the window to keep a lookout for any stragglers. Maybe he simply enjoyed being looked at and from a vantage point where he could look down on his admirers. Maybe he was getting ready to go out and was checking to see how big the queue for the Breakfast Club was. Finally, I decided that I was wrong on all counts. He wasn't on his way out at all. On the contrary, he had only just got in – from Cruz 101. And the reason he was standing in the window was that he had just thrown his keyring into the canal.

The following morning I rose late, thanked Charles for his hospitality, and scuttled off into the grey slanting rain, cursing myself for not having had the sense to bring an umbrella. I headed into the Village, where I was a little too late for the Breakfast Club but was still able to enjoy a very pleasant lunch at Manto. A meal consisting of pasta in a vegetable sauce, salad, bread rolls and a pot of tea came to £8, which I thought was fairly reasonable. Furthermore, my waitress, whose name was Rosie, was extremely attentive and even brought me a glass of tap water with ice and a slice of lemon at no extra charge. Speaking as someone who tends to associate gay café-bars with stroppy muscle boys on Ecstasy comedowns posing as waiters, I have to say that I was impressed. I cleaned my plate fairly quickly, left a generous tip and headed out into the street. I had a train to catch, but first I had somebody to see. Sunday being a holy day, dedicated to the contemplation of all things sacred, I had arranged to meet up with my good friend David Hoyle, otherwise known as the Divine David.

For the benefit of those who haven't yet had the pleasure, the Divine David is the most exciting cabaret performer to come along in a very long time. And that isn't just me talking – several national newspapers have said much the same thing. Described by one journalist as resembling 'a decomposing Liza Minnelli' (a reference to his matted black wig and runny mascara), David is best known for his vitriolic and very funny critiques of contemporary gay life and style. On one memorable occasion, he came on stage dressed in a rubber Nazi uniform, raised his arm in a Nazi salute and announced that he was looking for a Neo-Nazi skinhead with a big Nazi cock who would fuck him senseless and leave him feeling really positive about being gay. That same night, he treated the audience to a rendition of his latest song, a song he hoped to perform live on stage at Gay Pride, a song in which he repeats the two words 'Being gay' over and over *ad nauseam*, before finally finishing with 'is a waste of time'.

David Hoyle was born in Blackpool in 1962, lived in London for the best part of the 1980s and has been based in Manchester since 1988. He once joked that the first thing he missed when he got to Manchester was the underground – so he did the only sensible thing and started his own. Little short of a legend on the Manchester gay circuit for a number of years, he was recently forced to rechannel his energies back towards London, following a dispute with several Manchester pub and club owners who took exception to the content of his act and simply refused to go on booking him. The gay businessmen concerned were all members of the Village Charity, organizers of the Manchester Mardi Gras. It wasn't clear which element of David's act angered them the most. Was it another one of his self-penned songs, set to a manic techno beat and entitled 'Mardi Gras (Time to Die)'? Or could it have been his suggestion that really the men who ran the Gay Village cared very deeply when a person with AIDS died for the simple reason that it meant they were £7 down on a Saturday night?

When he isn't busy assaulting gay sensibilities, the Divine David lives in a bedsit in Whalley Range, on the borders of Moss Side, deep in the heart of Manchester's red-light district. David Hoyle, on the other hand, resides in a housing association flat in Longside. He's far more attractive in the cold light of day than he is on stage, with fair hair and twinkly blue eyes. But he's just as passionate in his attacks on what he regards as the dehumanizing effects of the commercial gay scene and equally polished in his delivery. I asked him to describe gay life in Manchester. He lit up a cigarette, took a long hard drag and said, 'I do think some people can be wilfully provincial, don't you? There's a bit of a stereotype if you're from the North where you're supposed to be suspicious of art, of creativity, of any kind of personal expression. And some people do seem very happy to live up to that stereotype, especially on the gay scene. These days, the gay ideal is to have huge genital organs and to act as if you've had a lobotomy, and that ties in very conveniently with the stereotype of being northern.' He grinned and slipped into a thick Manchester accent. 'I'm a bit thick, me. I don't know nothing about tha'!' Then he went on, 'Some people pride them-selves on their ignorance, don't they? For gay men, that means having no interest in anything outside of squeezing into a really tight pair of jeans, trying to make your genitals look colossal and standing around like cheese at fourpence in a gay bar.'

For a performer with David's rare attributes, Manchester's gay scene continued to provide a steady source of material. What it didn't provide were many opportunities to perform it. Partly, he attributed this to the fact that folk in Manchester were used to far safer stuff. 'There's a big northern drag tradition here, what I call traditional comedy drag mime, where all you do is stand on stage in a dress and false tits and mime to a record. It's hard if what you're trying to do is question that, or do something a bit more political. People always ask me why I don't do proper drag, and the simple reason is that to do so would be to support something I don't believe in. The whole traditional drag thing is all about confirming gender roles. It's symbolic of how the gay scene is so completely out of sync with cultural changes generally. I hate the terms "gay" and "straight", but if you look around today, straight men are the ones trying out new identities, thinking about what it means to be a man. Gay men are the opposite. Because they've got a chip on their shoulder about being gay, they overcompensate in an attempt to embody this illusion called maleness. They go to the gym, have their hair cut very short, act macho, all that. It has about as much substance as a puff of smoke. Gay men on the scene are being encouraged to be contemporary dinosaurs. That's why I describe myself as non-scene. Non-scene, straight-talking, that's me.'

Well, not entirely. David confessed that he did still go to gay bars in Manchester. In fact, he had even been known to pop along to Canal Street on occasion. 'The staff at Metz are very friendly,' he said, adding that the manager there was one of the few people who still supported him. 'But really the places with character are the older places like the New Union or Paddy's Goose. They don't pretend to be anything they're not. And you can meet all sorts of people there – travellers, rent boys, transvestites, married men. The one thing I'll say for Manchester is that you do find there are still plenty of people with character. Penny for penny, I'd say there's more character in Manchester than you'll ever find in London.'

'Really?' I said. 'But I thought character meant being able to quote every line from *Absolutely Fabulous*.' David grinned and lit another cigarette. 'Oh, well, now you're talking about very sophisticated London circles. I'm just a naïve boy from the North, but I would say that character means having your own opinions, your own slant on life. Of course, I could be wrong.'

In July 1997, five months after my visit to Manchester, Channel 4 screened a one-hour documentary about life in the Gay Village as part of its 'Queer Street' season. Overwhelmingly celebratory in tone, *Village Voices* was full of people making extravagant claims about the Village and its achievements. According to Chris Payne, head of Manchester City Advertising, the impact of the Village had been to transform Manchester into a major international centre, no longer in competition with London but on a par with Amsterdam, New York and San Francisco. Mardi Gras was hailed as probably the best street party in the world ever and the local gay businessmen who sit on the board of the Village Charity were praised (mainly by themselves) for their selfless efforts in raising vast sums of money for people with HIV and AIDS. The Village itself was variously described as 'a New Jerusalem', a community centre with something for everyone, 'the Amsterdam of the North' and a place everyone should feel proud to be a part of.

Thankfully, *Village Voices* did include one lone voice of dissent. It belonged to a local gay journalist in his early thirties named Toby Manning. And despite what seemed like a concerted effort on the part of the programme-makers to portray him as some kind of killjoy who wouldn't know a good time if it staggered up and waved a bottle of poppers and the keys to a loft apartment under his nose, his contribution made far more sense than those of the majority of the other participants put together. Filmed perched on the edge of a bed in a large, empty room (presumably to establish him as an isolated figure), he described Manchester as 'a provincial town with grand aspirations' and explained why, so far as he was concerned, the Gay Village was hardly a cause for celebration. Taking issue with the notion that the Village offered something for everyone, he criticized it for promoting a particular kind of aspirational lifestyle that was not only shallow, self-obsessed and vain, but also strictly off limits to those who didn't have the cash to afford it. He then committed the ultimate blasphemy of questioning the mood and purpose of events like Mardi Gras (and, by extension, Gay Pride), asking why anyone should feel 'proud' of their ability to have a good time.

I've known Toby Manning for a number of years. In fact, I had hoped to link up with him during my stay in Manchester, but he was out of town at the time. In light of his TV appearance, I thought it only appropriate to call him up and find out how his opinions had gone down in the local community. But first a bit of background. Toby was born in Manchester, grew up in Newcastle and returned to Manchester in 1988. Those were the days when it was better known as 'Madchester' and when the youth of the city were raving to the sounds of acid house and coming down from the second Summer of Love. Toby was a regular at the legendary Number One Club, a local gay venue and one of the key breeding grounds for the Madchester rave scene. He remembers it as 'a small underground dive, steaming with dry ice and smelling of poppers. You felt like you were off your head the minute you walked in there. It was amazing.'

So what happened to make him fall out with the Manchester gay scene, I wondered. At what point did he say farewell to all that summer love? Toby described his disenchantment as a gradual process, shaped by the influence of outside factors such as the underground queer fanzines he started reading a few years ago, but mostly prompted by the expansion of the Village. 'My negativity has definitely increased in direct proportion to the growth of the Village,' he said. 'For me, the Village is a microcosm of the gay community at large. As it's grown, it's become more and more narrow, more and more restrictive. It's not open to difference, to variety. I've always been very confused that a community which came into being on the basis of freedom of expression should have become so restrictive, so prohibitive about how people are allowed to express their gay identity. Also, I'm not sure that creating a gay ghetto where the rules of the real world are suspended is a particularly fruitful way to live. I know people argue that there is a positive function to having a safe nurturing space, but I do think that has been eclipsed by the fact that people are brought in to be put through the blender and to come out as identikit gay men.'

Toby himself is not what you would call an identikit gay man. Happy to describe himself as 'skinny', he has shoulder-length hair and a healthy aversion to gay uniforms, making him the very antithesis of a 1990s Village Person. In fact, his physical appearance has caused him problems. On more than one occasion, he has been refused entry to bars in the Village for the crime of not looking gay enough. 'It's ridiculous, I know, but if I do go to a gay bar or club in Canal Street, I don't get let in, presumably because I look straight. Ironically, the ones who do get let in are the typical gay stereotypes and the scally lads who are their nemesis and who, of course, look exactly like them.' Despite this, Toby was keen to stress that he does have an active social life. After years of living in the heart of

Manchester, he recently bought a house in a suburb called Chorlton. 'It's where all the media whores move, like Islington, or Camden without the teeny-boppers. It's a ten-minute bus ride from the centre of town. That programme gave the impression that I'm this sad figure who never goes out. In fact, I probably go out more now than I ever did before. I just don't go to the Village. I go to gigs and to clubs which are technically straight but where quite a few gay men are starting to show up. You can have a nice night. I think it's important that people know that. A lot of gays have got to the stage where they actually feel uncomfortable in anything resembling the real world. If they're not completely surrounded by faggots, they're either bored or they're uncomfortable. I find that a bit pathological, to be honest.'

Finally, I asked Toby whether his social life had been affected by his TV appearance. Did he get the sense that he could still be a part of the New Jerusalem if he wished, or was Canal Street completely closed to him these days? Was he *persona non grata* in Via Fossa? Had he been mauled in Manto or accosted in Castro? 'I've had a few snide comments,' he said. 'Someone remarked to a friend of mine that I was opinionated. He replied by asking them to explain why being opinionated was supposed to be a bad thing. I've had a few people tell me that I should lighten up and enjoy myself more. But I've been quite surprised at the number of people who have come up to say that they agreed with everything I said. This straight scally lad came up to me in the street and said, "Hey, mate, weren't you in that gay programme the other night?" I thought, oh my God. Then he said, "You talked a lot of sense."'

3

A WEEKEND WITH THE BLUES BROTHERS

Derbyshire

If you had told me ten years ago that I would spend a weekend holed up in a farmhouse in Derbyshire, surrounded by gay Tories, and that I would enjoy the experience, I would have beaten you over the head with a rolled-up copy of *Socialist Worker*, screamed 'Maggie, Maggie, Maggie – Out, Out, Out!' and sworn never to speak to you again – at least not until you paid proper penance by purchasing every record ever made by the Communards. Life is so much simpler when you're young. For years I refused to entertain the possibility that someone could vote Conservative and still be a decent human being. I was what you might describe as 'far righteous'. I firmly believed that 'people are their politics' – a line I picked up from Barbra Streisand in *The Way We Were*. These days I take a far more sophisticated view. People – gay people included – are made up of many things. The way a person votes doesn't tell you all you need to know about them. And people who need people are the luckiest people in the world.

My host in Derbyshire was Matthew Parris – parliamentary

sketch writer for *The Times* and an ex-Tory MP. Ex-MP, that is –
Matthew is still very much a Tory. And I have to say that I still
retain a hint of my old cynicism where gay Tories are concerned. It's
not that I think of them as being intrinsically evil, or stupid, or bad
in bed. It's not that I don't accept the fact that the Conservative
Party has a strong libertarian strain (as demonstrated by Edwina
Currie during the age of consent campaign of 1994), or that the
Labour Party isn't always as gay-friendly as certain people might
like us to believe (David Blunkett and Ann Taylor both voted
against an equal age of consent at sixteen). It's just that, to my
mind, being gay and voting Conservative still don't add up somehow. How can you be gay and support the people who gave us
Clause 28, who regularly launch attacks on gay men and women in
the name of family values and who sport some of the worst hair-
styles since *The Young Doctors*? On top of which, Matthew was a
great personal supporter of Margaret Thatcher – a woman who was
to gay rights what Hannibal Lecter was to vegetarianism. Still, as
an ex-boyfriend of mine is fond of saying, if we all thought alike and
shared the same tastes, we'd have much smaller shopping centres
(shopping being the one gay pastime even the most rabidly homophobic of Tories is happy to promote).

Anyway, Matthew's own track record on gay rights is pretty
exemplary. As the Right Honourable MP for West Derbyshire,
1979–86, he behaved, well, honourably. Even in the days when he
preferred to keep his sexuality private, he regularly stuck his neck
out to make public pronouncements about gay civil rights. He was
one of the first public figures to call for a change in the law surrounding the 'gay crime' of gross indecency and to condemn the use
of 'pretty policemen' in police entrapment operations. In 1982, he
voted in favour of the extension of gay rights to Northern Ireland.

The first time we met, he was on the managing committee of GALOP, an organization which offers legal advice and support to gay victims of violence and to those who've had the misfortune to be caught with their trousers down. These days, he regularly uses his position at *The Times* to raise awareness of gay issues. And besides, he's a thoroughly charming fellow.

We drove up to Derbyshire late one Friday night – Matthew, myself, a mutual friend named Jeremy and a young friend of Matthew's named Richie (I've altered names). What the exact nature of their friendship was I couldn't really tell you. Matthew tends to be quite coy about these matters, but it would be true to say that there was a fair amount of flirtation going on. I did notice, also, that Richie tended to bait Matthew rather a lot, with the kind of sadistic fervour that usually implies some degree of physical intimacy. A large part of the discussion revolved around politics and the media. Richie worked for a national newspaper, and was evidently quite proud of the fact. At one point in the conversation, he remarked that he thought it unfair that the *Daily Mail* had been voted Newspaper of the Year. Matthew agreed – it wasn't especially good that year.

We arrived in Derbyshire shortly after one a.m. and drove down a series of narrow, windy lanes until, finally, we pulled up at a large farmhouse. The first thing that struck me was how dark it was. Stumbling out of the car and practically falling into a ditch where the drive was supposed to be, I found myself wondering how anybody manages to survive in the country. The fact that there is no underground system I can just about contend with, but whoever decided to cut down on the electricity bill by not installing street lights seriously needs to have their head examined. What is the point of electricity if not to light our way in the darkness? In the city, people kick up a fuss if there isn't a streetlamp illuminating every corner – the argument being that a dimly lit street is an open invitation to muggers, rapists and criminals of all descriptions. In the country, people simply stagger merrily on their way, falling into ditches and fending off attacks by marauding livestock and assorted wildlife as if this were the most natural thing in the world. Perverse, I call it.

The farmhouse where I very nearly broke a leg is situated between two towns – Matlock and Bakewell. The nearest, Matlock, is six miles away. I could see the streetlights winking away in the distance, quietly mocking me. On the map Derbyshire shares a border with Manchester. But really it's a different world. Matthew bought the farmhouse back in the days when he was MP for the area and keeps it on as a sort of weekend retreat. He doesn't do much in the way of farming, although he does keep a few ducks and some geese. He recently had the cowsheds converted into holiday cottages, which helps pay for the upkeep of the building, and for the Italian housekeeper, Marta, who looks after the place while he's away. What can I tell you about Marta? She's a fairly large, very pretty woman in her early thirties, with a natural affinity for gay men, outweighed only by a deep, abiding love of cats. She and Matthew met a few years ago, while she was in London visiting her gay brother Stefano. They got along so well that Marta cancelled her plans to go back to Italy and moved to Derbyshire instead. I suppose there's only so much Mediterranean living a girl can take. I mean, who needs Italian sunshine and olive oil when you can have English drizzle and dripping?

The following morning, Marta demonstrated her skills in the kitchen, cooking up a none too traditional English country breakfast of scrambled duck eggs, sausages and kangaroo steaks. Over breakfast, Richie teased Matthew about being 'an uptight old thing'. Matthew took it all in good humour – even allowing that, yes, he probably was a bit of a cold fish. He put this down to his upbringing. At fourteen, he was packed off to boarding school, he says by choice, but he was terribly homesick. His first job was at the Foreign Office. Again, he felt homesick. Even now, at the age of forty-seven, he remained extremely close to his mother. He said he dreaded her death more than anything else – 'I can't even think about it without crying.' Old age doesn't worry him, though. He reckons he's more comfortable with himself the older he gets.

I asked Matthew how people in the area perceived him, a man regularly described as one of the forty most influential gay men in Britain? Was it even an issue? He said he thought not. Everyone in Matlock knew he was gay, even in the days when he was their MP, although no one ever brought the subject up – 'it wouldn't be polite'. This sort of English reserve wasn't always a good thing where gay people were concerned, he said, but it wasn't always bad either. 'It allows people some space.' Thus, if a gay person moved into the village and decided to flaunt their sexuality, they might feel a bit frozen out, but they wouldn't experience outright hostility. When I asked him about the local gay scene, he started by describing it as 'a cross between Mykonos and Ambridge'. By the time he'd finished telling me about the various gay people he knew and the various places they went, it sounded more like something out of Beatrix Potter.

This is largely down to 'The Rabbits'. This is the term Matthew and Marta use to describe their nearest gay neighbours – a couple who live 'just over the hill' in Marby. Let us call them Alistair and Peter, but Matthew and Marta took a vote and decided that 'The Rabbits' suits them far better. They moved into the area six years ago. For the first couple of months, they kept themselves very much to themselves. Every so often, Matthew would spot them pottering about in their garden, or arriving home with the groceries, and would drive by to say hello. As soon as they saw his car approaching, they would dash into the house and peer out of the window nervously – thereby earning their nickname. Matthew was clearly very taken with the idea of having a pair of rabbits for neighbours and had developed quite detailed character sketches of them (which, one day, I expect to see illustrating some children's book). Apparently, Alistair is 'the buck rabbit' and collects wind organs, which he stores in three large barns dotted around the area. Peter is 'the doe rabbit'. He lives and works in Nottingham, and spends the weekends with his lover of ten years, climbing mountains and scouring the local junk shops for wind organs. (Matthew ascribed the terms 'buck' and 'doe' on the basis of what he saw as the couple's respective masculine and feminine qualities – i.e. Alistair is the bossy one, while Peter tends to panic more easily.)

Naturally, I couldn't wait to meet them, and as luck would have it I didn't have to wait very long. Just after we'd finished clearing up our breakfast things, there was a knock on the door and two men in their mid-thirties appeared. Both were fairly handsome in a ruddy-faced, chunky-sweaters-and-hiking-boots kind of way and were carrying rucksacks. 'Hello,' they said in unison. 'We're "The Rabbits".' 'Hello,' I said back. 'I'm Mr Fox.' I didn't really say that, but, believe me, I was sorely tempted. Anyway, there was no need for me to take the piss out of them, since Matthew was obviously far better qualified for the job. Introducing me as a friend from London who was writing a book about gay lives around the country, he announced that he'd just been telling me his theory about which of them was the buck and which the doe. Alistair, the buck, smiled confidently and helped himself to some coffee. Peter, the doe, laughed nervously and insisted that it was really more of a give-and-take affair – that they each took responsibility for different aspects of the relationship and that they were both quite masterful in their different ways. Neither of them seemed particularly embarrassed about having their private affairs discussed in the presence of a total stranger. On the contrary, they seemed to enjoy it. For ten minutes or so, they stood there smiling happily. Then Alistair announced that it was time they were leaving, and within seconds they were gone. I hesitate to say that they bolted, but it wouldn't be so far from the truth.

The afternoon passed without much incident. Richie took a train back to London ('deadlines, sweetie, deadlines') and the rest of us took a drive around the local area, with Matthew pointing out places of historic interest. There was the George pub, where Prince Charles once took a pee and where there is now a plaque commemorating his royal highness's visit. There was Riber Castle, where we stopped for a while and stood around looking at ruins – something I am especially well practised at, having spent more hours than I care to remember at a pub in London called the Brief Encounter. Then it was time to go and collect the Christmas tree. Matthew wanted the biggest tree he could find; Marta was more concerned about the shape. By the time they'd agreed on which one to buy and we'd got the damn thing home, I had built up quite an appetite. Marta offered to whip up some more duck eggs, but I declined when Matthew announced that he, myself and Jeremy had been invited for dinner by Sean of the vicarage.

The vicarage is one of those grand, enormous, draughty piles that probably sounds like a great place to live if you're a bat, don't mind the occasional bout of hypothermia or still haven't recovered from watching *The Rocky Horror Picture Show* when you were very young and far too impressionable. The building is set well back from the road, with no driveway. Instead, you have to park your car on the roadside and walk through a very long, very narrow, very dark alley, across what looks like and – oh my God – is a graveyard, then down some stone steps thoughtfully encrusted with a particularly slippery variety of moss. By the time we made it to the door, I was half expecting Richard O'Brien to pop up singing 'The Timewarp'. Instead, the door was opened by a young, blond, slightly spotty gay man who bore an uncanny resemblance to one of the smaller members of the Muppet family.

Sean is twenty-four, and lodges with an older gay couple named Mark and Vince. Matthew had hoped that I would have the chance to meet them also, only they'd changed their plans at the last minute and had gone away for the weekend. Mark is rumoured to be something of a bully, which may have been a contributory factor to Sean's nervous disposition that evening. Then again, it could have been me. Call me old-fashioned, but if someone asks me if I'm cold and I am, then I say so. Sean asked me if I was cold as soon as I walked in the door and I answered yes, I was. I couldn't help it. It just came out – like the clouds of cold air that escaped from my mouth the moment I went to use the bathroom. Anyway, I was soon wishing I hadn't said anything. Sean was terribly sweet and a very kind host, but his embarrassment at the fact that his guests were slowly freezing to death really took the edge off the evening. I tried to make it up to him by enthusing wildly about the food – home-made tomato, apple and celery soup, followed by broccoli lasagne with roast potatoes and roast parsnips, topped off with a delicious chocolate mousse. I even tried taking my jacket off to reassure him that, hey, it really wasn't that cold after all. But to no avail. Sean spent the entire evening apologizing for everything – the cold, the food, the fact that Jimmy Somerville hadn't had a hit in years. In the end, I did the only sensible thing and got thoroughly drunk.

It seemed fitting that after dining at the vicarage we should go for a drink at a place called Marsden's. In Stephen King's *Salem's Lot*, the Marsden House is where nightmares come to life – home to a seven-foot vampire and his guardian, James Mason, who passes himself off as an antiques dealer. There were no seven-foot vampires at Marsden's and no sign of James Mason, but there were a few men who could have quite easily passed for antiques dealers. Five years ago, Marsden's in Chesterfield was the home of the local Conservative Club. These days, it's a gay club (so, little change there, then). We arrived a little before eleven p.m. – Matthew, Jeremy, myself and Sean, whom we had managed to drag away from the washing-up. The DJ, who looked a lot like Deirdre from *Coronation Street*, was trying to keep the party going with the latest remix of some old hit by George Michael. The crowd weren't impressed. The only person dancing was a cute boy in a tight black T-shirt – and he had his face to the wall and a bottle of poppers jammed up his nose. Finally, the DJ admitted defeat by announcing that the bar was closing. 'But you can go upstairs for another drink if you like. For now this is me, Sheena, wishing you all goodnight.'

We went upstairs. Upstairs was called the Warehouse. Upstairs was a notice saying 'Private Party'. We turned to leave, but were assaulted by a young woman coming up the stairs. 'Ignore me, then!' she said, very indignantly. It took me a moment to realize that her remark was directed at me. Apparently, we had met here last week. I had broken up with my boyfriend and had turned to her for a shoulder to cry on. By the end of the evening, she had persuaded me that there were plenty more fish in the sea and I had gone home happy, but not before thanking her profusely for taking the time to care and promising to be her friend for ever. And now here I was pretending I didn't recognize her – typical. I tried to explain that I couldn't have met her here last week, for the simple reason that I lived several hundred miles away and had never stepped foot inside this club before tonight. She stared at me for a moment, obviously not believing a word I was saying, then decided to let bygones be bygones and invited us to join the party, on the condition that we paid for our own drinks.

The party was something else. Apparently it was a joint cele-bration for somebody's engagement and somebody's twenty-first birthday. The man celebrating his twenty-first was very clearly gay. The man celebrating his engagement I wasn't so sure about. If I just tell you that he had long, heavily processed black hair tied back in a ponytail, wore a white shirt open to the navel with a pair of tight black trousers and silver-tipped cowboy boots, and made a point of dancing very energetically whenever we happened to look in his direction . . . well, you can draw your own conclusions. The two black men dancing next to him didn't look entirely straight either. One was dressed in a calf-skin waistcoat and very little else. Both had perfected the kind of wiggle that would have put Marilyn Monroe to shame.

The girls, meanwhile, were stomping around the dance floor in thigh-high boots, micro-skirts and rock-hard hairdos, oozing testos-terone and alcohol from every pore. It was quite alarming. One of their number, who said her name was Kirsty, grabbed Jeremy firmly by the waist and started flinging him around to the strains of some supposedly ironic hillbilly dance record called 'Cotton Eyed Joe'. (He still has the bruises to prove it.) Shortly afterwards, another girl (who would have been extremely pretty had she not been so drunk that her head was hanging to one side) shimmied towards me and started bumping and grinding to Tina Turner singing 'What's Love Got to Do with It?' I quickly discovered that she was the one engaged to marry the man in the cowboy boots, and immediately felt so sorry for her that I insisted we have one more trip around the dance floor. The biggest hit of the night was the dance version of 'Total Eclipse of the Heart', sung by Nikki French, with added backing vocals from every dizzy queen and scary fag-hag in the room. Just as I was really getting into the spirit of things, stomping around and wishing I was man enough to wear a pair of thigh-high boots and a micro-skirt, the lights came on and someone announced that it was time to leave.

On my way downstairs, I decided that it might be a good idea if I went to the toilet. As it turned out, this wasn't such a good idea after all. In the toilet there were a handful of gay men in tiny T-shirts, gossiping about some poor queen who wasn't there to defend himself, but who was apparently guilty of fancying someone who was the desired love object of someone else and who therefore deserved to be bad-mouthed all over town, or at least all over the walls of this public convenience. Apologizing for the interruption, I pushed my way through the bickering throng and stood at the urinal. Moments later, another man came and stood next to me, smiled and then broke wind extremely loudly. 'Sorry,' he said, still smiling away. 'I only came in for a fart.'

On the way out of Marsden's, I picked up a copy of *SP Mag*, a gay freesheet 'incorporating *Sheffield Pink*' and distributed 'across South Yorkshire and beyond'. The following morning, while Matthew was tucked away in his office writing his column for *The Times* and Jeremy was helping Marta prepare lunch, I lay in bed flicking through *SP Mag*. You can learn a lot about the gay character of an area from the local gay freesheets. Did you know, for example, that South Yorkshire is home to a woman who goes by the name of 'Decadent Dyke'? It's true. She has her own column in *SP Mag*. This particular column was all about the South Yorkshire police, who had recently placed a recruitment advert in *Gay Times*, sparking complaints from the Police Federation. One local detective chief inspector rejoicing in the name of David Bullett had 'slammed the plan to target homosexuals for recruiting'. Another officer, described only as the head of Rawmarsh CID, was reported to be 'ashamed and embarrassed'. Being a decadent sort of dyke, our columnist was none too happy with this state of affairs and was calling for readers to write to the Police Federation and complain – 'unless of course you have a different view or experience, then you should write to me'. It was encouraging to hear that the spirit of open debate was still alive and well in the pages of the free gay press.

And so it went on. A few pages later, I came across a lively little item about the use of the word 'Queer'. It began with a quip about how we're all into finding alternative labels these days, what with all the fuss about queer and so on, then went on to suggest a few more words lesbians and gay men might like to reclaim, like 'muff diver' and 'mattress muncher'. And there was a multiple choice thrown in for bisexuals – 'Betty bothways', 'catflap' or 'fence-sitter'. The item ended by saying that of course readers were under no obligation to choose any of these words – 'You could just be extra cool and decide not to define, as your sexuality is fluid'. Personally, 'fluid' is not a word I have much time for. I feel much more comfortable with the word 'aqueous'. Then again, I could just be being picky.

Next to this item was a larger opinion piece on the subject of cottaging. Entitled 'Domestic Bliss?', it opened by stating that very few subjects nowadays were likely to provoke outbursts of moral outrage in the gay community and cottaging remained one of the last taboos. Already, I was finding myself in disagreement. In my experience, there are still plenty of subjects likely to provoke outbursts of moral outrage in the gay community. Indeed, I know of dozens of lesbians and gay men who like nothing more than a good old moral outburst. They usually begin by saying, 'Speaking as a lesbian . . .' or 'As a gay man I think . . .', before going on to prove beyond all shadow of a doubt that they haven't really thought at all – at least not recently, and certainly not for themselves. Instead, they derive some perverse satisfaction from merely repeating the same second-hand, half-baked rhetoric they've been spouting for years, smug in the belief that this will be enough to guilt-trip the other party into submission and thereby win them the argument.

And the truly bizarre thing is, it usually works. Outbursts of moral outrage are still regarded as a legitimate form of debate within the lesbian and gay community – although not, I need hardly say, by the likes of me. I'll admit that, yes, there was a time when I would have quietly given in to any lesbian who declared that, as a gay man, I was a potential rapist and therefore not entitled to comment on anything. And there have been occasions when, confronted by a gay man hysterically screaming that I didn't know the first thing about AIDS because I hadn't been to half as many funerals as he had, I would have backed down rather than add to his grief. But not any longer. Outbursts of moral outrage are no substitute for reasoned argument. The sooner gay people stop behaving like small children, the sooner they'll start winning respect as adults. In the meantime, if someone takes issue with you by stamping their foot on the ground and threatening to scweam and scweam until they are sick, do as I do and laugh in their face. Believe me, it works every time.

Anyway, where were we? Oh, yes, the article about cottaging. Once I'd read beyond the first paragraph, I discovered a lot of things that I didn't know already. Were you aware, for example, that 'the parks, toilets and lay-bys of Sheffield are imagined to be the territory of dirty, raincoat-clad, pervy old men', whereas in fact 'some areas can be very popular with younger people' (hence, I would imagine, their appeal to dirty, raincoat-clad, pervy old men)? Did you also know that, far from being the exclusive preserve of those unfortunate souls who haven't yet seen the light and are still locked firmly in the closet, 'some scene queens also enjoy a quick trip to a popular toilet for a change of atmosphere and punters'? It makes you think, if only about what constitutes 'a popular toilet'. I picture a large, white-tiled room with porcelain hand-basins, gold taps and a steady supply of freshly ironed, neatly folded hand-towels. (Then again, given gay men's overwhelming loyalty to bars and clubs where even toilet paper is in short supply, I could be wrong.) The article gave a cautionary warning that cottaging is illegal and that, 'if arrested, you could be exposed', before ending on an upbeat note, suggesting that 'with care, cottaging can be fab' and 'we should give support to those who cottage, not condemn them'.

Now, I'm all for giving support to people who feel compelled to hang around public toilets looking for sex because this is their only means of expressing their homosexual desires. And I do think it's time the laws surrounding such activities were relaxed – if only to help the British constabulary make better use of their resources. It's quite absurd that police divisions all around the country continue to invest massive amounts of time and money in operations designed to catch the perpetrators of what are, after all, victimless crimes. I'm sure most reasonable people would much sooner see the police out patrolling the streets than hiding out in public conveniences for days on end.

However, I do find some of the things said in defence of gay public sex a bit hard to swallow. It's one thing to say that the law is an ass, quite another to claim the right to get your ass licked into shape wherever you choose. Call me old-fashioned, but I don't regard the freedom to have sex in public as a matter of civil rights, gay or otherwise. I have no desire to see heterosexuals bumping their uglies in full view of everybody, and I don't see why they should feel any differently where I am concerned. There are historic reasons why gay men go looking for sex in parks and public toilets, mainly to do with the fact that, for years, those were among the few places where they were likely to find it. These days, most of us have other options available. If we choose to indulge in what is, after all, antisocial behaviour, then we can hardly be surprised if other people take offence. And before anyone starts banging on about transgressive sexuality and all that nonsense, please remember the words of the great American pro-sex dyke activist and writer Pat Califia – we can't simply fuck our way to freedom. In other words, waving your willy in public doesn't make you radical, it just makes you a willy-waver.

Sorry to bore you with all of this. I was going to pop it down on a postcard and address it to *SP Mag*. Unfortunately, unlike my friend the Decadent Dyke, the author of this spirited defence of anonymous sex had chosen to remain anonymous and certainly wasn't encouraging readers to write in with their comments. That's radical willy-wavers for you – no balls.

*

Have you ever noticed how the most closeted gay men are often the most screamingly gay? Liberace was a case in point. So too is Matthew's friend David (not his real name). Matthew had invited David to join us for lunch – possibly out of sheer hospitality, although I suspect other motives were involved. Matthew is one of those people who likes putting potentially volatile combinations of people together, then sitting back and waiting for the sparks to fly. I don't condemn him for it – it's a game I quite like to play myself. Anyway, he was sorely disappointed that he hadn't managed to get me and the dreaded Mark into the same room, if only because he was so confident that there would have been a clash of egos. Inviting David to lunch may have been his last-ditch attempt at making mischief before the weekend was over. Certainly, nothing I had heard about him so far had led me to think that we would get along. He was a young Conservative at the local council and firmly in the closet. The night before, on our way to Marsden's, Sean had insisted we stop off at the restaurant where David was dining with some colleagues, so that he might pass on a message. The rest of us were instructed to wait in the car while he did so, lest we alerted David's workmates to the fact that he was gay (personally, I thought my leather chaps and pink feather boa provided the perfect camouflage for a night out at a former Conservative Club, but evidently I was alone in this). Sean was inside the restaurant for exactly two minutes before coming back with a flea in his ear. Apparently, he had embarrassed David by not being straight-acting enough. You'll forgive me, then, if I say that I had prejudged this person somewhat.

David arrived just after two p.m. He was, without doubt, the most effeminate homosexual I had encountered all weekend. He had plucked eyebrows and big bouffed hair with blond highlights. He had very tight jeans, designed by Jean Paul Gaultier – who, he wasted no time in mentioning, was one of his favourite designers. He sat with his legs crossed and flapped his hands a lot when he spoke. His voice was more camp than a row of tents. He talked about the outfit he was planning to wear to the works Christmas party – a sheer top, with John Richmond 'mirror-ball' trousers. Last year he'd worn a little something by Vivienne Westwood, with his hair tied into tiny pigtails as modelled by Björk. The sheer top he'd chosen this year was perfect because it revealed his pierced navel. No, it hadn't hurt as much as he'd expected it to, but even if it had it would have been worth it. After all, pierced navels are still quite unusual, aren't they?

I listened to all of this in total disbelief. If David's friends at the council really thought he was straight, then they were a bigger bunch of loonies than Lambeth has ever produced. I sincerely hoped they weren't ever asked to decide anything important – like whether or not to have biscuits with their tea. How can we be expected to have faith in government, even at a local level, when the people making the decisions can't spot a homosexual as obvious as David? Of course, I'm sure the reality is that they can. I've little doubt that David's colleagues knew full well that he was gay, or at least had their suspicions. His refusal to be open and honest about his sexuality merely saved everyone the embarrassment of having to talk about it. And I'm sure this suited them perfectly well. The British do like their homosexuals in their proper place – skulking in the shadows, not swinging from the chandeliers. Speaking as some-one who has been accused of swinging from the chandeliers in his time, I have to say that, on balance, I think it's a lot more dignified than cramming your life into a closet and your body into a sheer top and a pair of mirror-ball trousers.

I don't mean to sound so hard on David. After all, political life in this great country of ours is awash with people who say one thing in public and do another in private. Shortly before the last general election, it was estimated that there were between forty and fifty gay MPs in the House of Commons – nearly all of them closeted. Ian Greer, the gay former lobbyist at the centre of the 'cash for questions' affair described the situation on Radio 5 Live's gay news programme *Out This Week*. 'Some are married but are still gay,' he said. 'Many are actively gay. Others perhaps are not married but have chosen not to make any declaration as to their sexuality. I think it is very sad if you are an MP and you are gay, if you feel you have to get married to cover that sexuality [in pursuit of] an upwardly mobile career to the Cabinet.' Matthew himself was quoted in the *Guardian* as taking a more sympathetic line, stressing that one shouldn't rush to pass judgement on what is, ultimately, a personal decision. 'Whether or not you come out, or how far, is a moral decision for a politician to take. There are conflicting obligations, protecting the feelings and sensibilities of people close to you, for example. But balancing those obligations is something only an individual can do.'

Personally, I take the somewhat quaint view that people in public office have a responsibility to be honest with the people who put them there. This is why I could never understand all the fuss about outing. When Peter Tatchell and the gay rights group OutRage! threatened to expose the closeted gay MPs who had voted against an equal age of consent in the 1994 vote, people threw up their hands in horror, condemning the threatened action as barbaric and demonizing Tatchell as the most evil man in Britain, if not the world. Yet nobody complains when MPs who claim to represent traditional family values are exposed as adulterers, or when newspapers print the names of those MPs accused of taking cash for questions. In these instances, any invasion of a person's right to privacy is deemed to be in the public interest. Well, I am a member of the public and I regard it as being in my interest to know if a person empowered to vote on matters directly affecting me has a guilty secret which may affect the way they vote. Outing, as the late Vito Russo said, is simply a dirty word for telling the truth. Closeted gay MPs who vote in favour of anti-gay legislation and against the principle of gay equality have no right to expect other gay people to be complicit in their deception. It's as simple as that.

Thankfully, we appear to be entering an age when such arguments will soon be redundant, when being open about one's sexuality will be regarded as a possible vote-winner, rather than an automatic bar to a successful political career. One of the highlights of the last election was watching Ben Bradshaw, the openly gay Labour candidate for Exeter, beat his virulently anti-gay Conservative opponent, Adrian Rogers, into the ground. In the run-up to the election, Rogers had called on voters 'not to let the pink flag fly over Exeter'. The final leaflet of his campaign said, 'I ask every Exeter parent and everyone concerned about our country's children: Do you want an MP who wants to promote homosexuality in schools?' Come election day, the good people of Exeter answered with a resounding yes, giving Bradshaw the biggest swing to Labour in the South-West. When the results were announced, a grinning Bradshaw described the result as 'a victory for truth over bigotry'. Then there was the even lovelier sight of Michael Portillo, darling of the Thatcherite Right, losing his seat to another openly gay candidate, Stephen Twigg. Twigg, who achieved a swing of 17.5 per cent (almost double the national average) admitted to being 'quite overwhelmed at the time', though obviously not quite as overwhelmed as Mr Portillo, who appeared to have tears in his eyes when being questioned by Jeremy Paxman.

We now have four openly gay MPs in Parliament – including, for the first time in history, a Cabinet minister. I don't want to make too much of this, but I do think it is worth noting that they all got there on a Labour vote.

I left Derbyshire with a whole load of questions still unanswered. Would 'The Rabbits' ever tire of collecting wind organs? Would Sean ever recover from me telling him that his house was too cold? Would the couple celebrating their engagement in the upstairs room at Marsden's ever make it down the aisle? Would someone write a letter to the Decadent Dyke at *SP Mag* saying that, actually, they thought it only right and proper that the Police Federation didn't want lesbians and gay men joining the police force? And last but by no means least, would David wake up one morning and realize that, really, he wasn't fooling anyone?

I ended my meeting with David on a tender note. While Matthew was loading up the car for our return journey to London, David followed me outside for a cigarette. It was five p.m. and already pitch black. There was an awkward silence as we both stood sucking on our Silk Cuts. To ease the tension, I asked him what the traffic would be like tonight. 'The roads will be packed with people going back to London,' he said mournfully. 'They're the lucky ones. We have to make do with a trip to Matlock.' And at that moment, I felt immense sympathy for him.

4

HIGH LIFE AND LOW LIGHTS

Edinburgh

I went to Edinburgh to give a short talk at the Filmhouse cinema and stayed for three days. Well, I had to. Edinburgh is such a beautiful place. One of Britain's most dramatic and distinguished tourist destinations, it is a city full of steep hills and gentle lilting accents, a place rich in history and culture. For those with a passion for all things ancient and military, there is the Military Tattoo. For those open to all things new and different in the performing arts, look no further than the Edinburgh Festival. Picture the two events back to back and you have a measure of the city's character. Edinburgh, you see, is a city of two halves – the old and the young, the ancient and the modern. On the one side, you have the Old Town, with its stiff, strait-laced air and narrow, winding closes. On the other, you have the New Town, with its laid-back, populist appeal and breezy parallel avenues. Running between the two, unable to decide which side it's on, is George Street. Although not nearly as well known as neighbouring Princes Street, George Street is famous for its architecture – which, rather fittingly for a street on the borders of two worlds, reflects many different influences. Local guidebooks point to a bewildering range of architectural styles – Italian Renaissance, Edwardian, Corinthian, Doric and Baroque. Personally, I wouldn't know my Doric from my elbow, and the only thing I can tell you about Corinthian is that St Paul once wrote a letter addressed to two or more of them. If I'm truly honest, I have to say that my immediate love of Edinburgh had nothing to do with the drama of the landscape or the character of the buildings. It stemmed from the fact that my talk went down rather well and that I received a far warmer welcome here than I can recall receiving anywhere else.

My invitation to speak at the Filmhouse came about because of an essay I had contributed to a book of contentious gay opinion called *Anti-Gay*. The essay was entitled 'Confessions of a Gay Film Critic, or How I Learned to Stop Worrying and Love *Cruising*'. Partly an attempt to justify my love of one of the most notoriously 'homophobic' movies ever made, partly a critique of the whole 'positive images' school of 'gay film criticism' that was so popular in the 1970s and 1980s, and still stubbornly refuses to lay down and die, the essay focused on William Friedkin's 1980 thriller *Cruising* and the hysterical gay reactions to it in order to demonstrate the dangers of allowing your ideology to rule your common sense. For the benefit of those who haven't had the pleasure, *Cruising* stars Al Pacino as a New York undercover cop on the trail of a serial killer with a taste for Al Pacino lookalikes in leather. The film is set against the gay S&M scene and includes some pretty graphic shots of men doing the sorts of things such men do, including larking about in leather slings and having other men's hands shoved up their bottoms. A large part of the plot revolves around Pacino's attempts to pass himself off as a leather queen and his subsequent homosexual awakening. The killer is eventually identified as a young drama student who, unable to accept his own homosexuality and desperately trying to win the approval of his dead father, is going around killing the very thing he loves. The film ends ambiguously, with Pacino getting his man (in the old-fashioned, non-sexual sense), coupled with a few hints that, having been forced to confront his own homosexual desires, he may have experienced a homosexual panic and started carving up queers himself.

One of the many criticisms made of *Cruising* is that it represents gay men in a negative way by associating homosexuality with violence and death, while all the time portraying the gay scene as some kind of infernal underworld, with Pacino cast as the innocent abroad. Much of this may be true, but really, how could it have been otherwise? At the end of the day, *Cruising* isn't a self-help video for unhappy homosexuals, but a Hollywood thriller. It is in the nature of thrillers to make associations between sexuality and death. John Carpenter did it in *Halloween*. In that film, a child is traumatized by the discovery of two heterosexuals having sex and grows up to be a knife-wielding maniac with a nasty habit of slicing up sexually active teenagers. I don't recall any heterosexuals complaining that *Halloween* didn't represent them fairly. It is also a common feature of thrillers to take an innocent character with whom the audience can identify and put them in an alien environment where death might be waiting around the next corner. The fact that *Cruising* depicts the gay S&M scene as a world apart from the ordinary seems to me only reasonable. I mean, isn't that the point? You don't dress up in full leather gear and have people's fists inserted quite a long way up your back passage in an attempt to fit in with the rest of society. And if *Cruising* suggests that the world Pacino suddenly finds himself in is a little scary, well again that's only to be expected.

The reality is that homosexuality is a far scarier prospect than heterosexuality – at least until you get the hang of it. It seems to me that the real reason gay people didn't like *Cruising* wasn't because it was a distortion of the truth but because it was too close to the truth for comfort. That, and the fact that lesbians and gay men seem incapable of watching any film featuring a lesbian or gay character without demanding that the character in question be seen to set a good example, or at the very least act as a representative for every lesbian and gay man under the sun. Bloody childish, I call it.

Conveniently for me, my defence of *Cruising* happened to fit in rather well with a season of lectures the Filmhouse were hosting at the time, entitled '*J'Accuse*' and dedicated to reappraisals of films critically panned or otherwise condemned at the time of their release. Rather less conveniently, the Wednesday morning on which I was supposed to catch a train to Edinburgh happened to be the same Wednesday morning on which the IRA chose to plant a bomb in Manchester, with the result that train services were suspended for several hours and I was forced, kicking and screaming, to make my way to Heathrow, where a plane was waiting to deliver me to my destination in a fraction of the time. This being my first-ever experience of domestic air travel, I arrived in Edinburgh a few hours earlier than I felt I ought to have and with the distinct feeling that I had touched down in a different country. Which, given recent political shenanigans north of the border, I suppose I had.

A room had been booked for me at the well-priced but stylish Point Hotel on Bread Street. Rebuilt in 1995, the Point prides itself on combining modern elegance with old-fashioned service, making it the perfect place from which to explore Edinburgh. In light of the fact that I hadn't finished preparing my talk, I decided to leave any exploring until later, which was just as well. I had barely had enough time to unpack, jump in the shower, make myself a cup of tea with the modern, elegant yet strangely old-fashioned kettle in my room and settle down to complete my notes when the general manager of the Filmhouse, a man by the name of Charlie, rang to say that he would come and collect me in an hour. Exactly one hour later, he was waiting for me in the reception – a small, smartly dressed fellow with little round glasses who later told me that he was thirty-four but whom I immediately took to be at least a decade younger. As we walked the short distance to the Filmhouse, he filled me in on the evening's schedule. The cinema had managed to acquire a decent print of *Cruising*, which, naturally, they were encouraging people to come and see. Charlie thought it would be nice if I introduced the film with a few words. I could then sit through it if I so chose, or else return after the screening to give my talk and answer questions. Following this, I would be taken out for dinner and encouraged to get drunk.

As I think I may have already indicated, the talk went well. People asked questions and I did my best to answer them. Not everybody agreed with my interpretation of the film, but not everybody was expected to. One man recalled going to see *Cruising* on its original release in 1980 and compared the sense of moral outrage he felt at the time to the complete lack of indignation he felt seeing it again now. Interestingly, he said he never once doubted the authenticity of the film's depiction of the gay scene – he just didn't like seeing it in a movie that would be seen by people who weren't gay. Another man argued that, although the film's depiction of men in leather jackets acting out the rituals of S&M before being butchered to death was clearly intended to be homophobic, it was all far too silly to be taken seriously (which, I have to say, is pretty much how I feel each time I stumble across a leather bar). A woman compared *Cruising* to *Basic Instinct*, and said that she really couldn't see what all the fuss was about. All in all, it was a very enjoyable, very reasonable, very adult discussion. There were no hysterical outbursts, no accusations of internalized homophobia on my part and no death threats. Better yet, nobody stood up to say that while they were mature enough to discuss ideas which might call certain gay orthodoxies into question, there were other less fortunate people living in other parts of the country who would almost certainly be offended and whose feelings we really ought to consider before we went off having opinions of our own. I know it sounds ridiculous, but when your experience of gay public debates is largely confined to London, this is something you come to expect. Things are different in Edinburgh, obviously. Defending a film in which several gay men are brutally murdered and countless more are shown dancing badly may not be the most obvious way to ingratiate yourself to a group of gay men and women you've never met before, but what can I say? It worked for me.

One hour and two or three celebratory drinks later, I was sitting in a local French restaurant with Charlie and his good friend 'Ben' (not his real name). I feel I ought to point out that, up until now, I had assumed that Charlie was gay. Earlier, he had told me that his proudest moment at the Filmhouse was when he was given the opportunity to interview Derek Jarman. Stupidly, I had taken this as a thinly veiled reference to his own sexual proclivities. The truth was, he simply liked Jarman's films. And there was I, daring to lecture people on the subject of gay films and gay audiences, and the assumptions that even the brightest of gay critics often make. In my own defence, I would just like to point out that while Charlie may not be gay, nor is he entirely straight. Gay-identified in everything bar what he does with his genitals, he is what you might call a 'gay-acting straight male', or 'stray'. Or as he himself put it, 'I'm an asexual heterosexual wanker.' He told me that he had been in his current relationship for a number of years. His real love, though, was techno music. In fact, he made it perfectly clear that he enjoyed getting off his head on the dance floor far more than he enjoyed getting his rocks off in bed – which did start me wondering about what his girlfriend was getting out of the relationship.

Ben was far more straightforward. From the moment we were introduced, I had him down as a sexually active homosexual man who wasn't averse to the odd wank but preferred the company of other men while in the act. By the time I had spent an hour in his company, I was convinced that I was correct on all counts. Tall, dark and really rather handsome, Ben worked for a large bookstore in Edinburgh, where he was responsible for organizing talks and book-signings by visiting authors. I guessed that he was probably very good at his job, if his flirting skills were anything to go by. Flirting is an acquired art, and one that pitifully few gay men are any good at. The gay scene is generally too heavily sexualized and gay men generally too impatient for flirting to have developed as a mode of communication. By and large, gay men don't flirt – they cruise. The difference between flirting and cruising can't be stressed enough. It's the difference between someone catching your eye in a playful yet inviting manner and someone staring glassy-eyed at the bulge in your jeans. Anyway, Ben was a consummate flirt, one who understood that less is often more and who managed to make regular eye contact without assuming the appearance of something you'd find on a fishmonger's slab. After dinner, he kindly offered to take me on a guided tour of gay Edinburgh – an invitation which, being slightly drunk and more than a little curious, I graciously accepted.

The majority of Edinburgh's gay bars are situated in the New Town, in what is known locally as 'the gay triangle'. I have given this a lot of careful thought and I am convinced that calling the gay district 'the gay triangle' can't be a good thing for gay public relations. I mean, never mind *Cruising* – does no one remember Barry Manilow singing about the Bermuda triangle, where 'people disappear'? Think of 'the gay triangle' and you invariably picture a place which, once you enter, you can never escape from. It's an image that plays on every *Daily Mail* reader's worst fears – that their little Jasper will be sucked into the twilight world of the homosexual, never to emerge again. Now, I'm not saying that there aren't gay men out there for whom this pretty much sums up the experience of being gay. I'm sure there are. Indeed, there are people who were seduced into the shadowy world of the gay scene way back when *Cruising* was first released and haven't seen daylight since. And there are others who discovered the bright lights of the 1990s gay scene only a year or two ago and are having such a ball that they never want to re-emerge for as long as they both shall live. If my memory serves me correctly, Manchester seems to have more than its fair share of them. But really, such people are hardly typical. Most gay men I know spend their lives moving freely between different environments, dipping into the gay world as and when their mood (or, more often, their dick) dictates. Few experience any problems finding their way back out again – unless, of course, they happen to have taken far too many drugs that evening and are lost in a 'K' hole. Anyway, the point is that calling the gay area of town 'the gay triangle' doesn't do anybody any favours. It gives straight people the wrong impression and, even worse, it provides gay men with the perfect excuse not to find their way home of an evening. So, if all you Edinburgh queens reading would kindly take note and refrain from using the expression in the future, I would be most grateful.

The irony is that most of the bars in Edinburgh's 'gay triangle' couldn't be further from the image of a gay bar as a gateway to another universe (no leather slings here, thank you). They are the sorts of place where, if you were straight and didn't know that the licensee was gay, you would walk in, order a pint for yourself and a half for the wife, then go and sit on a couple of wicker chairs remarking to one another on how trendy the furniture was, how nice it was to see so many young men wearing their hair short these days and what a shame it was to see so many young girls following the same fashion. I swear I overheard a straight couple having a conversation much along those lines when Ben and I arrived at Café Kudos, a smart little venue on Greenside Place, just next to the Playhouse Theatre. It was a little after ten-thirty p.m. when we arrived and the place wasn't nearly as busy as I'd anticipated. I realized that it was a Wednesday evening, but even so, Edinburgh's gay scene isn't all that big and not everybody could have been at home watching *The X-Files*. Ben explained that ten-thirty was still fairly early for Edinburgh, where it is perfectly legal to serve alcohol twenty-four hours a day. None of the gay bars actually stayed open twenty-four hours, though one, the Phoenix, opened at six a.m. and the rest tended to be busiest between midnight and two a.m. The cliché about the Scots having a taste for alcohol obviously had more than a little truth to it, especially when the Scots in question happened to be gay. I discovered further proof of this when I popped down to the loo. There on the wall was a vending machine selling 'McCondom – Finest Scotch Whisky-Flavoured Condoms'. It didn't say whether or not McCondoms had been approved for anal intercourse, though when a condom tastes of whisky I suppose sticking it up your bottom is the last thing on your mind.

I was still savouring this thought when I returned to our table, to find Ben chatting with an attractive man at the table opposite. It turned out that they had met three years previously and hadn't seen each other since. 'He had a boyfriend at the time,' Ben explained when he returned to his seat. 'He still has. I remember he asked me if I had a problem with that. I said no. It was great. They both had very short hair. It was really bristly.' I deduced from this that young Ben had been the meat in somebody's sandwich, though he later told me that I'd misinterpreted what he'd said. Anyway, I blushed profusely and suggested we move on to a different bar. The place Ben took me to was a few doors down the street and was called C. C. Blooms. Of all the gay disco bars in all the cities in all the world that I have ever visited, this one will remain forever etched on my memory, if only because it is the one bar I know which has the distinction of having been named after the character played by Bette Midler in the hit film *Beaches*. Really, it's enough to make a grown man cry. The upstairs bar was empty, so we headed downstairs to the disco bar, where we stood around for an hour or so, sipping beer and watching a girl with bright red hair bopping about the dance floor with several gay male friends. Maybe it was the alcohol talking, maybe it was the lateness of the hour, or maybe it was the reminders of that great weepie of a movie, but suddenly Ben became terribly maudlin. He told me that he didn't really like going to gay bars. Try as he might, he always seemed to end up feeling awkward. In fact, the only reason he ever came to places like this was to get sex. The problem was, more and more these days, he really wasn't convinced that it was worth the trouble. Looking around at the range of men on display, I could see his point. We drank up and left.

Walking back in the direction of my hotel, discussing the short-comings of the commercial gay scene and the potential setbacks an attractive gay man of twenty-nine might experience in the search for someone to have sex with, we passed Calton Hill, the nearest thing Edinburgh has to London's infamous Hampstead Heath. Only unlike the Heath, which has the added attraction of a local chief superintendent who takes the view that there are far better ways of spending police time than running around trying to catch people with their trousers down, Calton Hill has been the focus of exten-sive police and local media interest. Ben claimed that the *Evening News* had even sent photographers out on to Calton Hill in the dead of night, with express instructions to take pictures of men having sex. Presumably, those same pictures would then be printed in the newspaper, so that any fine, upstanding citizens who hadn't been out walking on the hill that night could still have the oppor-tunity to be shocked and outraged and call for a police clampdown and stiffer sentencing. Ben couldn't tell me exactly how many arrests had been made, and to be honest I wasn't in the mood to push for further information. I don't mind admitting that all this talk of police surveillance operations and media witch-hunts was making me nervous. I mean, here I was wandering through a city I barely knew, with a man I had met only hours ago, in an area where two men seen walking together might be regarded as fair game for a gross-indecency charge, or a spot of good old-fashioned queer-bashing. Believe me, I can think of far better ways of getting my picture in the papers.

Fate being the cruel mistress she is, it was at this precise moment that a large, red-faced man appeared from out of nowhere, waving his arms around and hollering at the top of his voice. 'Hey, you!' he shouted as I prepared to run for my life. 'Are you drunk?'

Discovering that my feet had mysteriously attached themselves to the floor and stammering like a schoolboy, I replied that, no, actually, I wasn't particularly drunk right now, although if he'd asked me a few hours earlier . . . 'Och!' he said, smiling the way I am sure psychopaths do before they cut their victims' throats from ear to ear. 'You're a great guy!' Heaving a huge sigh of relief, I assured him that I thought he was pretty special too. And with that, I thanked Ben for my introduction to Edinburgh's gay scene and ran all the way back to my hotel.

The following morning I rose early, checked out of the Point and made my weary way to the Linden Hotel on Nelson Street, where I had arranged to spend the following night. The Linden claims to be 'Scotland's premier [sic] gay hotel', and for all I know it may well be. But compared to the Point, it was a bit of a comedown. There was no TV in my room for a start and although the ad promised tea- and coffee-making facilities, there was no evidence of a kettle. I then spent half an hour desperately trying to locate the shower, before finally realizing that it had been cunningly disguised as a child's wardrobe and deciding to walk up the hall with a towel wrapped around my waist and take a bath instead. Still, the staff were extremely friendly and very helpful, and the room, though not exactly elegant, was at least clean and tidy. The Linden also has the dubious distinction of being home to what is described as 'Scotland's first Thai restaurant', making it the ideal place to stay if you're gay, have a passion for all things oriental, never travel anywhere without your kettle and can fit quite comfortably inside a child's wardrobe.

Given that my time in Edinburgh was limited, I had planned my day down to the last detail, with a checklist of places to go and people to see. For some reason that I still can't quite work out, top of the list was a visit to the Lesbian and Gay Centre on Broughton Street. Undeterred by the rain (or by my previous experiences of lesbian and gay centres), I set off at the designated hour, clutching a map of the local area – available free of charge from the kind man at the reception desk and decorated with little black arrowheads highlighting all the local places of gay interest, or at least those who had bothered to advertise on the back. The Centre wasn't very far away, though I did wander past it two or three times, it was so small. I don't know quite what I was expecting – a large building with a rainbow banner outside, perhaps, and a selection of meeting rooms where people could hold gay self-defence classes and lesbian twelve-step recovery programmes? Possibly with a gymnasium on the first floor, plus a women-only space and a large front office where membership records and petty cash were stored, staffed by people with previous convictions for fraud? Anyway, it was nothing like that – just a small, discreet shop front, leading into a narrow hallway with a few doors on either side and a stairway down to the basement. All of the internal doors were locked shut, though I did bump into a young lad with straggly purple hair and a pierced nose who informed me that the shop would soon be open for the sale of T-shirts, badges and mugs with slogans such as 'Dykes Unite' written on the side. I decided to pass up this golden opportunity and headed down to the basement, which was basically just another narrow hallway, lined on one side with an exhibition of photographs celebrating the history of gay activism in Edinburgh and on the other with a row of noticeboards.

If the number of notices pinned to these boards was anything to go by, then the spirit of gay community politics is alive and well and currently residing in Edinburgh. A group called GROT (Get Rid of

Them) was encouraging people to vote tactically during the forth-coming general election, in a bid to get rid of local MPs who failed to support lesbian and gay rights. A poster advertising a conference on 'Changing Church Attitudes' asked people to consider whether individual churches were gay-friendly or not, and to come along and find out. A support group for lesbian mothers invited people to get in touch, care of the local One Parent Families Association. And Pride Scotland were calling for more lesbians to get involved in the organization of the annual Lesbian and Gay Pride celebra-tions, stressing that 'even in the "progressive" 90s, queer venues, campaigns and papers are still dominated by the boys'. Next to these notices, and highlighting a very different anxiety about the 'dominating' influence of gay men, was a series of newspaper and magazine cuttings relating to the recent tragedy in Dunblane, the demonizing of Thomas Hamilton as a suspected paedophile and the anti-gay hysteria that had gripped nearby Stirling and was felt to be gradually filtering down to Edinburgh.

The cuttings made sobering reading. In the wake of the Dunblane incident, in which sixteen primary school children and one teacher were killed before Hamilton took his own life, a Scottish Office minister by the name of Lord James Douglas-Hamilton ordered a review of the government's commitment to cracking down on sex offenders. Never ones to miss an opportunity to stir up hatred, a group of Christian fundamentalists and morality campaigners staged a protest outside the twentieth-anniversary cel-ebrations of the Lesbian and Gay Christian Movement in Edinburgh, waving placards invoking Dunblane and calling for 'a total ban on sodomy' in the light of what had happened there. Fears that Thomas Hamilton's crimes would result in a backlash, not just against suspected paedophiles but also against gay men involved in consensual sexual relationships, seemed justified. In the months that followed, a twenty-four-year-old man was jailed for three months after being found on school grounds in Paisley near Glasgow; a seventy-seven-year-old man was sentenced to four years for taking photographs of children at the seaside in Ayrshire; and thirty-seven-year-old Father Gerry Fitzsimmons faced shame and retribution after allegedly groping a sixteen-year-old boy. Of course, had the boy in question been a girl, then any sexual activity that may or may not have taken place would probably have been viewed rather differently. It is one of the peculiarities of British law that while a girl of sixteen is deemed old enough to consent to being fondled by an older man, a boy of sixteen is not. As the remarks made by certain members of Parliament during the recent campaign to reduce the gay male age of consent demonstrate, this inequality in law is partly a manifestation of British society's profound unease about the changing nature of masculinity and panic at the perceived horrors of anal sex. Hence the notion that, while a girl's vagina is a perfectly suitable receptacle for a man's penis by the time she is sixteen years old, a boy's anus should remain sanctified for ever – or at least until he is eighteen and legally entitled to get drunk, whereupon he can take it up the bum as often as he likes and simply blame the alcohol, as generations of allegedly heterosexual British men have done before him.

Not that this is any comfort to Father Fitzsimmons, or to the small gay community of Stirling who, in the period following the Dunblane tragedy, became the focus of a twelve-week police surveillance operation. Following complaints from the parents of a thirteen-year-old boy who suspected that their son was working as a rent boy, police mounted an extensive operation at a local public convenience, using hidden cameras. Questioned by the police, the boy claimed that he had been paid to have sex with a number of men frequenting the toilets. Allegations were later made that the police were using the boy in a deliberate ploy to entrap gay men, in the same way that so-called 'pretty policemen' had been used in the past. The operation resulted in a total of sixty men being questioned, eleven of whom were arrested. Some were charged with the specifically gay 'crime' of gross indecency, others with indecency with a child. In October 1996, one of the men accused of gross indecency, a sixty-year-old rigger named Michael Cummings, committed suicide by leaping from the Forth Bridge. One month later, Cameron Daisley, a forty-eight-year-old youth and community worker for Stirling Council, was found hanging by his neck in the woods near the toilets after being questioned by police about having sex with the thirteen-year-old. Prompted by this appalling turn of events, a local gay man, who wished to remain anonymous, rang Gay Times and spoke of his fears. 'A second man dies after the crackdown on cottaging,' he said, 'and the attitude here is well done police for smashing a paedophile ring. All of a sudden, gay men have become paedophiles. It's very frightening.'

Of course, the reality is that gay men in Scotland hadn't become paedophiles 'all of a sudden'. In the minds of some, that is exactly what they had always been. Charges of child abuse and the corruption of minors have been used to deny gay men equal rights for as far back as anyone can remember – regardless of the fact that the greatest risk of child abuse has always come from within the family. And while I am of the opinion that those who fail to distinguish between consensual gay relationships and the corruption of children clearly have dirty, narrow little minds and ought to look a little closer to home, I also recognize that gay men haven't always acted in their own best interests where such smears are concerned.

Think of the language we use to describe one another, the way we talk about someone being a 'sexy boy' when what we really mean is 'sexy man'. Think of the whole gay obsession with youth and beauty, the idolizing of male pin-ups with 'boyish' good looks, the pursuit of young men described by their elders as 'chicken'. Think of some of the nonsense spouted in the name of 'radical queer politics' – for example, when the Manchester-based queer anarchist collective Homocult produced a leaflet that read: 'Bring Us Your Children. What We Can't Fuck, We'll Eat!' I'm sure that really helped the mothers of Manchester live down the memory of the Moors murders and gain a far greater understanding of why everyone should be nicer to gay people. And while you're wiping the smile off your face, or condemning the actions of a bunch of loony lefties on the fringes of gay society, ask yourself why the most popular gay free paper in Britain happens to be called *Boyz*, and what that says about us to the world at large. I'm not saying that the likes of Lord James Douglas-Hamilton and the Christian fundamentalists who share his vision of the world would like us any better if we stopped being so youth-obsessed. But at least they would have a little less ammunition to throw at us.

By the time I had finished reading about the catalogue of injustices inflicted on the lesbians and gay men of Edinburgh and the surrounding area in the past twelve months (including, I noticed, an arson attack on the West and Wilde bookshop on Dundas Street), I was so thoroughly depressed that I decided to abandon my carefully prepared list of things to do and head back to my hotel – which, hopefully, would still be much as I had left it and not reduced to a pile of smouldering embers. Along the way, I stopped off for a swift pint at the New Town Bar. By night, the New Town Bar is frequented by older gentlemen in leather who act all intense and cruise the aptly named Intense Cruise Bar in the basement (somehow I doubted that there would be any Al Pacino lookalikes among them). By day, it is much like any traditional pub. I ordered a pint and sat at a table by the window. There were three other customers. To my left, a handsome young man was flicking through a copy of *Boyz*. To my right, a slightly older man with very prominent crooked teeth was doing his best to ignore the man next to him – a fairly young, fairly scary-looking fellow with a mohican hairdo and mad staring eyes. Every minute or so, the guy with the mohican would make some loud noise – coughing, clearing his throat or pretending to sneeze – in an attempt to draw attention to himself. Finally, when non-verbal utterances failed him, he resorted to words. 'How do you stop a wedding?' he shouted, in what I immediately recognized as being a Welsh accent. (It is one of the many trials associated with being Welsh that, no matter where you go in the world, however far you stray from the green, green grass and grey, grey skies of home, you will always be accosted by fellow Welshmen, whose only function is to constantly remind you of that part of your life which you had spent many years and many hours of therapy desperately trying to forget. If such people can't track you down, they will invariably pop up in the middle of your favourite television programme, overemphasizing their accents to make up for the fact that they can't be with you in person, and saying the stupidest of things in an attempt to embarrass you in front of your friends.)

'How do you stop a wedding?' the last of the Welsh mohicans shouted again, while I tried to figure out a way of sliding underneath the table undetected. Suddenly, the man to my left looked up from his copy of *Boyz* and shouted back, 'Well, you could try telling her you're gay!' As soon as the words were out of his mouth, I could tell that he dearly wished they weren't. This was the mad-eyed screamer's cue to unload his tale of woe on the assembled company. It began with the revelation that it wasn't he who was getting married but his sister. The problem was that the man she was marrying was a vicar – and not just any old vicar but a gay vicar. He knew this to be true because the vicar in question had tried to kiss him once and now he was going to have to spoil his sister's big day by telling her that the man she was marrying was a closet homosexual. Or at least he would do if he could only get to the church on time. The church, of course, was in Wales. And no, his sister didn't have a telephone, or maybe she did but it wasn't working. The tale ended, as such tales invariably do, with a plea for money – which, being sound of mind and generous of spirit, we all politely ignored.

I left the pub and headed off to the West and Wilde bookshop, where I browsed for half an hour or so, before retreating back to my hotel with a paper bag containing a handful of flyers for local gay clubs and a free copy of *Scotsgay* – 'the magazine for Scots lesbians, gays and bisexuals'. Back in my room, I read *Scotsgay* from cover to cover. This didn't take all that long since there were only twenty-six pages in total, and half of those consisted of listings and adverts for telephone sex lines. Generally speaking, the journalism used to fill spaces between ad sites was of a far higher standard than one normally expects to find in the pages of the gay free press. Possibly because the readership being addressed was far smaller and located in a specific part of the country, there was a sense that what was contained on these pages reflected the concerns of local lesbians and gay men (and bisexuals too, of course), without the usual guff about representing the entire queer community. I read an extremely good article by local gay activist Derek Ogg on the problems of

AIDS education, outlining the various strategies for encouraging gay men to play safely, and describing why in some instances they had failed. His basic argument was that playing on people's fear of contracting the virus was no longer a useful propaganda weapon, since new drug therapies had radically altered the lifestyles and life expectancy of people with HIV and AIDS. In Scotland, Ogg argued, the sexually upfront approach to gay men's health education recommended by experts in the field had been marred by compromise and fear of offending straight sensibilities. Interestingly, he ended by suggesting that those fighting the good fight against AIDS could take hope from the actions of the Gay and Bisexual Equality Network, who had recently stopped a proposal to include gay consenting adult 'sex offenders' as part of the paedophile register, proving that gay men were back fighting for their rights and not caught in a downward spiral of depression, as some might have thought.

As late afternoon merged into early evening, I realized that I hadn't eaten a thing since breakfast, and decided to pop upstairs and sample the cuisine at Buntoms – 'Scotland's first Thai restaurant'. Much to my surprise, it was really rather good. I ate like a pig before returning to my room in a seriously bloated state and collapsing on to the bed. On top of the cupboard next to the bed I found a stack of tourist information guides and turned to an article about the glorious city of Edinburgh and its noble history. It made for illuminating reading. Apparently, between the years 1479 and 1722, no less than 300 women were burned at the stake on Castlehill, accused of practising witchcraft. Soon after I finished reading this, I fell asleep and dreamed for the entire night about being chased across Calton Hill by marauding gangs of newspaper photographers and witch-finder generals, before being burned alive on the doorstep of the West and Wilde bookshop. A bad case of indigestion, obviously.

I spent the best part of my final day in Edinburgh in the company of a man named Aaron and I'm very glad that I did. Had it not been for him, I might have returned home under the misguided impression that the only gay men in Edinburgh were those having their pictures taken on Calton Hill, or those (like Ben) who were tired of the gay scene but didn't know where else to go, or those (like Charlie) who weren't really gay at all. I was given Aaron's number by a mutual friend who suggested that he would be a good person to talk to. All I knew about him was that he worked as a journalist at *Scotland On Sunday*, and was the author of a book, *Boy Soldier*, about the true case of two soldiers locked in an obsessive relationship, one of whom ended up murdering a taxi driver. Aaron suggested we meet at the Blue Moon Café, close to the Lesbian and Gay Centre. From the description he gave me over the phone, I recognized him instantly – a tall, dark, intense twenty-eight-year-old. He told me his father was Israeli (which accounted for his looks) and that he was born and raised in Swindon (which explained his accent). (Funnily enough, I met two people who pronounced their name as 'Arran' during my visit, and neither of them was Scottish. The other, a waiter at the Blue Moon Café, was actually from Gran Canaria.)

Over drinks, Aaron told me a little about himself. He moved to Edinburgh fresh out of university, at the age of twenty-two. Still firmly in the closet when he first arrived, he gradually edged his way out on to Edinburgh's emerging gay scene. He told me an extraordinary story about being picked up by a man named Billy, who invited him back to his house. In the living room was a model of a concentration camp, plus two shelves packed with videos. One shelf was devoted to films about the Holocaust, the other to Disney cartoons. 'The Holocaust was just like a Disney film to him,' said Aaron. 'It was all too much for a nice Jewish boy.' Back then, he knew of only one gay bar in the whole of the city. It was called the Blue Oyster Bar and it closed down shortly after he arrived (though film buffs will note that it was featured in the highly popular *Police Academy* series of films and that the depiction of leather queens dancing the tango didn't go down too well with gay audiences). In those early days, Aaron had one gay friend in Edinburgh, a guy called Mark who allowed him to sleep on his floor and offered to teach him the ways of the gay world. 'He hated the gay scene,' Aaron told me. 'He never went out. He found older men far more attractive than younger men and thought going to the gym was fascist. I felt embarrassed admitting to him that I was attracted to people my own age.' One night at a club, Aaron met a man who seemed to fit the bill. 'He was dancing shirtless and he had a very nice body. We had a week-long romance. I remember being very impressed by his taste in music, his books and his cat. Then one night he told me that he was thirty-nine. It put me off him straight away. I made up some story about not being able to deal with having a relationship at that time in my life and left. I never saw him again after that.' I asked Aaron why he thought he, like so many gay men, was so preoccupied with youth. 'I think it's because I never had romances when I was at school,' he said. 'So you want to make up for it later on.' I told him all this talk about lost youth put me in mind of a line from a song by Marc Almond, where the singer, who is gay and was all of thirty-one at the time, sings, 'I find I'm no longer chasing my youth. The truth is that I'm chasing yours.'

Shortly after breaking things off with the youthful thirty-nine-year-old, Aaron fell in with a group of gay men his own age who used to frequent the Blue Moon. 'They were all in relationships,' he explained. 'And they're all still in those relationships after five years. It gave me an incredible amount of confidence, knowing that gay relationships could work. I realized that there was such a thing as commitment. It wasn't all that dissimilar to my parents in a way. They don't have a lot in common. There are times when you think they can't really love each other. And you couldn't ever imagine them having sex. It was exactly the same with these gay couples. I couldn't imagine them being turned on by each other. They were so different. I couldn't imagine them ever coming together in the first place, let alone staying in the relationship. And in a strange way that was very comforting. It sort of signalled that there were imperfect gay relationships that worked, just as there were imperfect marriages that survived for years and years and years.'

Aaron's own imperfect but working gay relationship was with someone by the name of David. They'd met eighteen months ago when Aaron hired him to decorate his living room. A few weeks later, David moved in. Slightly older than Aaron, David had already served in the army, had a girlfriend and experienced the pressures of a six-year-long gay relationship before becoming a painter-decorator and meeting Aaron. Were they still monogamous, I wondered. 'Yes,' Aaron replied. 'It's harder to be a slag here than somewhere like London, because the gay scene is so much smaller and everyone knows everyone. You can't have a one-night stand in Edinburgh without everybody knowing about it.' Neither he nor David went out on the gay scene very much, he explained, partly because they socialized with heterosexual people a lot of the time and partly because they found most of the bars rather unappealing. 'It's like C. C. Blooms. I mean, it's a bit sad to take your straight friends to. I prefer mixed places, café bars that appeal to a mixture of gays and straights. There's a place called the Out House which is a sort of trendy mixed place, and there's another one called Baroque that we sometimes go to. I just think it's a much better atmosphere. It's far more welcoming in a way.'

From my conversation with Aaron, it struck me that my initial impressions of Edinburgh had been wrong in one vital respect. It may well be a city of two halves, with gay men running around inside 'the gay triangle' or being targeted by the local media, police and judiciary, while the heterosexual majority looks on and says nothing. It may also be a city in which the anxieties about relationships between the old and the young are running at an all-time high. But it is also a city in which gays and straights are coming together, in ways that mean as much as any amount of political campaigning. The thought of two openly gay men in a stable relationship enjoying a drink in the company of a mixture of gay and straight people may not sound particularly revolutionary. But at the very least it means that the next time somebody tries to whip up a bit of anti-gay hysteria by equating homosexuals with child abusers, there will be a few more heterosexuals in Edinburgh who know better.

5

THE GREAT DARK LAD

Essex

Here's a little piece of gay clubland history. Not so very long ago, there was a gay club in the heart of London called Sex. One of those hugely ambitious one-nighters the gay scene throws up from time to time, Sex ran every Friday night at the newly reopened Café de Paris in Leicester Square. It should have been a recipe for success. The venue had exactly the right air of faded glamour – all peeling gold paint and dusty red velvet drapes. The music policy was a fine balance between the credible and the commercial – serious underground house, interrupted by the occasional chart remix. And most importantly, the door policy reflected the early 1990s trend towards mixed gay clubbing, with just a hint of kinky queer fetishism, as modelled by Madonna in her *Sex* book and *Erotica* video. Go-go boys with come-to-bed eyes writhed about on their podiums, dressed in little leather G-strings. Girls in sequined bra-tops jiggled among the crowd. For a short while at least, Sex was the hottest thing in town. The cream of London's queer club scene could be found there, admiring the visuals (most of which featured Madonna striking one of her queer poses), sipping bottled lager or falling down the vast sweeping staircase that led on to the dance floor. Then, just as quickly as they had arrived, the gay glitterati gathered up their Gaultier skirts and left. Faster than you could say 'My name is Dita', Sex became a laughing stock. In a matter of weeks, it became a place no self-respecting scene queen would be caught dead in. In fact, people stopped referring to it as Sex altogether. They started referring to it as Essex.

I offer this story as an illustration of the fact that, for a lot of gay men especially, Essex represents everything that is hopelessly provincial, tediously straight and therefore – cue drumroll – *not at all sexy*! Of course, the irony is that those same gay men would probably drop to their knees at a moment's notice if a man with half a pulse and a strong Essex accent paid them the least bit of attention. It's hardly a coincidence that any male prostitute who places an ad in the back pages of *Boyz* describing himself as an 'Essex Lad' seems to do a booming trade. 'Provincial straightness' can be a powerful aphrodisiac – particularly when it comes knocking on your door in an Umbro top and Adidas trainers, ready to give you a good seeing-to in exchange for £60 cash in hand. Quentin Crisp once observed that the great tragedy of being homosexual was that gay men were all looking for the love of a real man – and yet by their own definition, a real man couldn't be gay. For years, the gay community has been trying to prove old Quentin wrong, but without much success. We may kid ourselves that he was simply a product of his time, imprisoned by his own internalized homophobia, and that we – free, gay, happy and simply bursting with Pride – have grown out of all that self-loathing nonsense. But go to any gay bar in the world and I guarantee you'll find plenty of gay men who get off on the idea of having a straight man to call their own – even if it means desperately trying to embody that straight man themselves. How else do you make sense of those gay contact ads that specify 'straight-acting'? How else do you account for the popularity of gay soft-porn videos with titles like *The Plumber's Mate* and *Rough Enough*? The plain fact is, gay men today are just as obsessed with straight-acting bits of rough as they ever were. Only being the contrary Marys we often are, we like to maintain the illusion that we are somehow above that kind of thing. So we make jokes about Essex in public and turn to the back pages of *Boyz* when our private longings become too much to bear.

Of course, homosexuals aren't the only ones given to making snide remarks about Essex and its people. Essex is the butt of more jokes than any other county in England, and they nearly all involve some monstrous image of heterosexuality. You've heard the sort of thing: 'Why do Essex girls wear large hoop earrings? So they've got somewhere to rest their ankles.' Or the allegedly feminist riposte: 'What does an Essex girl do with her cunt when she goes out? She leaves him at home.' You never hear any jokes about the good people of Essex which suggest they might be anything but heterosexual. In fact, you could be forgiven for thinking that there were no queers in Essex at all. Imagine, though, if you were to find one. What sort of man would he be? The 'Essex Lad' of small-ad fantasies? The 'Great Dark Man' Quentin dreamed of for so long? Or just another provincial queen with dodgy highlights and a chip on his shoulder? I decided to go and find out for myself.

I began my search in Chadwell Heath, Romford, on the London–Essex border. I was drawn to Chadwell Heath by an advert in the gay press for Essex Steam and Sauna. Now I have visited this sort of establishment before, and been overcome at the lack of sexual excitement on offer. Still I had high hopes for Essex Steam and Sauna, not least because it had the word 'Essex' in the title. Most gay saunas have names which try desperately hard to sound exotic and end up sounding completely naff – Tropics for instance, or Pacific 33. Compared to these, Essex Steam and Sauna sounded very straightforward – rather like the sort of man you might hope to meet there. The advert promised 'pleasure rooms', 'steam', 'sauna' and 'free refreshments'. It invited you to 'cum in for a tenner' and 'tan those butts for free'. What it didn't say was that Chadwell Heath is the arsehole of the world and that you might get your head kicked in by a bunch of lanky youths with lanky hair wishing to extend you a good old-fashioned Romford welcome. But hey, that's the power of advertising for you.

It all started pleasantly enough. The train from Stratford East took me via a place called Maryland, which sounded like a wonderful place to live, provided that your name wasn't Mary. I arrived at Chadwell Heath in the middle of the afternoon and what an immediate disappointment it was. The streets were strewn with litter. Worse still, the place was bustling with young men in Versace jeans, with no bums to fill them. I was always under the impression that men in Essex all had big, muscly bums on account of all that standing around discussing football, but obviously I'd been misled. Walking along the road that led from the station, I was verbally abused by two particularly sorry-looking specimens who were evidently obsessed with the thought of what men like me might do with our bums and willies. I put this down to the fact that they clearly didn't have much firsthand experience of either. Hopefully, the same wouldn't be true of the patrons of Essex Steam and Sauna. I had images of burly builder's mates with bottoms you could carry bricks on, soaping each other up in the steam room –

just to release the tension, mind, not because they were actually queer or nuffink.

It didn't take me very long to realize that I was being a little overoptimistic. A friend had given me detailed instructions on how to get to the sauna, insisting that it was right next door to a pub he used to frequent as a teenager. I could see the pub on the horizon – a huge square building with the sort of 'Tudor' finish the people of Essex clearly love so much. Drawing closer, I realized that the building was in fact a shell. The pub had obviously burnt down at some point. All that remained was the outer walls. And there, tucked away in the midst of this burnt-out charcoal ruin, was Essex Steam and Sauna. Well, at least they didn't have to go very far to find fuel for the sauna. And who knows, maybe they were having some building work done? Maybe the place would be teeming with workmen? I stepped gingerly over the rubble and pressed the buzzer. There was a moment's pause, then I was buzzed in. The smile was soon wiped from my face. Words cannot describe the sense of doom that descended on me as I parted with my £10. Inside, Essex Steam and Sauna was just like somebody's grandmother's house – all fluffy carpets and lingering smells. Really, it was as if grandma had gone away on holiday and her gay grandson had installed a sauna cabin and a catering size tub of KY in her absence.

The man responsible for this appalling breach of trust was named Eric. He was one of those camp, cuddly clone types you don't see too many of these days – except, of course, in the studio audience for *Gaytime TV*. 'It's a bit quiet right now,' Eric said as he handed me my towel. 'But it'll get a lot busier in an hour, when the workers start coming in.' He stressed the word 'workers' with a roll of the eyes and a knowing grin. Then he offered to take me on a tour of the 'facilities'. Basically, these consisted of a small sauna cabin, an even smaller steam room, a sunbed that looked as if it would fry you half to death if you were foolish enough to lie on it (I was and it did) and some showers with a few missing tiles and a lot of dodgy-looking wiring overhead. Oh, yes, and there were some private cabins upstairs, plus a wall that appeared to be held up with electrician's tape. Eric explained that he was still in the process of doing the place up. Still, at least he wasn't scrimping on the refreshments. Teas, coffees and glasses of fruit cordial were all included in the price, and there on the reception desk was a large glass bowl filled to the brim with the sorts of fizzy, chewy things children go mad for and gay men in their thirties would be well-advised to avoid.

I took full advantage of Eric's hospitality for the next two hours, even helping myself to a handful of fizzy, chewy things when nobody was looking. Well, I needed something to chew on. There were four other visitors that afternoon, and none of them could rightly be described as Essex lads – three white-haired old men with nimble feet, and a young Oriental chap with a well-developed chest, who spent most of his time running up and down the stairs dodging their attentions, before making a discreet getaway. 'The workers' Eric had promised me never showed up. I left Chadwell Heath a broken man. Then I decided to get over myself and plunge deeper into the heart of Essex in my search for the illusive gay lad.

There are some things that even the most detailed map can't show you. Take Chelmsford, for example. Pick up a map and you'll see that Chelmsford is a town populated by between 30,000 and 100,000 people, and situated right in the centre of Essex. But really it's so much more than that. Chelmsford is the archetypal Essex town – exceedingly suburban, completely characterless. The very place, in fact, where you might expect to find lads in abundance.

And imagine how perfect it would be if one of them happened to be gay.

I travelled to Chelmsford with my friend Steve Pitron. Steve used to live in Southend-on-Sea and spent a great deal of his spare time in Chelmsford before moving to London a couple of years ago. He works for a music company and is pursuing a career as a DJ (though if that doesn't work out, he could always try placing one of those ads in the back pages of *Boyz*. He won't thank me for saying this, but with those looks and that accent, he would never be short of business). Steve didn't come out as gay until he was twenty-one, though he was well acquainted with the Chelmsford gay scene long before then. The reasons for this aren't nearly as straightforward as you might expect. Several years ago, Steve was working in a local record shop. Steve's friend David had recently broken up with a girl called Zöe. Steve met Zöe and they became lovers. Not wishing to hurt David's feelings, or provoke a fight, our latter-day Romeo and Juliet decided to hide their love away in gay pubs and clubs. Well, it makes sense, doesn't it? What better place to conceal a heterosexual liaison from the rest of the heterosexual world than in a gay venue? The only foreseeable problem would be if the gay punters decided that that wasn't all you were concealing and took a bit of a shine to the man in question – which, of course, they did. Still, a bit of unwanted attention in a gay bar was a damn sight better than a brawl in the street. And as we now know, there was always a part of Steve that quite liked the attention anyway.

One day, Steve was offered a job as a DJ at the Army and Navy pub in Chelmsford, which is gay every Wednesday and Sunday night (the pub that is, not the place. According to Steve, the place was gay every night of the week. You had only to look at some of the people coming into the record shop to know that). Although he still identified as straight, Steve felt very much at home at the Army and Navy. The manager teased him about being in the closet, and when Zöe decided to shave all her hair off in honour of Sinead O'Connor, the rumour spread that she and Steve were some sort of radical queer couple. Still, as introductions to the gay scene go, Steve's was fairly painless. By the time he came out, he was already pretty familiar with the gay lifestyle – it was only the sex part he needed to get some practice at. Three years later, Steve still keeps in touch with the people he met during his Army and Navy days. And despite the fact that he is now happily settled in a gay relationship, Zöe remains one of his closest friends.

We caught a rush-hour train to Chelmsford, arriving shortly after six. Maybe it was just a trick of the light, or maybe it was a hormonal imbalance brought on by all the excitement, but my initial impression was that everything in Chelmsford was shiny and new. The university building opposite the train station was gleaming. The paved walkways around the shopping centre were spotless. The local branch of Habitat looked as though it had opened for business only yesterday. Compared to Chadwell Heath, Chelmsford was practically sparkling. And without wishing to discourage the people of Chelmsford in their efforts to keep Britain tidy, I have to say that it was actually quite sinister in a way. I mean, this is what Stepford looked like. In fact, I wouldn't have been at all surprised if Nanette Newman had floated by in a frilly frock, announcing to all and sundry that she'd simply die if she didn't get that recipe.

Obviously, my blood-sugar levels were dangerously low. I suggested to Steve that it might be a good idea if we went for something to eat. Minutes later, we were perusing the menu at a terribly inauthentic Mexican restaurant called Chi Chi's. Well, we had to! How can you go to a place like Chelmsford with the express purpose of identifying homosexual life-forms and pass up the chance to eat at a place called Chi Chi's? At first, I was disappointed. Looking around, it was evidently the kind of place where straight couples came for a special night out. Women with fluffy hairdos and white silk blouses sat opposite men with shaved temples and wide-shouldered suits, happily fulfilling their prescribed gender roles as they tucked into a taste of the exotic. Say what you like about heterosexuals, at least they know a thing or two about courtship. For your average straight couple, 'a special night out' means a romantic dinner for two, consumed by candle-light and preferably at the sort of restaurant where you place your order by pointing at the menu. For a gay couple, it means hanging around cruise bars and backrooms, and inviting a few new friends back for a gang-bang. I had a strong sense that our waiter would have known exactly what I meant. 'Where's the toilet?' I asked when he came to take our order. His reply was a dead giveaway: 'Do you know where Waitrose is? Well, turn left there, then walk towards Debenhams . . . Nah, only joking. It's just up the stairs.' All this, delivered with a knowing smirk and just the hint of a lisp. How very chi-chi. Satisfied that Chelmsford really was as gay as Steve had made it out to be, I tucked into my tostada with more enthusiasm than it deserved. See what a chance homosexual encounter can do to a man's critical faculties? It's almost frightening.

Thankfully, I had regained my composure by the time we arrived at the Army and Navy. Picture, if you will, an enormous mock-Tudor building set on the edge of a busy roundabout, normally populated by rock fans but tonight filled with the sorts of people whose idea of an exciting night out is a trip 'up town' to Benjy's. For the benefit of those readers who haven't experienced it for themselves, Benjy's is a gay disco held every Sunday in the heart of

London's East End. That's 'disco', not 'club' – if you catch my drift. Anyway, we were barely inside the Army and Navy when I overheard a skinny young man in a shiny blue shirt reporting back to his lesbian friends on what a wonderful time he'd had at Benjy's a few nights earlier. 'See, I told you, didn't I?' one of the lesbians said with a smug look on her face. 'I told you to go weeks ago and you wouldn't listen. I knew you'd enjoy it and I was right.' Credit where credit is due, but had I been in her shoes, I don't think I would have been quite so keen to broadcast the fact that I had sent a friend of mine to Benjy's, no matter how good a time they said they'd had.

The remaining thirty or so punters were a fairly mixed bunch. There were quite a few youngish women with brightly coloured hair and a handful of men who looked as though they would have been far happier chasing Oriental boys around Essex Steam and Sauna. But apart from a few gay couples huddled together in the corners, there was no sense of anyone having designs on fellow patrons of the Army and Navy. The atmosphere was completely devoid of sexual charge. Personally, I found this to be a refreshing change from the norm. However, I did wonder whether I would feel quite the same if this were my one chance in the week to pick up. That's the thing with gay sex – one minute you're having it shoved in your face from every angle, the next there's not a sniff of it to be found. Luckily, gay men have adapted to this situation remarkably well, to the point where they can go without sex for anything up to seventy-two hours before gorging themselves at the next available opportunity.

Steve had arranged for us to meet up with some friends of his – Zöe and a gay friend called Mark Dooris ('that's "Doris" with an extra "o"'). Steve explained that he'd known Mark for years and that he was the sort of person who really ought to be on the stage.

I've yet to meet a gay man who didn't act as if he really ought to be on the stage, but I didn't say this to Steve. Instead I said something like, 'Mine's a pint', before heading off to the toilets to scan the graffiti for evidence of any lad-type activity. There wasn't very much. Someone had scratched 'Rockers are Queer' on the back of the door and someone else had written 'Chas and Dave' below it. Whether this was a reference to those well-known cider-drinkers I couldn't say, but I can't imagine them going down very well in Chelmsford. One thing I do know for certain is that if my name was 'Luke from Leigh-on-Sea' I wouldn't go to the Army and Navy again in a hurry. 'Luke from Leigh-on-Sea has a tiny penis from you-know-who,' it said in one cubicle. 'Luke from Leigh-on-Sea is a fucking tosser,' it said in the next. And in the third and last cubicle there was yet another message: 'Luke from Leigh-on-Sea is a cunt by Ivan.' Evidently, poor old Luke from Leigh-on-Sea had done something to upset someone. I quite fancied the thought of making his acquaintance. Aside from having a tiny penis, Luke sounded like a bit of a lad.

By the time I'd finished scouring the toilets for further clues as to the nature of Luke's crime, or maybe just his phone number, Zöe and Mark were sat with Steve at the bar. I liked Zöe instantly. Maybe it was the prettiness of her face. Maybe it was the way she laughed at my jokes. Or maybe it was just the sense that she was a thoroughly decent human being. Zöe grew up 'in the middle of nowhere', which I took to mean anywhere that didn't have a branch of Habitat and a Mexican restaurant to boast of. To her, Chelmsford was 'like the buzzing metropolis'. She was very keen that I didn't get the wrong impression of the place. 'I'm singing Chelmsford's praises cos it gets a real knocking sometimes,' she said earnestly. 'It's not such a bad place really. It's got some nice recreational parks.' She went on to explain that she worked with mentally handicapped children. I asked her if she enjoyed her work. 'Oh, yeah,' she replied. 'And it's really secure – y'know, cos they'll always need you, won't they?' She blushed. 'I didn't mean that the way it sounded.' I assured her that I was certain she didn't.

Mark was a different story altogether. He was wearing a vaguely punky ensemble, topped off with a bleach-blond mohican. He explained that he had just returned from a day out in Brighton, where he'd taken a gram of sulphate. Even now, he was clearly speeding off his face. Luckily for all concerned, he possessed a brain that kept up to speed with his mouth. I asked him what he thought of Chelmsford and he launched into a series of one-liners. 'It's the sort of place where, at fourteen, girls have a pregnancy test instead of an IQ test. Then at sixteen they have a fertility test if they aren't already pregnant. And it's quite a rich area. People in Chelmsford get out of the bath to have a fart. The other rule is – the bigger the dog, the smaller the house. People who live in a small flat always have a Dobermann. The girls all get jobs in Debenhams and Habitat. They've all got babies a year old, a toddler called Justin at playgroup and a boyfriend who works in the City. The genetic throwbacks here are fabulous, though. You wouldn't believe it. You see these women walking around looking like Chrissie from *Man About the House*. Honestly, they all look as if their eyes are about to pop out of their heads. By the way, don't go for a makeover at Debenhams. They only do one eyebrow, cos they've only done half the course. They get some poor girl sitting there and then they promote a product they can't afford. It doesn't matter, though, cos everyone here goes shoplifting anyway. The housewives are all shoplifting for attention. Their husbands won't go down on them, so they go shoplifting all day. Either that, or they sit at home inhaling hairspray. Do you know what the best thing about Chelmsford is? The A12 to London.'

Mark's own personal history, when I finally managed to extract it from him, was a pretty colourful one. He was brought up in Epping before moving to Chelmsford with his mother (he never mentioned his father and it didn't seem polite to ask). At fourteen, he got into 'the whole New Romantic thing' and started sneaking off to gay clubs in the West End, dressed in leopard-print skirts and evening gloves ('I wasn't aware that I was gay,' he said. 'I was just into dressing badly.') One night at Heaven, he was chatted up by a man who offered him some head. 'I didn't know what it was. I knew I had to be cool, but I thought it was some kind of drug, so I just said, "Not tonight. I've got school in the morning, but any other time I'd love to."' I asked Mark if he could recall the first time he had gay sex. 'What, pleasurable?' he replied. No, I said, just the first. 'I'm just trying to remember when it was ever good,' he said, laughing. 'I can't stand all that "oh yeah fuck me" stuff. Get a life! I haven't got blue eyeshadow and a load of Dralon behind me. You can talk real!' Finally, he revealed that he first had gay sex at the age of eighteen. 'But I was still denying I was gay when I was twenty-seven.' He was thirty-one now.

A year after he began his forays into the London gay scene, Mark's mother received a call from the police. 'I was in Camden, pissed out of my brain. I was wearing my mother's evening gloves, some earrings I'd shoplifted and what I thought was a radical suit, one with big shoulder pads. It was my David Sylvian look – the suit anyway. The police picked me up trying to hitchhike home. I got abusive. They wouldn't believe me when I said I was eighteen. They phoned my mum. She thought I was at my friend's house doing homework. The thing was, my friend's mum was having a breakdown. She used to tell us about London and put make-up on us. Peacock-green eyeshadow – please! Anyway, the police called my mum and she came to pick me up. She was livid.' Was Mark any closer to his mum now, I wondered. 'I try not to be. We get on OK. She's a strict Catholic, though. Holy water, all that. She even started giving me pills to sort out my homosexuality. Personally, I think she was more worried about me wearing her frocks. I was born with her legs, you see. She always said that. She finds it very worrying. I always say she brought me up to be gay. When I was little she used to sit me on her bed and say, "What pendant shall I wear?" I was the one who taught her how to wear bouffant wigs.'

These days, Mark has developed a bit of a wig habit of his own. He has even been known to stagger around Chelmsford late at night dressed in full drag. 'I went out one night dressed as Patsy and fell over drunk on the bonnet of someone's car. I met this butcher a few days later. I was being very butch at the time. I can do butch. Anyway, he said to me, "You were pissed the other night, you were lying on my car. By the way, you've got great legs."' The way he described it, it seemed to me as though Mark enjoyed the attention he received from straight men when he went out dressed in drag far more than he enjoyed the company of other cross-dressers. 'I go to trannie clubs in town and they're all there sipping their little drinks and I'm there with a pint and a straw. They're all, "Look at her!" The thing is, I've got no problems with my femininity. Real women drink pints.' Egged on by Steve and Zöe, Mark revealed that he was considering doing a 'proper' drag act. 'I've had lots of different drag names. Nichola Teen. Sheila Blige. Gypsy Creme. I've decided I want to do a drag act called "Brenda Brown – More Than Just a Housewife". I'd just stand in a kitchen and make Brevils and Pop Tarts.' Somehow, I didn't doubt it for a moment.

By the time Mark had finished outlining his ambitions to be on the stage, it was time for Steve and me to leave. Zöe offered us a lift to the train station, which meant that we arrived five minutes before our train was due. Directly opposite the station was a fast-food place called Chicken DFC (I've no idea what the 'DFC' stood for – 'Dead Fried Chicken', maybe?). We decided to grab a bag of chips for the journey. Standing at the counter were two women in their late thirties, obviously heading home after a night out on the town – both drunk, both with tight perms, both wearing fake-fur jackets and what looked suspiciously like peacock-green eyeshadow. The man behind the counter was sitting staring into the deep-fat fryer with a far-off look on his face. I asked him whether we'd have to wait long for a bag of chips. The woman nearest to me almost bit my head off. 'We were first,' she snapped. I explained that I was well aware of this fact. I was merely asking if there was going to be a delay because my friend and I had a train to catch. 'Yeah, well, we've got to get a taxi,' she snapped again, with a smile to her friend that said she was pleased with the sharpness of this retort. Obviously, somebody had inhaled far too much hairspray that day.

There was nothing else for it. I had to go all the way – all the way to the furthest reaches of Essex. Then, perhaps, I might finally find what I was looking for. Together with my good friend Carl Miller, I caught the Great Eastern Railway from Liverpool Street to Southend-on-Sea. Carl is an Essex boy born and bred. Our train journey took us through Seven Kings, a commuter town where he spent the first eighteen years of his life. Seven Kings wasn't a bad place to grow up gay, he reckoned, largely because everyone living there seemed to be on their way somewhere else and was far too preoccupied with their own upward mobility to even notice when the next-door neighbour's son started acting a bit funny. Carl started acting a bit funny around the age of fourteen. This consisted of skipping games lessons and sneaking off to the West End to watch matinée performances of popular musicals. At fifteen he started hanging around bookshops and flicking through pamphlets about revolutionary gay consciousness. He would then relay this information to his schoolmates, who were somewhat bemused by all his talk of autonomous teenage sexuality and demands for an end to the age of consent. While other boys were picked on for being effeminate, Carl was running around shouting, 'I'm a poof! Shag me now!' Not surprisingly, this tended to intimidate people. Carl finally had his wish granted following a performance of *Twelfth Night* – his high school production, in which he starred alongside the boy who became the object of his affections (and who is now, incidentally, a well-known and very closeted stage actor). Later, he discovered the joys of hanging around Southend bus station, waiting to be picked up by older men with nice warm cars and a wife tucked away at home. It might not sound like the obvious route to becoming a happy, well-adjusted, self-assured homosexual, but it was a lot cheaper than hanging around gay bars. And, as Carl says, by the time he was in a position to go out on the gay scene, he had a strong sense of who he was and what he wanted, and was therefore far better equipped to deal with some of the situations a young scene queen can find himself in. The fact that Carl has been in a stable relationship for the past fourteen years seems to bear this out.

As well as being a place where young homosexuals are encouraged to blossom and grow, Seven Kings is a stopover point for people getting out of the East End and moving on to an altogether more beautiful life in Chigwell. The way Carl described it, it's also a pretty multicultural place – home to a mixture of Irish, Asian, Jewish and black families. Or, as Carl put it, 'a melting pot of half-melted commuters'. Our train stopped for a few minutes at Seven Kings before moving on to Shenfield (where Carl's grandfather once lived in a blacksmith's cottage), then Billericay (Harvey Proctor's old constituency), Rayleigh (named after Essex's first gay couple, Ray and Leigh, or so Carl said), Hockley ('home of a little-known Essex painter'), Prittlewell and finally Southend. By the time the train pulled into Southend Victoria we were both pretty desperate for the loo (Great Eastern Railways clearly didn't see the point of such facilities) and headed straight for the toilet on the platform, closely followed by two officers of the law. Now I don't know about you, but I find it pretty hard to pee when there's a police officer breathing down my neck. Really, it's a wonder I wasn't arrested, standing there with my penis in my hand and not so much as a drop of proof that my intentions were lawful. Meanwhile, Carl had locked himself in a cubicle and was chatting away to me quite happily. Maybe it was the tone of our conversation that finally convinced our friendly policemen that we weren't about to re-enact scenes from a Roman orgy, or maybe they simply decided that they had better things to do. In any event, we left Southend Victoria station without handcuffs or loss of liberty, and stepped out into the street, just in time to see the light fade over the Royal Shopping Centre.

Is there anything more depressing than a seaside town out of season? I have it on good authority that Southend can be quite beautiful in the summer. Tonight, though, it was pretty grim. In fact, it put me in mind of that Morrissey song, the one where everyone's favourite miserablist goes 'trudging slowly over wet sand' in 'the seaside town they forgot to close down', praying for a

nuclear war to come and blow the whole damn thing away. We
were still half a mile from the seafront and already it felt as if the
nuclear war had come and gone. It was barely six o'clock and there
was hardly a sign of life. We walked along Victoria Plaza and we
didn't see a soul. We strolled down Queen's Mall and up Princess
Walk and we didn't hear a thing. We passed half a dozen shops
with signs that said 'Anything for £1' and they were all empty.
Clearly, there was life in Southend – shops with names like House
Proud and Kid's Stuff gave some indication as to the kind of life it
might be – but tonight it felt as if the entire town had shut down
for the winter.

   We wandered into Woolworths. The girl at the cash desk didn't
look very pleased to see us. I assumed that this was because we
were the only customers and she was about to lock up and go home.
I could feel her eyes boring into the back of my neck as we wandered past the Pick 'n' Mix, but I didn't care. I was determined to
find some proof that not everyone in Southend was obsessed with
keeping their house nice and having children. And lo and behold,
I found it – a pile of Marc Almond CDs and a Barbra Streisand trib-
ute book, complete with a cover line that read, 'I don't feel like a
legend. I feel like a work in progress.' I left Woolworths feeling
thoroughly vindicated. I even bought a packet of batteries and
some Mint Imperials on the way out, just to show that there were
no hard feelings. Next stop Waterstone's, where Carl wasted little
time in locating the gay section. We spent a very pleasant ten minutes scanning the shelves for the most entertaining titles (*How to be
a Happy Homosexual* still gets me every time) and rearranging the
books to our own satisfaction. Just as we were about to leave, my
eye was drawn to a display close to the door. Some enterprising
member of the Waterstone's sales team had taken the trouble to

arrange two neat piles of special offer books right next to one another. The first was entitled *A History of Phallus Worship*; the second was called *The Goblin Companion*. If the man who put that little display together isn't a cocksucker, then my name is Barbra.

You probably don't know this, but Southend prides itself on the fact that it has 'the longest pleasure pier in the world'. I know because there's a sign right next to it, emblazoned with those very words. As we stood taking in the sea air, Carl and I agreed that there was something really rather poignant about that sign. The pier certainly looked very long, though from where we were standing there didn't appear to be much in the way of pleasure taking place on it (proof, I feel, that it isn't the length of your projectory that matters, but what you do with it. Luke from Leigh-on-Sea please take note). The kiosks where one would normally expect to buy ice creams and candy floss were all boarded up. Huge stretches of the pier were completely empty. All in all, it looked pretty desolate. I suppose this was to be expected. In places like Southend, the pleasure only really begins when the summer season starts, and families flock to the British coastline to relive dreams of the kinds of golden seaside holidays that only ever existed in the mind of Enid Blyton.

Still, I did find it rather odd that the pier in winter wasn't the focus for a different kind of pleasure. I mean, everyone knows the old adage that when the hets are away the homos will play. The area surrounding the pavilion in Brighton is rumoured to be a favourite haunt of gay gentlemen in search of a bit of company. I once paid a visit to an old lady in Brighton – the grandmother of a close female friend – who left me in little doubt as to the peculiarly gay character of the place. 'Look what they've done to it,' she said, gesturing out of the window. 'They come here with their funny clothes and their funny voices and then they hang around the pavilion all night, getting up to all kinds of mischief. It's a wonder the police don't just lock them all up. Brighton used to be the Queen of the South, you know. Now it's just Sodom by the Sea!' Somehow, I couldn't imagine anyone describing Southend in such florid terms. And for some reason, that saddened me.

We walked along the seafront, which was open for business but didn't appear to be doing any. Mostly, it consisted of noisy, brightly lit amusement arcades with names like New York and Las Vegas in pink neon, and the sorts of amusing games where you insert £17.50 into a glass box with a mechanical claw in the middle in the vain hope of winning a little teddy bear holding a red cushion with the words 'I Wuv U' on the front. In my limited experience, amusement arcades are precisely the sorts of place where you might expect to run into attractive young lads who will gladly offer you the pleasure of their company in exchange for whatever funds you haven't already invested in the pursuit of less satisfying amusements. But not here. Every now and then a man with a baggy shirt and a stumpy little ponytail would walk up to one of the machines, put some money in, then stare really hard at it for a few minutes before walking away again. And as if that wasn't enough excitement for one evening, there was always the Rainbow Funfair, which, like the amusement arcades, was pretty empty but insisted on sounding like it was having the time of its life. Somehow, it reminded me of a life not so very different from my own. It was like a gay theme park without the sex. It was ghastly.

Walking on, we passed a guesthouse called the Hope Hotel (which sounded about right) and a pub called the Cornucopia (which didn't). Further along, there were a series of restaurants and takeaways. I suddenly realized that I was feeling rather hungry and that some good old British seaside fare would be just the thing. Carol's Licensed Restaurant sounded promising, as did the Kingfisher Diner ('fish, chips, kids meals served all day') and the Neptune Fishbar. Sadly, all three were closed. The only seafront restaurant open was the Orient Express, which sold pizza, pasta, grills, steaks, kebabs and chicken burgers – everything, in fact, apart from the kind of food you might describe as Oriental in origin. Clearly, we weren't going to find anything resembling a traditional fish bar open at the ridiculous time of seven p.m., so we did the next best thing and headed for the Chinese district, where we enjoyed a true taste of the Orient at the Chinatown Restaurant. If you're ever in Southend, I strongly recommend you pay this place a visit. You shouldn't have any trouble finding it. It's right next door to the Southend offices of the South East Essex Chinese Association.

There is one gay bar in Southend. It's called the Cliff Hotel and it has a listing entry in *Gay Times* which says 'music, drag, DJ'. It should really say 'lesbians, perms, pool table', but I suppose that would be considered offensive. We arrived at the Cliff around eight-thirty, stuffed to the gills with shark-fin soup and chicken chowmein and having made a quick detour via the bus station for old times' sake. Inside, the Cliff was much like any other provincial gay pub. There were about forty men and women distributed pretty evenly around the place, although it would be fair to say that the older ones tended to hide themselves away in the snug at the back. The main bar was dominated by a pool table, which in turn was dominated by a group of lesbians with big perms and waistcoats. In one corner of the room was a small cabaret stage, with a chalk noticeboard to one side announcing forthcoming attractions in large, swirly, multicoloured lettering. 'Fancy Dress Charity Night!'

it said. 'Raffle and Prizes! Golden Oldies Music, '50s–'80s! Proceeds to Charity!' It was all too much for some people. In the bottom left-hand corner of the noticeboard, someone had inserted a little announcement of their own. Scribbled in plain white chalk were two words: 'Tracey's birthday'. I never found out who Tracey was, but Tracey, love, if you're reading this – happy birthday.

The one thing distinguishing the Cliff from most gay pubs was the choice of music on the jukebox – '90s indie, rather than '80s disco. The moment we arrived, someone put on 'The Female of the Species' by Space. I really can't emphasize strongly enough how thoroughly appropriate this record turned out to be. The female inhabitants of the Cliff were indeed more deadly than the male – at least where the pool table was concerned. They may have had the biggest, fluffiest, girliest perms I had ever seen on a group of lesbians, but they were old-fashioned butches at heart. And boy, could they play pool. They were slaughtering the men left, right and centre. I watched in awe as one male contender after another marched up to the table to try his luck and was ritually humiliated. I confess I took particular pleasure in the defeat of one man with bleach-blond hair and jeans pulled half-way up his back, who made a point of bending over the table at every opportunity, while simultaneously tilting his head back so that the assembled company could admire the enormous lovebite on his neck. He obviously had fantasies about being fucked over a pool table. He was, but not in the way he'd hoped. Mark my words – somewhere in this great country of ours there is a factory churning out pool tables especially designed for gay pubs, with a pair of killer lesbian pool players free with every purchase.

We sat at the bar and ordered a drink. A double vodka and tonic cost only £1.65, which included a five-pence donation to a local hospice for the terminally ill. (Oh, well, I thought, drink enough of these and I'll recoup that five pence one day.) At the end of the bar was a pile of newspapers. I picked up a local freesheet, the *Yellow Advertiser*. The headline was rather bewitching: 'Woof Justice? Council tight-lipped over police allegations.' The story involved some local mayor or other who was facing prosecution for 'a public-order offence involving a dog'. At no point in the article did it say what the exact nature of the offence was, merely that the mayor denied all allegations and that his fellow Liberal Democrats on the council were standing by him. 'This does not affect the party because it is to do with the individual,' one councillor was quoted as saying. 'What they do in their private lives is nothing to do with politics at all.' And people accuse the Lib Dems of having no principles to stand on.

I flicked through the *Yellow Advertiser*, pausing over such headlines as 'Handbag theft', 'Barracks future under microscope' and 'Have you seen a Space Ranger?', until finally I reached the property guide. This was divided into sections, with the name of an estate agent above each one. There was 'Town & Country', which seemed to have an awful lot of properties in places called Thundersley and Benfleet. Below it, there was 'Tudor', which specialized in Tudor-style homes in and around Southend. A two-bedroom flat was advertised for £35,000, a three-bedroom house with 'period kitchen' for £49,000. I was about to relay all this to Carl when I was interrupted by a couple of men in their early thirties, both dressed in business suits. 'Anything interesting in there?' one of them said. I replied by offering him the paper, and asking if he was looking to buy somewhere. 'Oh, no,' he said. 'I'd just like to see whether anyone I know has got their house in there, and what they reckon it's worth.'

Thanks to Carl's extraordinary procuring capabilities, I did manage to talk to one person at the Cliff who wasn't obsessed with the value of his friends' homes, didn't have a lovebite on his neck and hadn't been publicly humiliated by lesbians. His name was Jamie, he was twenty-one and he was without a doubt the nearest thing I'd seen to a gay lad since embarking on my tour of Essex. My, was he handsome – short blond hair, dazzling blue eyes, a strong jaw and a complete lack of self-awareness that made his many physical attributes all the more attractive. Clearly, I wasn't the only person in the room who thought so. If looks could kill, I'd be festering under Southend pleasure pier by now. Jamie had spent most of the evening talking on the payphone, smoking like a true labourer and declining offers of drinks from unwanted admirers. Largely due to Carl explaining that I was writing a book and that he would be immortalized in print, Jamie was willing to accept a drink from me. (And they say a writer's life is a lonely hell. Trust me, there are compensations.)

Jamie had been coming to the Cliff since he was sixteen, though for the past year he'd been living in London and working as an 'operations manager' at one of the swish gay café-bars in the West End. Unfortunately, he was forced to give up his job when his employer decided to do everything by the book, which meant that he would have had to pay tax – the salary just wasn't enough to live on. He moved back to Southend two months ago and was living with his nan. Southend was boring, he said. Carl's and mine were the first new faces he'd seen at the Cliff in years. He didn't plan to stay around for very long. He'd recently enrolled on a management training course. The first chance he got, he'd be back in London.

I could have talked to Jamie for hours – if only to watch the looks on the faces of the Cliff regulars become more bitter and twisted with each passing moment. Unfortunately, we had a train to catch. Heading back to the station, we passed the local tourist information centre. Displayed in the window were a number of promotional videos about life and leisure in Southend. One was dedicated to local wildlife and claimed to show 'surprising features of interest in Southend's parks, gardens, roadsides, villages, church-yards and even wasteground'. Another was entitled *Southend – the Playground of the South*. Well, yes, I thought, if your idea of a play-ground is a ghostly pleasure pier, a few amusement arcades and a room full of lesbians playing pool.

Sitting on the train, my thoughts turned to Jamie and his predicament. Naturally, I could understand why someone in his situation would want to get out of Southend as fast as they could. But the thought of him moving back to London worried me deeply. At this moment in time, Jamie possessed something that most gay men spend half their lives trying to recapture. And I don't just mean his youth. There was something very special about him, something unstudied, something rare and precious. He was real in a way that men who place ads describing themselves as 'Essex Lads' are never quite real, and all the more sexy for it. Moving back to London would be his undoing, I was certain of it. Six months from now, he would be dancing on a podium in a little leather G-string, working hard at being sexy and wondering where all the hordes of admirers had gone. And it just didn't seem right somehow.

6

SEX, LIES, RELIGION

Belfast

In Belfast there are many strange forces fighting for possession of a man's soul. Are you a Loyalist or a Republican? A Protestant or a Catholic? Do you swear allegiance to the Queen, the Pope or the IRA? Are you an Orangeman or is emerald green more your colour? And pray pardon me for asking, but which side of the church do you sit on? It's hardly surprising, given Belfast's special significance in the history of the Irish conflict, but this is a city where questions of identity linger in the air like gunsmoke. Even in these times of peace talks, cease-fires and dreams of an end to the violence of the past thirty years, deciding who you are, what you believe in and how far you're prepared to go to stand up for it can still mean the difference between life and death. In Belfast, people truly know the meaning of 'identity politics'. God forbid that, on top of all the other questions of identity a person is forced to consider, they might also turn out to be gay.

On paper, Ireland as a whole has one of the worst records on gay civil rights in the whole of Western Europe. Prior to 1993, all forms of gay male sexual activity were completely illegal in the Irish Republic, where the teachings of the Catholic Church continue to mould public opinion, if not the law. Indeed until very recently, the Republic represented one of the last model Catholic states anywhere in the world. Abortion, contraception, divorce and homosexuality were all severely frowned upon – and to some extent still are. Things are slightly different in the largely Protestant stronghold of the North, although here again the influence of the Church shouldn't be underestimated. Catholicism may not be the most progressive of religions, but nor is Ulster Unionism in its many varieties particularly liberal in its outlook. When homosexuality in Britain was partially decriminalized in 1967, the change in the law wasn't extended to Northern Ireland. In fact, it took fourteen years and a prolonged European Court battle before those British gay citizens living in Northern Ireland could begin to enjoy the same degree of freedom as those on the mainland. Opposition came from many quarters, but none so vociferous as the Reverend Ian Paisley, leader of the Democratic Unionist Party, who will go down in history as the man who tried (and failed) to 'Save Ulster From Sodomy'.

Historically, attitudes towards homosexuality in Ireland have been closely tied up with the conflict, in all its political and religious complexity. The story of the Irish conflict is a very long and highly emotive one – far too long and far too emotive for me, a Welshman who upped and left his homeland at the first opportunity, to even attempt to sum up here. But there are a few key dates and people that deserve a mention, especially as they relate to the history of homosexuality in Ireland and the public perception of it. It is generally thought that Christianity was first exported to Ireland from England in the fifth century AD. In the years that followed, monasteries sprang up everywhere and Christian laws were extended to cover all aspects of life – including what people did in the privacy of their own mud hut. The first recorded reference to homosexuality in Ireland was made by a seventh-century Christian abbot named Cummean Fota. In fact, so obsessed was our man Cummean with homosexuals and their evil ways that he didn't just make a passing negative reference to homosexuality and leave it at that. Oh, no. He actually spent the best part of his life compiling detailed tables in which he described various gay sex acts (e.g. sodomy, oral sex, mutual masturbation), before indicating what he thought their appropriate punishment should be. These days, a man with Cummean's obvious talents could earn a modest living publishing self-help manuals for gay sado-masochists. What satisfaction his activities brought him back then is anybody's guess.

The monasteries may have been a breeding ground for men like Cummean and his kind, but they did at least provide the basis for some sort of state education, not to mention a relatively stable form of government. This, combined with easy access to the Continent, meant that Ireland soon gained a reputation for being at the forefront of European thought. Sadly, it couldn't last. Invasions by the Vikings and Anglo-Normans set a trend that was to continue for centuries. Gradually, Ireland was subjugated to English rule. The English invasion gathered pace during the sixteenth and seventeenth centuries, during the lengthy reigns of Henry VIII and Elizabeth I. The monasteries were dissolved and Irish land carved up and distributed among English settlers. The so-called policy of plantation remains the most lasting legacy of this period and is often cited as a direct cause of 'the Irish problem'. Significantly, it was also during this period that the English laws on buggery – 'an abominable crime', punishable by death – were directly transposed to Irish law. This was largely thanks to the efforts of one Reverend John Atherton, an English cleric who was making quite a name for himself in the emerging Irish Protestant Church. Unfortunately for the reverend, his glittering career came to an abrupt end when he was hoisted by his own petard and hung for the crime of buggery in 1640.

Thankfully, not all of the homosexuals associated with Ireland and the Irish conflict were such unprincipled buggers. For one thing, there was Oscar Wilde of course. Although he is remembered more for his wit than for his political passions, Wilde was always acutely aware of his own Irishness and what it signified. 'I am not English,' he once said. 'I am Irish, which is quite another thing.' On one occasion he boasted that 'rhyme, the basis of modern poetry, is entirely of Irish invention'. As for the question of the conflict, he made it abundantly clear which side he was on. 'We forget how much England is to blame,' he told an American reporter. 'She is reaping the fruit of seven centuries of injustice.' Asked to describe his politics, Wilde insisted that he was a Republican, since 'no other form of government is so favourable to the growth of art'. Under the English, he claimed, 'art in Ireland came to an end, and it has had no existence for over seven hundred years'. The reason for this, he said, was that 'art could not flourish under a tyrant'.

It's hardly surprising, then, that following Wilde's fall from grace and the harsh treatment he received at the hands of the English prison system, the Irish people claimed him as their own – a victim of English barbarism, a martyr to the Irish cause. In other words, he may have been a sodomite, but he was their sodomite and the English had no business locking him up like that. Significantly, the man who led the prosecution against Wilde, a Dublin-based Protestant lawyer by the name of Edward Carson, MP, frequently acted on behalf of absentee English landlords in evicting Irish tenants. Presumably, this didn't help discourage people from viewing the Wilde case in purely nationalistic terms. Whatever the reasons, the fact is that Wilde's reputation as a writer and social critic never suffered quite so much in Ireland as it did in England. Today, while gay activists in London await the results of their campaign for a statue of St Oscar to be erected in the heart of the West End, in Ireland his image can be found everywhere – on T-shirts, in bar rooms, even on tea towels.

The most famous homosexual in the history of Irish nationalism was Sir Roger Casement, one of the men behind the Easter Rising of 1916. Born in Ireland in 1864, Casement grew up in a family which ardently supported the cause of Irish independence. At the age of twenty, his job as a ship's purser took him to the Congo, where he was appalled at the treatment of the native Africans by European colonialists. For twenty-six years he fought against these conditions and in 1911 was knighted for his work by the British Foreign Office. Casement then turned his attention to the Irish nationalist cause. When war broke out between England and Germany, he urged his Irish compatriots to support the Germans, and arranged for German arms to be shipped to Ireland for use against the British. Following the 1916 uprising, he was arrested for treason and put on trial. Casement's argument that he was Irish, not British, and that his actions were therefore not treasonable, won him the support of many prominent world leaders. This changed when extracts from his personal diaries were circulated by the British government in an attempt to blacken his good character. The diaries, dubbed 'The Black Diaries', contained explicit accounts of Casement's homosexual activities, describing the men he slept with and even referring to the size of their penises. Sympathy for Casement evaporated and he was sentenced to be hanged. The authenticity of the Casement diaries has since been hotly contested, with many Irish Republicans refusing to believe that a man so noble, so heroic and so strongly associated with their cause might also have been a size queen.

Even today, the suggestion that there might be gay men and women involved in the Irish Republican movement is a tough one to swallow – for Irish Republicans, and for many gay people as well. Still, they do exist. I recently came across an extraordinary letter, published in a book entitled *Lesbian and Gay Visions of Ireland* and written by Brendi McClenaghan, a gay man serving a prison sentence for his involvement with the IRA. In an attempt to 'present the links that exist between the Republican and gay/lesbian struggles,' he harks back to the Stonewall Riots of 1969, comparing them to scenes he witnessed as a child on the streets of Belfast. 'There are many similarities between both these struggles,' he writes. 'In America it was about rights and liberties denied on the basis of sexuality. Here, the struggle was being waged by people discriminated against in every aspect of their lives because they were Catholic/Nationalist.' The only difference, of course, is that the Stonewall queens didn't run around blowing up innocent bystanders. Wisely, McClenaghan acknowledges that there will be many lesbians and gay men who won't share his view of the Republican struggle. He also admits that, within the Republican movement, the position on lesbian and gay rights has been 'pretty dismal'. In 1980, six years after the emergence of a lesbian and gay rights movement in Ireland, Sinn Fein finally adopted a motion at its party conference in support of lesbian and gay rights. The reason there was no support before this, he suggests, is that nobody within the Republican movement saw any connection between their struggle and that of lesbians and gay men, and that it was generally assumed that lesbian and gay Republicans simply didn't exist. The reality, however, was rather different. 'I have no doubt that there were Republicans who were lesbian or gay both before and after 1969,' he writes. 'They just weren't visible, either out of fear or from choice. While choice may have been a luxury, fear was the greater force (and possibly still is for many). To understand this fear you have to realize not only the nature of the movement at that time, but also the history of Republicanism during those years since 1969. The perception was that to be a Republican was to be Catholic, Nationalist and very much the upholder of "traditional family values" as dictated by the Catholic Church.'

But not any more, apparently. In June 1993, homosexuality in the Irish Republic went from a state of total illegality to one of total equality. All previous laws criminalizing gay activity were abolished, replaced by a new, gender-neutral law with a common age of consent at seventeen, and no special privacy conditions pertaining to gay sex. What's more, it was made clear that there would be no exceptions from this law for the armed forces, thus putting the Irish Republic several steps ahead of Britain in the fight for gay civil rights. Inevitably, the repercussions have been felt in Northern Ireland, where the gay male of consent is still unequal at eighteen, and where a person can still be discharged from the army for being lesbian or gay. The Nationalist-run Derry council has been heard to make a lot of pro-gay noises in recent years, while Sinn Fein has extended its commitment to lesbian and gay rights and even has a lesbian and gay subgroup. To top it all, in Ireland there is evidence of the Catholic church toning down some of its pronouncements on the subject of homosexuality in a bid for more popular appeal. Proof, if it were needed, that there is nothing more political than religion.

*

I flew to Belfast one cold winter afternoon in January, amid growing fears that the peace process was breaking down. In the weeks preceding my visit, the Sinn Fein leader Gerry Adams had paid his first historic visit to Downing Street and several people had been killed. On New Year's Eve, members of the Loyalist Volunteer Force (LVF) opened fire on a bar in north Belfast, killing a thirty-one-year-old housing worker. Shortly afterwards, a twenty-eight-year-old community worker and father of two was shot dead outside a Belfast city nightclub. He was the fourth Catholic to die since the Irish National Liberation Army claimed responsibility for the death of the LVF leader Billy Wright at the Maze Prison a few weeks earlier. Most political commentators seemed to be of the opinion that the attacks were designed to provoke a Republican backlash and that the pressure was now building on the IRA to avenge the killings.

All in all, it didn't seem like the best time to visit Belfast. I don't know quite what I was expecting. Riots in the streets, I suppose. Or scenes from *Mad Max*, with battered army vans and men in balaclavas. In fact, it was nothing like that. Belfast today is a city desperate to live down its past, despite the efforts of a small number of extremists to continually rub people's faces in it. For now, those with peace in mind and their sights firmly on the future appear to be winning – at least in the city centre. Here, in the secular heart of Belfast, beloved by bold property developers and timid tourists alike, there seems to be a concerted effort to live as normal a life as possible. And what could be more reassuringly normal than the sight of young urban professionals going about their business? Here you will find the so-called 'Golden Mile' – an impressive row of swish shops and smart restaurants so bright and shiny, they practically dazzle you. Which, presumably, is the point. In the short time I spent exploring Belfast, I heard it said again and again that this is a city much like any other – that really you could be anywhere. I'm not sure that I agree. The city centre is certainly a far cry from the Belfast you think you know from *News at Ten*. But it doesn't feel quite right somehow. It's all too clean and polished to look entirely normal, almost as if someone has been frantically trying to wash away the evidence of a past crime.

Gay life in Belfast is concentrated around two bars – the Crow's Nest on Skipper Street and the Parliament on Dunbar Street. I had a gay guidebook and a local street map at my disposal, but I decided to try a different approach. A friend had told me that one of the best things about Belfast was that you could stop a total stranger in the street, ask them where the gay bars were and they would not only know exactly where to go but probably offer to walk with you half the way. I decided to put this theory to the test. The first person I tried, a man of about fifty, smiled at me benignly and hurried off, looking back over his shoulder every couple of seconds to check that I wasn't following. The second, a younger man of about thirty-five, stopped, scratched his head and said he thought there might be 'one of those places' somewhere in the vicinity of the Albert Memorial, but he wasn't sure where exactly and I would probably be better off asking somebody else. Sure enough, the next person I stopped came up with the goods. A middle-aged woman heavy with shopping, she sat her bags down for a moment, had a good look around and then pointed me in the direction of the Crow's Nest, with what I took as a friendly warning to 'mind how you go'. I thanked her profusely and headed off, amazed that I hadn't encountered any hostility and wondering whether I would have dared stop a stranger in the streets of Manchester, Cardiff or Edinburgh and ask them the same question without first checking that I had an offensive weapon concealed about my person.

The view from the Crow's Nest was nothing much to write home about. Given the Victorian splendour of so many of Belfast's pubs, with their elaborate stained-glass windows, dark wooden beams and polished brass fittings, it was somewhat disheartening to go along to a gay venue and find it so completely lacking in local character that it really could have been anywhere. I left after ten minutes and hurried around the corner to the Parliament, which, according to my guidebook, was 'a bauble of glitter amongst a fairly unprepossessing landscape'. This, it turned out, was by far the more popular of the two venues – something I immediately put down to the fact that it had stained-glass windows. Now it may have been the pressures of the day, or relief at not having found myself in the middle of a war zone, but I began to see all kinds of things in those windows. At last, I thought, a gay bar where the past and the present coexist in perfect harmony, where you can have stained-glass windows and alco-pops, where diversity isn't perceived as a threat but as something to be celebrated. And in Belfast of all places! I bought a celebratory drink, stood at the bar and spent the next few minutes wondering whether there was anything remotely significant about the fact that the venue I had already fallen in love with happened to be called the Parliament. Did the name really mean what I thought it meant? Was it in some small way a declaration of Irish gay independence – a stubborn refusal to be part of the steady globalization of gay consumer culture, whereby every gay bar in every city in every part of the world ends up looking exactly the same, and populated by men who seem to have emerged, ready-made, from the same Boyz 'R' Us factory somewhere in Chelsea, New York or West Hollywood, Los Angeles?

Evidently not. I was woken from my reverie by the arrival of two men in their early thirties who came and stood next to me at the bar. My first thought was that the one closest to me looked distinctly Irish, but this was probably due to the fact that he bore an uncanny resemblance to the cheeky-faced one from Boyzone. The other was of mixed race, with cropped black hair and a gold tooth. Both were dressed in figure-hugging T-shirts and combat trousers. Both clearly knew their way around a gym. 'So, you both go to the gym,' I said by way of an opener. They both smiled nervously and swelled with pride. The boy from Boyzone told me his name was Robbie. His boyfriend's name was Adam. They had just returned from a trip to London, where they were looking to purchase a house which they planned to let. 'You can't charge the same rents in Belfast,' Robbie explained, before pointing out that his brother owned several houses in London and was living quite happily off the proceeds. During their visit, Robbie and Adam had found time to explore London's gay scene. They'd been to Trade ('The best club in Britain,' according to Adam), and visited a number of the city's gay saunas. 'There's nothing like that here,' Robbie said wistfully. 'There was one we went to, with a really good gym and everything. We made a total night of it. It was fantastic.' (Irish boys seem to have quite a passion for gay saunas in London. I once met a beautiful boy from Donegal in a London sauna. He told me he came there to have sex, but never to the point of orgasm. 'It's a mind thing,' he said, though he later admitted that it was more of a Catholic thing.) Returning from London, Adam and Robbie felt that Belfast was rather dull by comparison. 'There isn't really a scene here,' said Adam. 'We don't go out much. We tend to keep ourselves to ourselves.' Still, they were able to quote me a price on a tab of Ecstasy (£7, compared to £15 in London) and they clearly weren't averse to a pint at the Parliament every now and then. 'It's OK,' Robbie conceded. 'The trouble here is the people. You hardly ever see anyone attractive. Gay men here don't know how to make the best of themselves. It's better than it used to be, but it's still pretty bad most of the time.'

No offence to Robbie and Adam, but one of the things I liked about the Parliament was that it wasn't full of preening queens radiating attitude with every flex of their bicep. Still, such are the indomitable power of the pink pound and the general weakness of the gay spirit that it surely can't be long now. Already, people are starting to talk about the city's two gay bars as the beginnings of 'a gay village'. Give it a few more years and every gay man in Belfast will be standing in front of the mirror, worried that his pecs aren't quite pert enough and his abs not quite firm enough – worried, in fact, that he doesn't look exactly like everyone else.

Some parts of Belfast remain forever locked in the past. To see them, you have to leave the safety of the shopping malls and the gay bars and travel to the west side of the city. Here you will almost certainly find men in balaclavas – at least you will if you take time to study the vast, ferocious murals with their martyrs and their gunmen, and the slogans that read 'For God and Ulster' and 'Ready for Peace, Prepared for War'. This is the part of Belfast that most people are vaguely familiar with, where locals declare their political allegiances by painting the kerbstones red, white and blue, where Catholics and Protestants live on separate sides of the same street (as they do in Duncairn Gardens) and where different teams of dustmen collect the rubbish on different days. It is often said that Northern Ireland is a world apart – a reference to the way the province is cut off from the surrounding landscape, and to the parochialism that flourishes there. Nowhere is this truer than in west Belfast. In fact, it's probably more accurate to say that west

Belfast is 'worlds apart' – two worlds, Catholic and Protestant, divided by mutual suspicion, rarely daring to occupy the same space. For years, Falls Road has served as the focus for the Catholic community, while Shankhill Road is Protestant territory – and always will be if the people who live there have anything to do with it. Walking around these streets, never knowing exactly where the territorial boundaries lie, is an unnerving experience – even if, like me, you have no religious affiliation whatsoever and really couldn't care less whether someone is a Catholic, a Protestant or a fully paid-up member of the twenty-four-hour church of Elvis.

I know I shouldn't joke about this, but I can't help myself. Christianity has always struck me as a pretty ridiculous religion. Lord knows I've tried to make some sense of it. I went to Sunday School as a child. I studied religious education at A-level. I even attended a Catholic college, where I spent another year poring over the Bible. And I'm still in the dark. So far as I understand it, the story goes something like this. In the beginning was God and God was love. In fact, so full of love was God that he sent his only son into the world to save mankind from eternal damnation, and to give young children the opportunity to dress up as angels and shepherds at Christmas time. The name of God's son was Jesus. Despite the fact that his mother always insisted that she was a virgin, and that he bore absolutely no resemblance to the man who claimed to be his father, Jesus grew up to be quite a well-adjusted fellow, give or take the odd encounter with the devil and the ability to perform miracles. When he wasn't busy turning water into wine or resurrecting the dead, he spent a lot of time hanging out with his alternative family, identifying with eunuchs, making friends with prostitutes and generally telling people to stop judging one another and start loving one another instead. Unfortunately, Jesus didn't prove too popular with the religious or political leaders of the day and eventually he died a nasty death on the cross. Shortly afterwards, the Christian Church was founded and, to cut a long story short, it's been nothing but trouble ever since. Throughout the past two thousand years, people calling themselves Christians have gone around waging wars in the name of a man who turned the other cheek and damning people to hell for daring to live a lifestyle or express an opinion remotely different from their own.

Maybe you think I'm being unnecessarily harsh, but I really don't think so. Broadly speaking, my attitude to Christians is this – I don't care what they do, just so long as they keep it to themselves. They may be only a small minority, but if they want to dress up in funny clothes and perform bizarre rituals, then of course they should be entitled to do so. All I ask is that they leave me out of it. If they do insist on ringing my doorbell first thing on a Sunday morning, or trying to co-opt me into their weird, alternative lifestyle, then I think I'm perfectly within my rights to tell them where to get off. And if they will go around quoting ancient scriptures inciting violence against perfectly rational people who pay taxes and are entitled to love whoever the hell they want, then frankly I think they should all be locked up. I mean, there are laws against that kind of thing. For the record, I know perfectly well what it says in the Book of Leviticus about men who lie down with other men. I also know what it says about men who touch the skin of the pig, and I don't hear Christians of any denomination calling for all butchers and football players to be rounded up and sent on a one-way journey to hell. Of course, things may be slightly different in west Belfast. For one thing, practising Christians are by no means a minority. Walking up Shankhill Road, I was overwhelmed by the sheer number of churches and religious meeting halls. There was practically one on every corner. And on those few street corners where there wasn't a church, there stood a pub. Between them, these two institutions pretty much sum up what it means to be a man in a place like this. God knows what it must be like for anyone growing up gay. Fortunately, I didn't have to rely on God to give me this information. I knew just the man to ask.

Gay journalist John Lyttle was born in Larne in 1959. His family moved to Shankhill Road when he was very young. His father, Tucker Lyttle, was a prominent member of the Ulster Defence Association (UDA) and was something of a local 'godfather' figure. In John's own words, 'He basically ran west Belfast for the UDA.' In 1974, John moved to London and has remained there ever since. He writes a weekly column on gay issues for the *Independent* newspaper and recently completed a book about his father, who died a few years ago. I asked John what it was like growing up on Shankhill Road. 'It's a bit like living in the twilight zone,' he said, laughing. 'Growing up as part of that generation who were witness to "the troubles", you don't realize how bizarre your life is. If you happen to be gay, it's even more bizarre. Living in west Belfast, well, let's just say it's the exact opposite of loving your fellow man. You can kill him, but what you can't do is love him, at least in the sense of sucking his dick. There's this incredibly old-fashioned, blue-collar, working-class idea of what a man is. It doesn't matter whether you're Protestant or Catholic. It's a very Irish thing, very "devolved" rather than "evolved".' In spite of this, John's growing awareness of the fact that he was gay wasn't quite as traumatic as one might have imagined. 'In some ways, being gay was incredibly helpful. Very early on, I began to see my life in parallel to myself. Once you feel isolated, you start to see life from a distance. It's something that you're part of and yet not part of at the same time.

I felt that very early on. I knew I was different. Funnily enough, when I heard my family talk about Catholics, I always compared it to the way they talked about queers. I always thought, "Well, you're wrong about me, so you're probably wrong about them too."'

John came out at the age of fifteen. 'It was bizarre, simply because of my circumstances. I was the only queer on Shankhill Road who never got beaten up. If anyone came near me, I'd shout, "My father is Tucker Lyttle", and they would back off. Or somebody would be coming towards me and someone else would intercept them and whisper in their ear. I knew exactly what was being said. So that worked out quite well. But me being gay was a terrible blow to my family – not just the immediate family, but the extended family too. Because it was the first time there'd been a queer in the family, nobody could say, "Well, it must come from your side of the family." There was nobody to blame.' When John sat his parents down and told them he was gay, they reacted quite well – far better than he had expected them to, in fact. Then they hauled him off to see a psychiatrist. 'I later discovered that the same was true for so many Belfast boys. As soon as you utter the words, they drag you off to the NHS. I knew a guy called Charlie who was sectioned in the end, because his parents demanded it. He was so stressed out by the bullying, rather than the fact that he was gay, and they locked him away in a mental hospital for three months. Lots of men I knew, at the age of fifteen or so, they were taken to see a psychiatrist. It seldom worked out to the parents' satisfaction. In my own case, I told the psychiatrist, "Look, I can cope with this." He said, "Yes, but it must be difficult. You're working class, living on the Shankhill Road." I said, "I know, but the people who really need help here are my parents. So how about me leaving the room and you calling them back in and seeing if you can help them?" He did exactly that. A few minutes later, they burst out of his room, grabbed me by the hand and we never went back.'

John has fond memories of gay life in Belfast in the early 1970s. 'One of the nice things about the gay scene in the beginning was that everybody knew one another. What was really good was that it was a place where Protestants and Catholics could meet. The only thing that mattered was whether you fancied a person or not. It didn't matter what their religious beliefs were. There was the occasional blow-up – a very Irish thing. I used to get a bit of stick because of my father. Someone I'd been friends with for two years would get really pissed one night and say, "You fucking Proty cunt" and start singing "The Men Behind the Wire". But mostly it was a very supportive environment. I remember there were always lots of private parties, gatherings at one another's houses. The pubs closed early, so you had to conduct a large part of your social life in private homes. People were always crashing out on each other's sofas. There were a lot of gay organizations too. I remember there was one that owned a house near the university. Every Sunday it was open house. You'd go along, talk to people. It was very fortifying. It was my ideal vision of gay life to a certain degree. But always, always, there was this sense that you could die, that your life could be taken from you at any moment. A car could come around the corner and you could be just blown away.'

Or otherwise disposed of. Shortly after he came out, John was cornered in the toilets at the College of Business Studies and told that his life expectancy would increase greatly if he left Belfast for good. He moved to London shortly afterwards. 'The big thing back in Belfast was that you had to go to London. I used to say, there'll always be a Belfast, but it will be in London. Everyone I knew went over there for a while, and a lot of them came back again. They couldn't hack it in London. A lot of them said they felt rejected on the gay scene for being Irish – unless they happened to run into a potato queen. They hated the coldness of it. I know I did. I missed Ireland tremendously. Migration doesn't always work for the Irish, contrary to cultural stereotypes. Now when I go back, it's like there's been a reverse process. London has gone to Belfast. One of the things I used to like about the gay scene in Belfast was that it was shabby. You go over now, and everyone is pumped up and dancing to cover versions of songs by the Teletubbies. You have the younger ones standing around like prime beauties and the women tucked away in the back bar. The feeling of unity that used to be such a strong feature of the gay scene in Belfast has just gone.'

John's experience of growing up gay in Belfast was in many ways unusual, shaped by the fact that his father was actively involved in the conflict. But his strong sense of his own identity as 'a Proty', his early awareness of what it might mean to be 'different' in ways other than the purely sexual, the 'feeling of unity' he found on the gay scene – these are things that many gay men of his generation tend to refer to. 'Robert' (not his real name) was born in 1959 and raised in Porterdown, the Protestant stronghold of Ulster. His parents were staunch loyalists, with a love of the British royal family that bordered on religious devotion. From a very early age, Robert shared this strange passion. At the age of four, he had a scrapbook filled with pictures of the Queen. 'I loved the royal family,' he explained. 'It was very exciting when any of the royal family had babies. It was all bound up together – Ulster and truth and justice and happiness and our Queen. We loved our Queen.' In fact, young Robert loved his Queen so much that he and his friends used to play a game in which they pretended to be, for want of a better word, queens. 'We would dress up in our mothers' dresses and walk up and down in the living room with the test-card music on, being queens. I was always encouraged to dress up as a child. My parents thought it was rather sweet.'

Robert was what you might call a somewhat precocious child. At the age of five, he read an article in one of his mother's magazines, on the subject of whether or not parents should tell their children the truth about Santa Claus. Horrified at his discovery, he confronted his parents with the magazine, demanding to know why he had been lied to. Then, when he was ten, he found a copy of *Woman's Own* which included a pull-out colour supplement devoted to the many 'different faces of love'. He remembers two faces in particular. 'There was a photo of two men with blazers and big bouffant hairdos and big wide ties, one standing behind the other with his hand on his shoulder. I thought they seemed quite nice. I couldn't quite understand what this different love was, but I thought it sounded nice. I thought it sounded like me.' Robert didn't become fully aware of his sexuality for another three years, but he was already aware of the concept of 'otherness'. He knew that he was different from the other boys at school. 'I was very conscious of the fact that I wasn't butch, that I didn't play rugby. I was in the school choir and had a queeny circle of friends. If we were ever forced to do sports, we would do cross-country running. We used to walk most of the way, eating Spangles.' It was also around this time that he began to develop an interest in Roman Catholics. Robert's mother had been sent to a Catholic school as a child and was determined to teach her own children that Catholics weren't the devils some people said they were. Although he attended a predominantly Protestant school, Robert would sometimes travel to school on the Catholic bus. 'We didn't really mix with Catholics,' he explained. 'At my school there were three Catholic boys out of maybe four hundred. I became very interested in otherness and taboos. I was very keen to meet people from hard-core nationalist areas, Catholics especially. To me, homosexuality and Catholicism seemed equally naughty, equally transgressive.'

By the age of thirteen, and following the untimely death of his mother, Robert had become totally obsessed with religion. In fact, he reckoned that he might have gone on to become a proper Bible basher, had he not been too busy bashing a part of his own anatomy. 'I found it hard to justify my homosexuality and I thought it might just go away if I took Jesus into my heart. But I was an absolute inveterate masturbator. I'd get up in the morning and have a wank. At breaktime, I'd have a wank in the school toilets. Sometimes I'd even do it on the bus home. Of course, this was the express bus. Then I'd be overcome with guilt and would throw myself into the Bible. I remember going to an American-style evangelist rally with this man saying Billy Graham-type things about how we must all be washed in the blood of the lamb, and calling for everyone with Jesus in their heart to come forward. Well, I was there. I was really swept up in it all. Then I found a copy of *Forum* magazine, with an article on how to suck cock without gagging. From then on, I was torn between the Bible and pornography.'

By the time he was sixteen, Robert was well versed in the art of sex – at least in theory. He spent many a long hour at the local library, looking up every reference to homosexuality he could find. One day he spotted a news story in the local paper about a lesbian and gay rights group in Belfast. He phoned the Samaritans for advice and was put through to a man who happened to be involved in setting up the group. They arranged to meet. 'He was English, in his thirties,' Robert recalled. 'I thought he was terribly old. He thought I was terribly well read for my age. I'd read Genet, Gide, Forster, everything. He took me along to the Belfast Gay Liberation

Society youth group. I was intensely shy. I could barely speak.' In spite of his shyness, Robert became a regular at the group. 'I felt like I was a member of a secret society. I told my father that I had joined the Humanist Association, or that I was doing extra studying.' In reality, he was meeting people who encouraged him to put all those hours of library study into practice and who confirmed his suspicions that homosexuals weren't the only sexual outlaws in Northern Ireland. 'There was this boy who told me that his brother had threatened to kill him if he ever went with a Catholic girl. Well, at least there was no danger of that.'

It was through the group, also, that Robert met the man who was to initiate him into gay sex. 'He was older than me, about thirty. He used to catch the same train as me. One night we were on the train and he said, "Let's have a snog." I was really scared. We kissed and cuddled all the way from Belfast back to my home town. When we got off the train, he said, "Come on, there's a park near here", and off we went. He pushed me up against a tree. He kept saying things like "You're so hot" and "You're such a lovely young chicken." I remember thinking that was a funny thing to say. He kept trying to suck my cock, which was completely flaccid. Eventually he got angry and said, "What makes you think you're gay anyway? What's wrong with you?" I said I was cold and a bit nervous, and we carried on. Then, just as he was about to come, a branch fell off the tree and on to my head. He came. I didn't. I remember this in such detail because I went home that night and wrote a twenty-page entry in my diary. I was late home. My father had gone to the station to pick me up. He was furious. He told me I was never allowed to go to Belfast again.'

But he was allowed to go to Paris. The following year, Robert went to gay Paris on an exchange trip. He borrowed a copy of the *Spartacus* gay guide from someone at the gay youth group and spent his time exploring the city's gay bars and saunas. When he returned home, his father found a copy of *Gay News* in his bag. 'I told him I'd found it on the plane. He said, "You've got to be careful, you know. There are homosexuals in big cities all across the world."' Armed with this knowledge, Robert decided to pay a visit to London. One of his abiding memories of this trip is of visiting a gay commune and watching someone pick crabs out of his pubic hair while delivering a lecture on the politics of cottaging. But it wasn't an entirely wasted journey. In London, Robert saw productions by radical gay theatre companies such as Hot Peaches, Bloolips and Gay Sweatshop. He also attended the infamous *Gay News* trial, in which Mary Whitehouse charged the editor of Britain's fortnightly gay newspaper with blasphemy for publishing a poem by Professor James Kirkup. The poem was entitled 'The Love That Dares to Speak Its Name' and described the sexual feelings experienced by a Roman centurion on seeing Jesus suffering on the cross. The prosecution won, making this the first successful blasphemy case in fifty-five years. Robert returned to Northern Ireland a very angry, very gay young man.

He remembers the Belfast gay scene of the mid- to late 1970s as being extremely tightly knit. 'All the men who worked in the best clothes shops were very big on the gay scene. There was one shop called Trampas, after the Doug McClure character in *The Virginian*. It seemed as if all the assistants there were gay. I remember one of them winning a prize for impersonating Liza Minnelli in *Cabaret*. Several people were arrested for cottaging. A boy from my school left and got a job at a gentleman's outfitters. He was interviewed by the police over possession of some cannabis and his address book set off a police investigation into about thirty people. It was very scary. Back then, homosexuality was still illegal. The maximum sentence for homosexual sex was life imprisonment. This boy was only seventeen at the time.' Undeterred, Robert wrote to his MP, explaining that he was seventeen and that he'd experienced gay sex and that the law ought to be changed. He left copies of *Gay News* lying around in the school library and handed out leaflets in the centre of Belfast, calling for a change in the law. 'Looking back, that was perhaps rather a foolhardy thing to do. I remember a woman who came up to me. I handed her a leaflet. She said, "Oh, my God, what are you involved in? You're not one of those awful people. I know you're not. I've been a midwife for thirty years and I can tell from your face that you're just not one of them." I said, "But I am, I am." '

Breaking the news to his father took a little longer. Shortly after his son had left Belfast to attend college in Brighton, Robert's father came across his diary. 'He was quite good about it really,' Robert said. 'I remember I was very cold. I'd read *How to be a Happy Homosexual*, so I gave him the party line. I was very bolshy. I said there was a whole gay world out there and lots of gay people who were happy, healthy and successful in their lives. I really shouldn't have used the word "healthy", because I actually had syphilis at the time. Anyway, he cried a bit, then he said I would always be his son and there would always be a home for me.' Despite his father's good nature, Robert visits Northern Ireland less and less these days. 'The last time was two years ago. I went to a gay club in Belfast. There was this sixteen-year-old blond disco bunny boy. I told him I used to go to gay discos in Belfast twenty years ago. He couldn't believe it. That's the trouble with gay youth. They have no sense of history.'

Because the gay youth of today have no sense of history and because my visit to Belfast left me in a peculiarly religious frame of mind, I have decided to draw this chapter to a close with a sermon.

And the subject of today's sermon is 'gay identity'. For what profit it a man if he loves another man, but has no sense of identity? Without identity, his love is like a pink balloon or a whistle blowing in the wind – full of air, signifying nothing. If a gay man has love, but no identity, then he can never truly enter the kingdom of gay goodness and everlasting pride. Or to put it another way, keeping faith in the redemptive power of identity is what being gay is all about. Of course, it wasn't always thus. In the years BP (Before Pride), there were no such things as gays, only homosexuals. And what's worse, identity wasn't really something that people thought about very much. In those dark times, homosexuals were truly lost in the wilderness – a disparate group of individuals, spread out all across the globe (but mostly in America), each pursuing his own interests and never sparing a thought for the plight of his fellow homosexuals, or even liking them very much. Then lo, it came to pass that the wise queens at the Stonewall Inn did take exception to the police pushing them around and did fight back against their oppressors. And for five long days and nights they fought, with tooth and nail and six-inch heels. And through their good fight, the modern gay rights movement was born and gay identity forged.

And the forefathers of the gay movement looked on and saw that it was good. And the gay merchants looked on and saw that it was a good way to make money without a great deal of investment, and so everybody was happy. And so it continued for many years, until the day came when the youngsters of the tribe did start to question the wisdom of their elders, and ask if this thing called gay identity wasn't just a little bit restrictive, and did it come in a different size? And the elders were sore afraid and said, 'Who has put these words into your mouth? Surely it is the work of the devil, for only one possessed by the devil could question the goodness of such a holy thing. For a man can say that there is no one gay identity but many gay *identities*. Or he can say that there is no one gay community but many gay *communities*. But he can never, ever say that to be gay is not good. Goodness and mercy shall follow the children of Stonewall always. For thus it was written, and must remain for ever and ever, amen.' And the youngsters listened carefully to the words of the elders. And when they had finished listening they turned to one another and said, 'Fuck that, we're going shopping.'

You'll appreciate, I hope, that my little sermon isn't entirely serious – although, God knows, there are enough people out there delivering sermons like this for a living, and they're not all raving Bible bashers. When it comes to making a virtue out of victimhood, or demonstrating how a little bit of history can go an awfully long way, gay-identity politics has far more in common with Christianity than the representatives of either party are prepared to admit. Historically speaking, we gays have tended to think of ourselves as a peaceful, loving people. Unlike Christians, we have never gone in for armed combat on a large scale – though it's fair to say that some of us do take an extraordinary amount of pleasure in dressing the part. Nor are we in the habit of rounding up people who don't happen to share our beliefs, tying them to wooden stakes and setting fire to them – at least not in the literal sense. But as anyone who has ever attended a gay political meeting will know, there is a ferocity and a meanness of spirit which often pervades gay identity politics, and which is on a par with anything the Christian Church can throw at you. This can be summed up as: Love me, love my dogma.

Like devout Christians, devout gays love a bit of dogma. And why not? After all, it's so much easier to learn one fixed set of rules and apply them to all situations than be forced to constantly reappraise one's beliefs in the light of new experiences, new information. As well as being confident in the knowledge that 'Gay is Good', devout gays also know that anything which suggests that gay might not be quite as good as they say must by its very nature be 'homophobic' in origin and can therefore be dismissed out of hand. This is all part of 'the fight against oppression'. Devout gays also know that shaved arseholes are sexy and that lesbians are invisible – even when they're standing in front of you at Gay Pride, larger than life, with their breasts exposed. There's never any point in asking them how they know these things. They just do. If you do insist on applying some sort of intellectual rigour to the argument, then you will find that devout gays have many comforting little myths to fall back on. Many of these sound almost religious in tone and describe that holiest of days when they saw the light, declared their 'true' selves and were welcomed into the fold. Like anyone possessed by blind faith, devout gays rarely evolve beyond this primitive stage of consciousness. Instead, the coming-out narrative takes on greater significance with each retelling, until it ceases to be merely the story of how a person announced to the world that they were gay and becomes instead a kind of gospel. As with Christians, it tends to be the case that the later in life the gay man in question discovers his 'true' self, the more devout he becomes. Just think of St Paul if you need an indication of how irritating this can be.

None of this would be quite so annoying were it not for the fact that, like the most devout of Christians, the most devout believers in the gay world religion often have an unshakeable faith in their own moral righteousness. This is why, for example, there is a tendency for self-appointed 'gay community leaders' to attempt to pass themselves off as Old Testament prophets or modern-day saints. This is most noticeable in the case of larger-than-life American gay political figures such as Larry Kramer (who, incidentally, tends to speak and write in the exact same upper-case invective as the religious right). But it is also true of some of the smaller, far less colourful characters who populate British gay politics – in particular those who, despite having no medical training or history of involvement in social work or any of the caring professions, have managed to carve out a highly lucrative niche for themselves in the fight against AIDS. Their only real qualification for the job is that they are gay and prone to seeing themselves as victims. Their only real talent is for delivering sermons. This they do with monotonous regularity, climbing up on a mountain of corpses and waving away all dissenting opinion with a shroud. For men such as these, AIDS has been a blessing of epic proportions, providing the perfect excuse for a lifetime of voluntary martyrdom, not to mention a wealth of opportunities for sanctimonious self-congratulation.

Like devout Christians, devout gays often claim to have made enormous personal sacrifices in dedicating themselves to the cause. The reality, as often as not, is that dedication to the cause has given them a position in life they would never have had any hope of achieving in the world at large. Like religion, identity politics narrows the world down, makes it a smaller and less challenging place. The only trouble is, it can't make it go away. How ironic that it was a black gay man with AIDS, the late American activist and health educator Phill Wilson, who highlighted the dangers of a gay world religion when he observed that identity politics was a cul-de-sac. Come to think of it, I wonder if he ever visited Belfast.

7

A COTTAGE IN THE COUNTRY

Somerset

Somerset is breeder country. This isn't meant as an insult; it's simply a statement of fact. Breeding is what the good people of Somerset do best. They breed sheep. They breed cattle. And they breed among themselves – rather enthusiastically, I might add. In Somerset, it isn't unusual to find four generations of first cousins interwed and interbred, with seven children to a household and another one on the way. Occasionally, the breeding cycle is disrupted when the one on the way turns out to be a homosexual. But this is merely a temporary setback. Gay men born and raised in Somerset tend to uproot themselves and move away at the first opportunity. Most of them, anyway.

Take my friend Andrew Loxton. Born in 1961 in a tiny village called Dinder (population 110), Andrew is the youngest of eight children. His family come from a long line of farmers and take their name from the village of Loxton, six miles from where he was born. Andrew knew he was different from other boys from the age of six. He had three sisters – each of them at least ten years older than himself, all with boyfriends. Even as a small child, Andrew used to fantasize about his sisters' boyfriends, imagining what lay hidden in the crotches of their purple flared trousers. Had he been heterosexual, Andrew would probably have grown up to become a farmer. He would have married his cousin and carried on the family tradition by producing lots of little Loxtons and the odd herd of dairy cattle. Instead, he left home at eighteen and went to study sociology in Plymouth, before finally settling in London, where he now works as a housing adviser for people with HIV and AIDS. It was Andrew who suggested I pay a visit to Somerset – to find out why he left, but also to meet some of the gay people who continue to make a life for themselves there.

We left London at noon one crisp Friday in December, with Andrew at the wheel, a packet of Mint Imperials for the journey and a short-list of people who had been forewarned of our visit. The drive from London to Somerset takes about three hours – longer if you stop off on the M4 to peruse the menu at that purveyor of fine service-station cuisine known as Julie's Pantry. I have never quite understood the appeal of Julie's Pantry. I think it might have something to do with the name, and its suggestion of good old-fashioned, no-nonsense British wholesomeness, cunningly disguising the fact that most items on the menu were first invented in places even further afield than Lancashire. In any case, it is extremely popular – so popular, in fact, that the queue extended for miles and we were forced to forgo Julie's tantalizing offer of vegetable lasagne and pomme frites and settle for a veggie burger and a piece of battered chicken in a bun from a nearby fast-food counter, staffed by a spotty youth who obviously hadn't learned the meaning of 'fast-food'. Since there were no seats available, we decided to eat our lunch in the car, where we could at least avoid being stared at by people in shell suits. If people who hang around motorway service stations paid half the attention to their own attire that they do to other people's, the shell suit as we know it would soon cease to exist.

At four we arrived in Bradford-on-Avon, a small but thriving market town near the borders of Somerset, Avon and Wiltshire, home to about nine thousand people and the first stop on our gay tour of the area. We parked the car alongside a gang of shifty-looking schoolchildren and made our way along a winding road called the Shambles, laughing merrily as we went. (It's amazing, the capacity gay men have for finding pleasure in the simplest things. Take two London queens, plonk them down in the middle of the country and they'll amuse themselves for hours.) Soon we arrived at an old seventeenth-century country pub called the Sprat and Carrot (cue more hysterical laughter). There are eighteen pubs in Bradford-on-Avon, one for every five hundred people. The busiest of these is the Sprat and Carrot, or, as it's known locally, the Queer and Faggot.

The landlords of the Sprat and Carrot are called John and Mark. They share the same, double-barrelled surname, although they aren't brothers in the usual sense. They took over the pub in the summer of 1994 and live together above the bar, with three large dogs (a boxer, a retriever and a Rottweiler) and one average-sized cat. The room we sat and chatted in was decorated in that rather fussy, country-cottage style decried in the recent television ad for Ikea. Dotted around the room were little teddy bears in denim shorts and leather chest harnesses, mementoes of some gay weekend away, looking rather out of place amid the plump sofas and ruched curtains. Evidently, John and Mark had no intention of chucking out their chintz. In fact, I doubt if they'd have understood the well-worn joke, 'What's a gay man's favourite w(h)ine?' 'Take me to Ikea.'

John is the less extrovert of the pair, with fair hair and a soft Devonshire accent. Mark is more gregarious, with dark spiky hair and a perma-tan. Both have moustaches and smoked more or less constantly during the hour and a half that we were together. They met in 1992, in Exeter. ('I'm from Exeter originally,' John explained, 'and he's from all over the place.' Mark jumped in immediately: 'I've been around.'). A year after they met, they decided to do what growing numbers of gay people are doing nowadays and get married.

Marriage has become one of the key debating points for gay rights campaigners in the 1990s. In his virtually unreadable book, *Virtually Normal*, Andrew Sullivan claims that opening up the institution of marriage to lesbian and gay couples would strike right to the heart of homophobia. For Sullivan, lesbian and gay marriage is not only a question of legal protection but also a way of sending a message to the world that lesbians and gay men are just the same as everyone else. The only problem is, we aren't. Sullivan's argument is based on the naïve assimilationist assumption that the only thing distinguishing us from heterosexuals is what we do in bed, and that our sexual orientation has no bearing on how we function as social or political beings. Others take a more pragmatic approach, arguing for gay partnership rights which would afford the same legal benefits as marriage but without the connotations of a marriage ceremony. And then there are those free queer radicals who hate the very idea of gay marriage and want to defend the right of every gay man to fuck himself stupid – as if he weren't quite capable of exercising that 'right' already. For my own part, I wouldn't get married if you dragged me to the altar in a wedding dress with the offer of a world cruise for a wedding present, but I would defend the right of anyone to do so if they really thought it would make them happy.

In any case, the argument is purely academic. In 1997, Britain was named the divorce capital of Europe. The divorce rate in this country is six times what it was thirty years ago. If the family-values brigade want the institution of marriage to survive into the next century, they should let the fags and dykes in before it's too late.

Discussing the subject with John and Mark, there was little to suggest that they regarded gay marriage as being in any sense political; they simply saw it as a way of demonstrating their commitment to one another. Mark's mother offered to fly the entire family out to Amsterdam, but in the end they settled for a Metropolitan Community Church wedding in Exeter. They had a cake made, with two grooms on the top, and they swapped surnames. Following the service, a number of locals turned up to throw confetti and were disconcerted when they couldn't locate the bride. There was also a photographer present. A photograph of the happy couple stood on display next to one of the teddy bears. Neither John nor Mark looked particularly happy. Neither of them liked the photograph very much.

Before moving to Bradford-on-Avon, they ran a small hotel in Somerton, where, according to John, 'They're all interbred even more than here. We had a disco every Saturday and there was always trouble. Windows put in and everything.' To date, no windows have been smashed at the Sprat and Carrot, despite the fact that everyone within a twenty-mile radius knows that the landlords are gay. Shortly after John and Mark arrived, a reporter from the local newspaper came to interview them. 'We're animal lovers, you see,' John explained, somewhat unnecessarily. 'So it was supposed to be an article about how animal lovers had taken over the local pub.' Only that wasn't how it turned out. 'The article appeared and the opening line was "Married homosexual couple take over Sprat and Carrot." There was just a couple of lines about the dogs. Sort of, "By the way, they have a Rottweiler, a retriever, a boxer and a cat." Us being gay has nothing to do with the business, or how we run the pub. My thought was, if anyone asks if we're gay, then I'd say yes, we are, but if they don't ask then there's no need to tell them. Then this article appeared. I was horrified.'

He needn't have worried. The day the article appeared, the pub was busy as usual. One of the local lads came over to the bar, said that he'd read the piece in the paper and congratulated John and Mark on having the courage to be so open. When they responded by saying that, actually, they hadn't intended to be quite so open, he promptly offered to track down the reporter responsible and teach him some manners. 'A lot of people really like the fact that we're gay,' said John. 'A lot of them don't know any other gay people, so it's a novelty to them. And women love it anyway, don't they?' Mark added, 'The lads like it too. When the lads come in I say, "Who am I tonight?", which is my way of asking them if there's going to be any trouble. They say, "You're the landlady tonight. We'll behave ourselves."' I asked if there had ever been any occasion when people didn't behave themselves. 'We've had a few comments,' John said. 'As a rule, they come in once and then they never come back again. There's one bloke who comes in. He told us his wife wasn't very keen on him coming here, but he keeps coming back. As soon as they realize you're not going to jump on top of them and rip their clothes off, they're fine. And it's not as if we're mincing around in stilettos, carrying handbags.' Mark laughed. 'Not all the time anyway.' John frowned. 'What I mean is, we're just ordinary people. As soon as people get that into their heads, they're fine.'

Like a lot of ordinary gay couples, John and Mark lead a fairly conventional life. They take five weeks' holiday a year. Shortly before our meeting, they'd been to Gran Canaria (Mark would like to open a bar there one day, though John isn't so keen). Arriving back from their holiday, they stopped off in London to see Celine Dion at Wembley, which is about as ordinary as you can get. They have a lot of heterosexual friends. In fact, they reckon the majority of their friends are straight. Every so often, they take an evening off to visit one of the gay bars in nearby Bath or Bristol, where they're greeted as local celebrities. I wondered whether their reputation had had any impact locally, whether gay people actually came to the Sprat and Carrot. 'We've got one or two,' Mark replied, looking to John for confirmation. 'There's the Welsh one, and there's that one with the beard.' John went on, 'Well, they were a bit strange, weren't they?' Then, turning to me, 'We do get quite a lot of gays, I suppose. Since we took over here, it's like everybody came out of the closet. Most of the gays in Bradford are out. It's couples mostly. And they come here from Bath and from Bristol. It's a lot more cosmopolitan.'

Than what, I wondered. A damp weekend in Skegness? Charming though Bradford-on-Avon was, I have trouble picturing it as anything other than a small rural town with a refreshingly tolerant attitude towards homosexuality. If this is middle England, then the *Daily Mail* has obviously got it wrong. But it is hardly what you would call a cosmopolitan place. There is no cinema, for example. Once a month, films are shown at the town hall. For those who like nothing better than to be surrounded by old things, there are a fair number of antiques shops. But for the vast majority of people, the social life of the town revolves around the pub. The popularity of the Sprat and Carrot owes something to the personalities of the landlords, but it is also a reflection of the amount of respect the people of Bradford-on-Avon have for tradition. There is only one fruit machine in the pub and a dartboard. There are no quiz nights, no karaoke nights, no live music, none of the things one associates with a modern pub. There is absolutely nothing wrong with this, of course. It makes a nice change not to be assaulted from all sides with amplified music and overpriced bottled beer. But cosmopolitan? Hardly.

Much as I liked John and Mark, I found myself quietly disagreeing with a lot of the things they said. At one point, I asked whether there was much homophobic violence in the area. 'There was one guy who got beaten up recently,' Mark replied. 'But he was cruising for a bruising.' Apparently, the man in question had been hanging around a public toilet in the town that was well known to be a cottage. He was attacked by two men, dragged to his car and beaten up. One man took his credit cards, cash card and pin number, and went off to the nearest cash dispenser, while the other man held him at knifepoint. Attacks like these take place all over Britain. More often than not, the victims choose not to report the crime to the police, for fear of what might happen to them when they reveal where the attack took place. It isn't unheard of for a gay man who has been brutally attacked in a public toilet or an outdoor cruising area to go to the police and find himself charged with importuning. Rarely are the victims of such crimes shown much by way of sympathy. The attitude of the police tends to be that they were asking for trouble. This is akin to saying that a woman who walks down the street in a short skirt deserves to be raped. To hear a gay man expressing much the same opinion is disheartening, to say the least.

I ended my conversation with John and Mark on a happier note, with an introduction to 'gut-barging'. Reports on this strange local phenomenon have appeared in several national newspapers and on morning television. And they all stem back to the Sprat and Carrot. According to the newspapers, 'gut-barging' is a traditional Somerset sport in which two men of ample girth strip off their shirts and literally 'barge' into one another. Before the contest begins, the floor is liberally strewn with Bombay Mix. The winner is the man who remains standing the longest. Needless to say, this 'ancient' sport was invented all of a year ago. 'It's all down to this chap who comes here,' John explained. 'He claims that he's a gut-barger and he put out a press release about this completely made-up sport. People think it's real. He's been on Richard and Judy and everything.' As we left the Sprat and Carrot, John pointed the guilty man out to us. He was a large fellow with a long beard, sat cradling a pint. I desperately wanted to go up and ask him what Richard and Judy were really like, but I didn't dare.

We left Bradford-on-Avon just after six p.m. and drove to Bristol. Andrew had arranged for us to meet up with an old schoolfriend of his, but he wouldn't be home until after nine. In the meantime, we decided to while away a few hours on Bristol's gay scene. Before I go any further, I should point out that I had been warned about the gay scene in Bristol. A friend of mine once visited a gay pub there and was informed by some stupid queen that they didn't want Londoners coming up and infecting them all with AIDS. Arriving at the Griffin dressed in tell-tale London gay garb (i.e. blue combat trousers and silver Schott jacket), I braced myself for a similar confrontation. I needn't have worried. It may have been no later than seven p.m., the pub may have opened only an hour before, but everyone in the Griffin was so drunk that they barely noticed our arrival.

Once we'd recovered from the shock of being ignored, we

ordered some drinks, found ourselves an empty table and took in the scene. And it was a scene. A sign at the bar said that tonight was fetish night, but aside from the barman, who had gamely taken off his shirt and suspended an ill-fitting chest harness from his bony shoulders, there was no evidence of it. Unless, of course, you have a fetish for school caretakers. I'm not joking. Just about everybody in the pub looked like a school caretaker. Those who didn't fell into one of two camps. A few looked as if they might possibly teach geography and the rest seemed far too young to be out drinking, which may explain why they were falling around the place. The overall effect was of a school disco gone completely out of control, with the new geography teacher snogging the old caretaker, while the pupils helped themselves to sir's illicit stash of booze. It was really quite terrifying.

I drank two vodkas and tonic very quickly and soon found myself in need of a pee. Feeling a bit like Jamie Lee Curtis in the last reel of *Halloween*, I wandered off on my own to find the toilet, which was situated down a narrow flight of stairs and could be located quite easily by following the smell of floral disinfectant. Hovering at the urinal were two very young, very drunk men. One had a small dog at his side. The other had a nasty-looking scar on his forehead. As I walked in, they both turned and stared at me, then shuffled along the urinal, making a space for me to come and pee next to them. I am pee-shy at the best of times and the presence of a small dog, hovering at knee level, didn't exactly help matters. I smiled weakly and dashed into the cubicle. Within seconds, I heard urgent whispering outside the door. 'Go on,' one voice was saying. 'Go on.' The dog barked. The other voice giggled. It was the sort of giggle people emit when they are about to do something they know they shouldn't. I pressed my foot firmly against the door and quickly finished my business. As I opened the door to leave, scarface came tumbling into the cubicle, grinning sheepishly. Suddenly, I had a fair idea of how he might have acquired that scar.

Making my way back to the bar, I spotted a poster on the wall, headlined 'Queerbashing at Tog Hill Picnic Area'. The poster described a recent assault on a thirty-year-old gay man which sounded suspiciously like the incident Mark had described earlier. According to this version of events, the victim was ambushed by two men, struck across the head with a torch and robbed of his wallet, watch, car keys, two mobile phones, a lap-top computer and a dictaphone. (What he was doing lugging all this stuff around at four a.m. in a place described as a picnic area, I've no idea. Come to think of it, there was no mention of a picnic hamper, but I suppose egg sandwiches are the last thing on your mind when you've just had your entire mobile office stolen.) The poster was produced by an organization called Avon and Somerset Lesbian and Gay Policing Initiative. Leaflets outlining their aims and objectives were piled up on a shelf nearby. An informal body, comprising representatives from the local police service and members of the lesbian and gay community, the Initiative aims to 'build better relationships, greater trust, understanding and communications between the police service and the lesbian and gay community by encouraging a partnership approach'. To this end, the local police had recently appointed a Lesbian and Gay Community Liaison Officer, one Sergeant Martyn Thompson. Without having met Sergeant Thompson, I nevertheless felt rather sorry for him. It can't be an easy task, trying to build better relationships with a community embittered by years of police harassment. In my experience, gay men's attitudes towards the police range from suspicion to outright hostility. The members of the Initiative seemed to acknowledge this. At the bottom of the leaflet was a paragraph urging people to put the past behind them: 'We hope you will have the confidence to approach the police to report any breach of the law in the knowledge that the matter will be dealt with in an impartial and sensitive manner. If not, we want to know about it!'

The lesbian and gay community has a long and noble history of producing leaflets. You can tell a lot about the gay population of any given area from the selection of leaflets on display at the local gay watering hole. The Griffin boasted quite a collection. There was a green one advertising Bristol Young Lesbian and Bisexual Group – which offers support, videos, arts and crafts, and 'cuppas' to 'girls and young women up to the age of twenty-five' (what do they offer those over twenty-five, I wondered. A bottle of sleeping pills?). There was a black and white one for a club called Heresy, 'first Sunday of every month', at a venue called Club Loco. There was a pink one packed with information about GayWest, a social and support network based in Bath, 'working towards an integrated gay community as an alternative to the commercial scene'. And next to these, a bright orange leaflet with the words 'Wake up Bristol. HIV is Here.' Obviously, the author had been talking to that man my friend had told me about.

The Griffin isn't the only gay pub in Bristol. Nor is it the most frightening. That distinction goes to the Elephant. There is a tendency in gay male circles to refer to any gay pub frequented by older gentlemen as the Elephants' Graveyard. In the past, I have always regarded such remarks as unnecessarily cruel, downright ageist and not at all funny. Since visiting the Elephant, I have had to revise my opinion somewhat. We arrived around eight p.m., shaken from the school disco up the road but with an hour still left to kill. Within ten minutes, I would have happily killed half the people in the place. By half, I am referring very specifically to the three beady-eyed, visibly drunk old queens hunched at the bar who chose to mark our arrival by serenading us with a chorus of 'Don't Cry for Me, Argentina', sung very loudly and accompanied with lots of waving of arms and thrusting of hip replacements. This wouldn't have been quite so alarming if 'Don't Cry for Me, Argentina' had been the record playing on the jukebox. Instead, they were competing with Shirley Bassey singing 'I Am What I Am' – and losing, horribly. We smiled politely, found ourselves a couple of stools at the opposite end of the bar and waited for the storm to subside.

Only it didn't. The singing continued and, once the song was over, the insults began. At first I thought I was being paranoid. I mean, we had never even met these people and all we'd done was go and sit by ourselves. Hardly the greatest injustice a gay man has ever had to suffer, is it? But gradually the voices got louder and the words clearer – something about people who obviously thought they were better than other people, and who needed a good shafting to put them right, but first I'll have another triple whisky, barman, and don't you dare tell me I've had enough already, I'm a paying customer, you little bastard. Clearly, this display of gay male pique was directed at us. Apart from the barman, we were the only other people in the place. What was a man supposed to do? I did what I always do in these situations: I stared at the bar in what I hoped was a quietly confident manner and prayed for it to be time for us to leave. Half an hour later, that time came. On the way out of the door, Andrew turned to me and made some crack about our three suitors being 'The Witches of Eastville'. Eastville is a suburb of Bristol. It is not a place I have ever visited. And no, I don't have any immediate plans to do so.

Question: What do you do when you're the wrong side of thirty-five, a little overweight, living on the outskirts of Bristol with the man you've spent the past fifteen years of your life with and in need of some extra cash to help pay off the mortgage? Answer: Sell your body, of course. Meet David and James, probably the busiest masseurs in Bristol, most ages and tastes catered for. Actually, David and James aren't their real names. They are names they invented for the purpose of this interview – not because they're closeted (quite the contrary, in fact – both are out to their families, their friends and their work colleagues), but because they don't want the tax man knocking on the door. Or the police, I shouldn't wonder.

David went to school with Andrew and was reputed to be the sort of chap who gives good copy. 'You have to meet him,' Andrew had said to me some months before. 'He's had the most extraordinary life.' Arriving at David and James's place that Friday evening, I began to see what he meant. We were met at the door by James, who is in his early forties, has short cropped hair with a long ponytail at the back and a dangly earring in one ear. Explaining that David wasn't home yet, he invited us to take the weight off our legs and join him in a cup of tea. Before we had even had time to put our bags down, he was flashing a series of photographs at us, telling us to take a good look. We did. I, for one, soon wished that we hadn't. Pictured in the photographs were a selection of young men in various stages of undress, many of them stark bollock naked, usually with pimply bottoms. Evidently, James was very proud of these photographs, although they weren't the sort of thing you would send in to *Amateur Photographer – Readers' Husbands*, maybe.

James insisted that we pay particular attention to the ones featuring a pale, skinny lad with red hair, no clothes and a vacant look on his face. Obviously not the brightest boy in the world, he was under the impression that only the lower half of his body was being photographed and that his face wouldn't be seen.

By the time David arrived home and the four of us sat down to dinner, I had successfully blotted the memory of those photographs from my mind and was beginning to enjoy myself immensely. Partly this was due to the vast quantities of wine we managed to put away over dinner. But it was also the company. Once those photographs were safely inside the sideboard, it didn't take me long to decide that David and James were among the nicest, most interesting gay men I had ever met. It's a tough lesson for a gay man to learn, I know, but just because someone's taste in pornography is different from your own, it doesn't make them a less valuable human being. Besides, apart from being wonderful hosts, David and James were one of the greatest double acts I have ever witnessed. They finished off one another's sentences. They called each other 'Mary'. And they each had a story to tell.

David was brought up in Wells, a small town deep in the heart of Somerset, close to where Andrew was raised. 'It was vile,' he said simply. 'Really quiet, small-town, hicksville, Bible belt, all that. Somerset is very redneck.' He had his first gay experience at the age of eleven, with a boy from his school. 'We used to have this ritual,' he explained. 'Our school was on two different sites and we'd meet at lunchtime. We had this parting ritual where we'd rub noses, touch tongues and kiss. We did it to shock people, really. The teachers would come and break it up.' Undeterred, David pursued his interest in boys well into secondary school. At fourteen, he picked someone up in a public toilet in the village and had his first real sexual experience. 'I'd read about cottaging in a sex education book, which said that homosexuals were disgusting. I thought they only existed in America. I went to this toilet every day after school. Nothing happened. Then one day I was sitting in the cubicle, watching through a hole in the door. This guy came in and started waggling it about. He was nice. I think I got lucky, really, cos he was under seventy. He was about twenty-five, twenty-seven. Anyway, we did it, and then I went home and had a bath.'

For the next year or so, David's life revolved around 'a long series of impersonal screws'. Then, at fifteen, he met a man he really liked. 'His name was Peter (not his real name) and he was a married man from Shepton Mallet. There are two things I remember about him. He had a nine-inch cock and he was a bastard. He had this friend called Mark (not his real name) he used to hang around with. He used to meet me during school lunchtimes and we'd have sex in Mark's office. Mark was always trying to get me to have sex with him as well, but I didn't want to. Anyway, the next big thing that happened was that Peter got divorced. His wife knew that he was gay and that he was hanging around with people much younger than himself. He told her a lot of stuff he shouldn't have told her, basically. I felt as if I was to blame for breaking up his marriage. She was going to name me in the divorce court, but I was too young so she wasn't allowed to. He was the worst, though. He threatened to tell my parents about us. Once he told me he had told them, just to see what my reaction would be. I went ballistic. Another time, he offered to put me up in a flat of my own. He changed his will and said that he was going to leave me all this property. He had some land on some island in the Caribbean and he said he was going to leave it to me. I made him rip the will up. I couldn't handle it. The whole thing really screwed me up.'

So much so that, at sixteen, David had a nervous breakdown. At seventeen, he discovered religion, met a girl who knew all about his past life and married her. The marriage lasted five years. During that time, David and his young bride moved to Bath and became involved with an extreme right-wing religious sect who claimed that they could cure him of his homosexuality. Every couple of months, the elders of the church would subject David to an exorcism in which they would attempt to cast out the evil demon of homosexuality. 'I look back at it now and it's like I was a different person. I thought that if I committed myself enough, it would work.' It didn't. A few years into the marriage, David resigned from his job at the local bank. 'My wife was still working, and I found I had a lot of spare time to fill, so I went back on to the gay scene. This was in the early '80s. There weren't many pubs and clubs around here then, so I went back to my old ways, cruising and cottaging. I'd never really stopped it completely. It was off and on. I'd have cold showers for three months and then rush off to a cottage.'

The marriage came to an abrupt end when David contracted syphilis from a man he met during one of his sexual escapades. 'Thankfully, I didn't pass it on to my wife. We were using condoms. I only found out I had it because I used to give blood. They wrote and told me. I told my wife and we split. I remember her leaving, closing the door, and me thinking, "Let's get on with it, then." It didn't really hit me for a while. I went out, found a gay club in Bath. I didn't do anything, cos I still had syphilis, but I hit the scene in a big way. I had a couple of short-term relationships and then, in August 1983, I met James. We've been together ever since.'

I asked David how his family reacted to all of this. Most parents have enough trouble coming to terms with their offspring being gay, let alone dealing with exorcisms, broken marriages and venereal disease. 'It wasn't easy,' he said, laughing more at himself than anyone. 'My wife's parents told them I was gay when the marriage ended, before I could tell them myself. Mum didn't want to talk about it at first. Dad took it much better. Mum was on tranquillizers for months. Things are much better now, though. About six years ago, Mum and I went on that television debate programme, *The Time, The Place*. She was asked how she felt when she learned that her son was gay. She said, "Well, I wasn't exactly throwing my bonnet over the windmill."'

While David was busy getting married and contracting syphilis in Bath, and his mum was wondering what to do with that bonnet of hers, James was living a few miles away in Saltford with his mum and dad. 'I had a very sheltered, Catholic upbringing,' he explained. 'Living in Saltford was very middle class and quiet. Too quiet for me.' These days, the only evidence of James having been raised a Catholic is a dildo shaped like the Virgin Mary (again, something he was proud to wave before our eyes). Like David, James knew he was gay from an early age. And like David, he soon knew his way around the local cottaging scene. 'My first cruising experiences were hanging around public toilets on my pushbike. The first man I ever picked up was overweight, not very attractive, but had a really big cock. We had it off in the bus-station toilets. It was vile. I still see him around. He drives a bus in Bristol. Basically, I spent the whole of my teenage years in cottages. I never had a relationship. I was too frightened for that. I just wanted sex. I was still very closeted, still living at home. At twenty, I started telling a few people I was gay. I went to my first gay club at twenty-one – the Oasis in Bristol. They wouldn't let me in. You had to have an active knowledge of the gay scene and I didn't have one. I knew all the cottages, though. I used to spend six or seven hours a day in one cottage on the Downs, near Clifton suspension bridge. I'd get six guys in a day – only guys my age or younger.'

James was still living at home when he and David first met. 'Still living with Mummy at thirty, can you believe it?' He worked as a car salesman, before joining the large financial firm where he continues to work part-time. He remains very close to his mother, who sounds like rather an exceptional lady and has always treated David as one of the family. When James's father died a few years ago, his mother wrote a new will. In it, James and David are treated no differently from James's brother and his wife. James and David have discussed the possibility of moving away from Bristol. David is currently enrolled at university there, studying the history of art. When he qualifies, there is the chance that he'll be offered a job in Glasgow. The only thing holding James back is his mother. 'She's very old and not very well.'

One of the few things James and his mum don't talk about is the massage business. He and David were first introduced to the idea five years ago by a friend of theirs, a fifty-seven-year-old who set himself up as a masseur in the hope of raising a bit of extra money for his retirement. Much to everyone's surprise, it worked. 'He made a bomb,' said David. 'Every time we met him there'd be another eighteen-year-old rugby player in tow, or a twenty-five-year-old businessman. Then, in January 1995, James went part-time and we had to find a way of bringing in more money. It was either this or become benefit queens, living off the national handbag. And James has always wanted to work in a caring profession.'

As well as providing care in the community, David and James are also shining examples of the enterprise culture the Tories were always banging on about. In the space of a few years, they have turned the skills they acquired trawling Bristol's cottages into a thriving cottage industry. They are fortunate in that they have so few overheads. Their house is large enough to accommodate a lodger, plus two massage rooms. They also have a separate phone line strictly for business – a sort of Bat-phone, if you will – which never stops ringing. The night I spent at their house, several men called to place bookings for the following day. 'About 70 per cent of the men who come here are in straight relationships,' said David. 'But the biggest irony is the ones you recognize from out on the scene. I used to go out cruising and I'd see someone I liked, usually someone youngish and quite butch. I'd cast my net in their direction and they'd tell me to fuck off. Now they come here and pay me to have sex with them.'

Neither David nor James would deny the fact that they mix the massage business with pleasure. Like a lot of gay men involved in the sex industry, they aren't simply in it for the money – they're in it for the sex as well. They rarely have sex together these days ('About once a year, on my birthday,' David joked) and having men ring you up offering to pay for sex is so much easier than having to go out looking for it. 'The gay scene here isn't very good anyway,' David said. 'It's really tiny and everyone knows everyone else. There aren't many bars to choose from. It's more social groups, support groups. On the social side, there's the Clifton Set, which are like the A Gays from Tales of the City, but they're too dressy for us.' James chipped in, 'We don't dress to impress.' And David finished, 'No. We dress to depress.'

I'm sure David and James won't mind me saying that they are the unlikeliest sex workers I have ever encountered. I know this because at one point during our conversation I asked David how he would describe himself in a small ad. 'Twenty-eight, good-looking, slim, gorgeous, huge dick,' he said at once, and then burst out laughing. 'That's a lie. Overweight and underpowered would be closer to the truth.' But happy, obviously.

We rose late the following day, thanked David and James for their hospitality and then drove off in the direction of Shepton Mallet. Before that day, I had never spared so much as a thought for Shepton Mallet. Suddenly I had an image of a place seething with young married men with secret lives and nine-inch penises. Sadly, we drove through the place in less time than it takes to unzip a man's flies. Somerset is a bit like that. You're approaching a fork in the road, the person next to you says, 'There's Shepton Mallet' (or Williton, or Wells, or Evercreech, or whatever), and before you've had time to get a good look it's gone for ever, lost in a cloud of exhaust fumes. Soon we hit on a spot in the road called Canard's Grave. Canard was a nineteenth-century highwayman. According to local legend, he was hanged right here on this spot and buried in the middle of the road, so that he might never rest from the sound of passing traffic. Obviously, things have got progressively worse for poor old Canard over the years. Once, there was only the occasional cart-horse to disturb his sleep. Now, there's a steady stream of trucks, tractors and homosexuals in Vauxhall Astras.

We stopped for lunch at the Little Chef. It wasn't our first choice. Just before we sped past Shepton Mallet, we spotted a pub with a sign outside saying 'sizzling rump, £2.99'. Unfortunately, sizzling rump was available only between the hours of noon and two p.m. It was already two-thirty and the only place open for business was the Little Chef. We sat next to a table of five teenage boys who spent half their time whispering about the girls sat at another table and the other half talking very loudly about the sorts of thing teenage boys talk about when they're not getting enough sex –

football, fights and the number of pints they could drink without throwing up. The food was no better or worse than you'd expect. We lined our stomachs and headed back to the car. Parked outside the Little Chef was a delivery van with the words 'The Puritan Maid, Complete Food Service' painted on the side. For some strange reason, it made me think of Chaucer.

It was four p.m. when we pulled in at the Manor Farm guesthouse, a gay establishment on the outskirts of Shepton Mallet. I was amazed to discover that Shepton Mallet was large enough to have outskirts, but there you go. The Manor House is an enormous building. As its name suggests, it was once part of the farm next door. The owners, whom I'll introduce in a moment, bought it from the farmer in 1988. The farmer has a gay son, apparently. He's thirty years old, very open about his sexuality and lives just up the road. Unfortunately, this hasn't had a very good effect on his father, who is as homophobic as they come and doesn't care who knows it. I learned all this from Harry, who runs the guesthouse with his boyfriend, Joe, and likes nothing better than to sit down and chew the ears off his guests. Harry isn't really his name, but his gravelly voice reminded me so much of Harry H. Corbett that I couldn't possibly call him anything else. Harry is in his sixties. He is a retired magistrate, ex-military, and very fond of gliding. His boyfriend is far younger, in his mid-thirties, and comes from Sri Lanka. Before taking over the guesthouse, they lived in Dulwich, south London. Harry moved here for the gliding. I don't know what, if anything, attracted Joe to the place. The night we stayed, he was in hospital having his appendix removed. His presence was everywhere, though. Dotted all around the guesthouse, propped up on bookcases and pinned to walls, were dozens and dozens of ornamental fans.

Our room was really quite special. The walls were papered blue and gold, with Regency stripes, and a couple of gilded fans for added interest. Above the bed was a shelf with a candlestick and three candles, a painting of a dog, a painting of a cat and three pictures depicting classic cars. Standing on the bedside table was a pile of books: *The Christmas Vision* by Patience Strong, *Reflections* by Patience Strong, *Beautiful Days* by Patience Strong, and some others by people you won't have heard of but will almost certainly want to rush out and buy – *What's the Point: Finding Answers to Life's Questions* and *Uphill and Its Old Church*. Next to these was a magazine called *The Australian Women's Weekly*. I've no idea how many Australian women pass through the Manor Farm guesthouse, but I'll bet it's not that many. The visitors' book suggested that most guests came from London, Manchester and the Home Counties, although I was pleased to note that there had been someone from Bridgend. By and large, the place seemed to attract gay male couples in the summertime and groups of lesbians on walking holidays during the winter months. The fact that we were obviously not lesbians and had not come dressed for a walking holiday clearly made old Harry a bit suspicious. Just as we were leaving to go out that evening, he intercepted us at the front door. For five minutes we listened politely as he went on about nice quiet guests who don't like to go out clubbing and people who drive into Bristol after the hours of darkness and invariably have their cars stolen. The moment he paused for breath, we thanked him for his words of warning and drove off to Bristol to go clubbing.

Actually, 'clubbing' is too strong a word for it. There are no proper gay clubs in Bristol, merely a pub, the Queen's Shilling, which has a late licence and a small dance floor. We arrived around nine p.m., just as the place was filling up with girls in smart blouses and men in casual jackets with red ribbons on the lapels. (Given everything I had been told about the lack of AIDS awareness in Bristol, I found this rather surprising – until I remembered something a friend once told me about how red ribbons are used as a secret code among gay men in rural areas. Apparently, it isn't unusual to be sat on a bus in the Yorkshire Dales, quietly minding your own business, while the youth opposite you attempts to grab your attention by quickly opening and closing his coat to reveal the red ribbon pinned inside. Meanwhile, of course, the two old ladies in front are busy discussing the latest queer goings-on in *Emmerdale*.)

By ten-thirty, the Queen's Shilling was heaving. David and James had arrived and were filling us in on the latest gossip. According to David, the skinny man stood at the bar with the receding hairline and the ill-fitting jacket was a local drag queen known as Margo. He was very rich, part of the Clifton Set, and definitely not somebody to be messed with. Personally, I wouldn't have messed with anybody there, with the possible exception of the dark, olive-skinned chap in the black shirt who stood directly opposite us for most of the night, managing to look extremely cool and self-possessed while peering over at regular intervals to check that we were still aware of his presence. I was impressed. Sadly, just as we were leaving, he went and spoiled it all by rushing to the door and shouting 'Come back!' in an accent that was more Weston-super-Mare than Mediterranean. In any case, there was no question of us going back. By midnight, the music at the Queen's Shilling was too loud to bear and we were longing for the sanctuary of the Cottage.

It makes perfect sense that Somerset and Avon's only licensed gay sauna should be called the Cottage. It was a little surprising, however, to find that it was situated in the middle of a busy Bristol street and that the front of the building had been decorated with a rainbow flag. David and James had warned us that we probably wouldn't make it past the door, at least not without our birth certificates, passports, national insurance numbers, two household bills and at least three other forms of identification. In the event, it was easy. We each paid the £6 entrance fee, signed a piece of paper swearing that we would abide by the rules of the club and were in. Now I have visited a few gay saunas in my time. I have sat in steam rooms in Paris and spread myself out in sauna cabins in Berlin. I have even sampled the dubious delights of Brownies sauna in Streatham (once, and it was an awfully long time ago). And, of course I have had the dubious pleasure of Essex Steam and Sauna in Chadwell Heath. But I have never in my life seen anything quite like the Cottage.

The first person we encountered was Geoff, the owner, who explained about a few of the facilities (i.e. pointed us in the direction of the sauna cabin). Geoff was short and squat, had a thick Scottish accent and was dressed in a pair of white nylon running shorts so thin that you could see the shadow of his pubic hair. Sat behind him, dressed only in towels, were seven or eight men in their late thirties and upwards, silently staring at a computer screen. Someone had been downloading porn from the Internet and people were gathering round to get a good eyeful. I had never visited a gay cybersauna before, and the last place I expected to find one was Bristol. It didn't take long to discover that the reception area was the most heavily populated area of the building. The sauna cabin, which would have held three at a squeeze, was empty, while upstairs was a dark labyrinth of playrooms and private cabins, all of them apparently vacant.

And thus it was for the next half hour or so. Then all eyes turned to the door as a middle-aged man entered, accompanied by a much younger boy – no older than eighteen. Everyone held their breath as they disappeared into the changing area. A few minutes later, they re-emerged. The man, who was the spitting image of Jack Nicholson, led the boy upstairs. Purely in the interests of research, I followed. I found them standing together in the middle of a passageway lined with cabins, Jack holding on to the lad as he gently removed his towel. Slowly, the doors of the cabins opened and a handful of men came creeping forward. They attached themselves to various parts of the younger man's anatomy, as Jack snogged the face off him. It was like a scene from *The Hunger*, an early 1980s vampire flick starring Catherine Deneuve and David Bowie, only a shade more scary. My fears for the boy were unwarranted. Afterwards, he and Jack joined the rest of the gang downstairs, where they all sat around drinking tea and discussing property prices. They could have been at an estate agents' convention.

Driving back to our guesthouse, Andrew and I decided that tonight we had truly seen the other side of gay life – the side that doesn't draw attention to itself by dressing prettily or talking wittily, the side that will never make it on to *Gaytime TV*. I was reminded of something said to me by the Divine David during my visit to Manchester. According to David, the gay scene of the future will amount to half a dozen men crammed into a gym in Slough. Tonight, Andrew and I felt that we had seen the future. It was a gay sauna in Bristol. And it wasn't very pretty.

I couldn't visit Somerset without seeing Glastonbury. Growing up in South Wales, I had always pictured Glastonbury as a place filled with magical people who wore colourful clothes and went to sunny rock festivals. It was somewhere I had always longed to visit. And besides, we had an appointment to meet someone there.

We drove into Glastonbury at noon the following day. The sun was shining and there were lots of people with colourful clothes, but aside from that it was quite different from the way I had imagined it all those years ago. At fifteen, shops filled with crystals and wind chimes sounded strange and exotic. At thirty-one, they just seemed naff. We wandered along the main street, past shops with names like Dragon, Rainbow's End and the Gothic Village. We stopped at a place called Starchild, which dealt in 'fine aromatics'. Inside, it smelt as if someone had left a bottle of poppers open all night. Next door was a shop called Stone Age with a sign outside which read: 'To Promote the Practical Use of Crystals and Gem Stones For Healing and Transformation'. All around, people wandered by in New Age traveller garb – combat trousers, chunky rainbow-coloured sweaters, vegetable dye in their hair – the kind of people who actually bought magazines with names like *The Green Man* and *The Druid's Voice*. It was all so crushingly worthy and hippie-dippie, I almost cheered out loud when I spotted an older woman strutting up the street in a fuck-off fur coat. Yeah, I thought, transform that!

Andrew had already briefed me about Glastonbury – how it was a tiny enclave of progressive thought in a county full of rednecks, a place where gay people could take refuge from the horrors of Breedersville. Still I found myself wondering whether any gay people actually lived in Glastonbury and, if so, whether they practised Tantric sex. I came away none the wiser on that score, although I did discover a few things that surprised me. For one thing, Glastonbury used to have its own gay clubnight. It was at a place called Jaspers and it was called 'Pulse' (a clever name that, drawing together the twin associations of pulsating gay music and a local population who live on pulses). Sadly, Pulse didn't pulsate for long. The manager of the bar wasn't the problem. So far as he was concerned, Pulse was good for business. Unfortunately, the owner of Jaspers is a local Tory county councillor, slightly to the right of Genghis Khan. He was outraged when he discovered that homosexuals were using his property as a meeting place and ordered that the club be closed, leaving the local gay community without a place to call their own. Happy to report, they didn't take this lying down. On learning that the man who pulled the plug on Pulse also owned a local haulage company, they made a tour of the sites where his vehicles were stationed and plugged the locks with super-glue.

I learned about this from Leighton, the friend of a friend of Andrew, whom we met at a café called the Global Coffee Shop. Aged twenty-three, Leighton had been in the area all his life. He lived with his family in a town called Street and was employed as a care worker for the disabled in Glastonbury. He spent a large part of his time with his boyfriend in Bristol. Within minutes of us meeting, he explained that neither he nor his boyfriend went out on the gay scene very much these days, on account of the fact that they were both recovering alcoholics. Leighton started drinking heavily during his late teens. By the time he was in his early twenties, he realized that he had a problem. He went to see a counsellor, who referred him to a gay alcohol support group in Bristol. It was there that he met his partner. They have been together ever since. Some of Leighton's friends had suggested that alcoholism was all that held the relationship together, although he disagreed. 'But obviously, it does help that we're both avoiding alcohol.'

Leighton knew he was gay from the age of five. He was picked on a lot at school and learned how to deflect attention by making himself the butt of the joke. 'I played on the fact that I was effeminate to make people laugh. They weren't laughing with me. They were laughing at me.' But at least while they were laughing they weren't beating him up. In Leighton's opinion, Glastonbury was no less homophobic than the rest of Somerset. 'People in Glastonbury might seem a bit more liberal, but there's still a strong yobbo element. People will beat you up because they're bored or drunk. You have to protect yourself, mostly by not being completely open about it.' Still, he somehow managed to survive, despite the fact that his cropped hair and facial piercings proclaimed his queerness to the world. 'This is nothing compared to how I used to dress,' he explained. 'My family do worry, though, especially if I go out wearing PVC trousers or something.' He came out to his parents a few years ago. 'They weren't surprised in the least. They've been a great source of support, particularly with the drink thing.'

I asked Leighton whether he ever thought of moving away – to London, maybe, or to Manchester. 'If you'd asked me that six months ago, I would have said yes. But now, no, not really. Now that I've stopped drinking, the gay scene doesn't really hold much appeal to me. Giving up booze was the hardest thing I have ever had to do. Much harder than coming out. And there's a lot of problem drinking on the gay scene. I still feel a bit vulnerable in those situations. Before I faced up to the fact that I had a problem, I had some really terrible experiences, waking up with people I couldn't even remember meeting. It was dreadful.' I pointed out that for a large number of gay men, this would be regarded as normal behaviour. He grimaced. 'Yeah. I know.'

We chatted away for an hour or so, discussing why he had never been to Gay Pride ('It clashes with the Glastonbury Festival and I can't afford to do both') and whether he thought there was much local AIDS awareness ('My boyfriend used to be a buddy, but most people here don't think it's an issue'). Just as it was nearing time for us to go, I made a joke about all the chicken hawks Andrew and I had encountered over the weekend, in particular the man we'd seen at the sauna with his barely legal boyfriend. Leighton fell silent for a moment, then looked me straight in the eye. 'Actually, there's a twenty-three-year gap between me and my boyfriend. He's forty-six.'

I was still thinking about this as Andrew and I began the long drive back to London. Part of the reason why we encountered so many gay couples with twenty years between them is purely logistical. The most striking thing about Somerset was the almost total absence of any gay men between the ages of twenty and forty. It was almost as if, sometime in the not too distant past, an alien ship had come down, abducted all the eligible young things and whisked them away to Planet Compton Street. Those who remain are simply making the best of things. Whether this is terribly sad or terribly heroic, I haven't quite decided yet. But it strikes me that it's no worse than spending the rest of your life worrying about the size of your tits.

8

FUN CITY?

London

London is a city of exiles. It is estimated that anything between a third and a half of all the gay men in Britain are based in the capital – and very few of them are Londoners born and bred. Of course, you wouldn't know this from their accents. The only gay men in London encouraged to speak with regional accents are those advertising their services in the back pages of the gay press – 'Irish John', for instance, or 'Billy Sexy Northern Lad'. Let your average gay man loose in London and the chances are that within a few years he will be speaking 'The London Queen's English' – a strange, often strained dialect that defies the basic laws of phonetics, but can be attributed to prolonged exposure to a combination of American gay-porn movies, Madonna songs and favourite snatches of dialogue from *Absolutely Fabulous*. Converse with him for more than a few minutes, and you'll probably find that his true origins lie in some remote corner of Britain – or some other, more distant part of the world. There are currently more gay Europeans residing in the capital than there are gay café-bars selling overpriced imported beers or handing back customers' change, 'Continental style', on a saucer. The reasons gay men give for moving to London are many and varied. Some come to work, some to study, some to access the city's enviably large network of gay and AIDS service organizations, some to pursue the dream of living in a place where few people know your name (or your mother) and nobody cares who you went home with last night.

I moved to London in September 1984 – fresh out of South Wales and under the pretext of furthering my education, but with a secret desire to get as far away from my home town as possible, to a city far better suited to a nineteen-year-old on the verge of coming out. As Mr Daniels, the school careers officer, was fond of reminding me, my final year at school wasn't just about passing exams. In a much broader sense, it was supposed to prepare me for the dramatic changes ahead. And do you know what? It did. Alone in my room, I listened to records by Bronski Beat, Soft Cell, the Smiths and Frankie Goes to Hollywood, and fantasized about leaving my 'Smalltown Boy' life behind, fleeing to the city of neon lights and non-stop erotic cabaret, where the streets were filled with handsome devils eager to be held and anything was possible. 'We're a long way from home, welcome to the pleasuredome', like the song says. Two months after arriving in London and before I had confided to a single living soul that I was gay, I found my way to Heaven – the most famous gay nightclub in the world, the one where Holly and the boys had shot the video for 'Relax'. Standing on the corner of Villiers Street and the Arches, smoking furiously, I watched the men go by with their moustaches and their flannel shirts and their faded, five-button Levi's, waiting for someone who looked vaguely like me to assure myself that I was welcome too. Eventually he appeared, dressed in baggy black trousers and a crisp white shirt, clean-shaven, with an impressive quiff and a slightly worried expression. I followed him inside and was overwhelmed by the sight of so many men ('so little time'), and the smell of sweat and poppers. They say that everyone remembers their first night at Heaven. I don't remember all that much, except that I stood in a darkened corner on the edge of the dance floor, too tongue-tied to order a drink from the bar, terrified that someone might actually come up and talk to me. I tried telling myself that 'Frankie Says Relax', but to no avail. I left an hour later, still nervous and alone, but certain that I would be back soon.

My self-confidence has grown a lot over the years and gay London has grown too. In the mid-1980s, there were only a handful of gay venues in the West End. I dimly recall the excitement that surrounded the opening of the Brief Encounter on St Martin's Lane – now considered one of the naffest bars in the capital, despite regular attempts to rekindle people's interest with a fresh coat of paint and better lighting. Sadly, even the the best makeover and the most flattering lighting can't disguise the fact that, like me, the Brief has been a part of the London gay scene for well over a decade – which in gay terms makes us both rather old and jaded. In London, the gay money tends to be on whatever is new or pretty, as demonstrated by the recent growth of gay Soho, where new bars and clubnights continue to open up on what seems like a monthly basis, providing fresh talking points for the men whose lives revolve around Old Compton Street and who seem to have very little else to talk about (except porn movies, Madonna and *Absolutely Fabulous*).

The Soho I used to associate with Soft Cell and seedy films has changed beyond all recognition, as straight sleaze has given way to gay enterprise. Streets that were once lined with darkened doorways into a world of (hetero)sexual opportunities and 'live nude girls' are now lined with brightly lit windows into a world of (homo)sexual opportunism and deadly dull, scantily clad 'boyz'. In some respects, it's still business as usual. Gay men who spend the best part of their lives hanging around Soho may not be paying for sex directly, but they are certainly paying for the privilege of socializing in that part of gay London where the best-looking men (and therefore the best sex) are generally assumed to be found. A night out in Soho doesn't come cheap and heaven forbid that you shouldn't look the part. Having the right wardrobe is just one consideration. Add to that the costs of joining a gym, getting a regular haircut, and having your chest waxed, and all that disposable income is soon disposed of.

Meanwhile, areas like Vauxhall, Islington and Earl's Court continue to provide safe havens for those too poor, too old, too fat, too hairy or simply too busy to compete with the Old Compton Street queens with their designer sportswear and smooth, gym-toned bodies, maintained by daily workouts at the Soho Athletic Club and displayed each week on the dance floor at Heaven, or Love Muscle, or Trade, or wherever the music and the men are deemed sufficiently 'hot' and the drugs are in ready supply. Earl's Court in particular tends to get a bad press these days. Once the throbbing epicentre of gay life in the capital, it is a place many people associate with ageing leather queens and '70s Castro clones – a reputation based largely on the fact that it is the site of the infamous Coleherne leather bar and is a favourite destination for American gay tourists of a certain generation, who return time and time again to the gay guesthouses and hotels in Philbeach Gardens. It is certainly true that leather queens and clones do seem more at home in Earl's Court than they do in any other part of London. The Coleherne is still enormously popular, despite the fact that this was a favourite haunt of Colin Ireland, the London gay serial killer who, between March and June 1993, brutally murdered five gay men. The Coleherne has also been raided by the police more times than any other gay bar in London, resulting in some quite nasty clashes on occasions. They're a thick-skinned lot, those leather queens.

Still, my guess is that even they will have been hit pretty hard by the greatest tragedy to befall the Earl's Court scene. I am referring, of course, to the recent closure of Roy's Restaurant. London's first-ever gay restaurant, Roy's will be remembered for many things. The ads, featuring a drawing of a hunky waiter and the slogan 'Check out the dish of the day at Roy's', were classics of their kind. The menu, which always included something enveloped in a cave of filo pastry and floating in a sea of pink champagne sauce, was never less than breathtaking. The waiters, who always made a special point of thrusting their groins in your face as they presented you with the bill, were charm itself. They will be missed, but not as much as the many rare and precious moments that I and others enjoyed at Roy's. How can I forget the night when, sitting next to a crowded table of American cloney types, I overheard them debating the literary merits of one 'Gory Vidal'? And you can make all the jokes about leather queens you want, but at the end of the day who could fail to be touched by the sight of two men in their forties, dressed in studded leather biker's jackets, lovingly brushing the crumbs from one another's moustaches?

Of course, not all of the gay men in Earl's Court are in their forties and look like members of the Village People. A decade ago, when I lived in a gay flatshare near Putney, I spent a large part of my moderate income in Earl's Court – most of it in an attempt to seduce an otherwise unremarkable young man with a razor-sharp 'flat top' haircut who worked at a bar called Banana Max. (Perhaps I should explain that in the mid-1980s, every gay man in London either had a flat top or wanted to have sex with someone who did. I had a friend at the time, a man called Lawrence, who seemed to think that finding a boyfriend with a flat top would be the key to everlasting happiness – until he had his own hair cut into the style and found that, suddenly, everybody wanted to take him home. Ah, the wonders of being gay and discovering that one can actually become the object of one's own desires!) I never did manage to seduce my barman, but that's not the point. The point is that there were always plenty of other young men available and willing to tickle the fancy of an eager twenty-one-year-old who would rather run his fingers over someone's flat top than pick filo pastry out of their moustache. Even ten years ago, Earl's Court attracted a wide range of gay men, including some who were just as pretty as any you'd find in the West End and tended to have a lot less attitude. The picture remains much the same now, although Banana Max has long gone and the barman I was so fixated on has become another casualty of the E generation, last seen gibbering in the darkened corner of a club, with pupils the size of saucers and skin like a pizza. His hair was still perfect, though.

It used to be said that if you couldn't pick someone up in Earl's Court, then you might as well just throw in the crusty towel and forget sex altogether. Not any more. These days, there are plenty of places for gay Londoners to go in search of sex when all else fails – and some of them even provide fresh towels. It's comforting to know that whichever part of London you happen to find yourself in, you're never too far away from the nearest backroom. Though technically illegal, many clubs provide an area set aside for sexual activities or turn a blind eye to what goes on in the toilets when the light is mysteriously switched off. Some venues even advertise themselves as glorified backrooms with a bar and DJ booth attached. The clue is usually in the name. Visit a club called Glory Hole or Cum and you know pretty much what to expect. Underwear nights are also extremely popular, especially now that gay men have been successfully programmed to go weak at the knees at the sight of a Calvin Klein waistband. Personally, I have always found underwear nights rather intimidating. Once upon a time, being seen out in public without your trousers on was something that only happened in your worst nightmares. These days, gay men do it for real, in the pursuit of pleasure and in the name of sexual liberation. Amazing, isn't it, this capacity we have for turning every shameful situation into a source of gay pride? Obviously, a lot of people think so. One bar in south London used to hold underwear parties every night of the week and twice on Saturdays. The ads in the gay press featured a photo of a large penis and the slogan '541 feet of penis can't be wrong.'

If the thought of wandering around in your undies and being attacked by a giant penis doesn't turn you on, you can always take the more relaxed option and visit a gay sauna. Bristol may boast the only gay cybersauna in Britain, and Essex Steam and Sauna may lure you in with the promise of meeting real Essex lads, but London offers more opportunities for steamy encounters than anywhere else. The advantages of gay saunas over underwear parties and backrooms are obvious. You don't need to fork out for expensive underwear, you won't get spunk stains on your jeans and, if you do end up spending two hours or more in the steam room, at least your skin will look fabulous afterwards.

You're probably thinking that my view of gay London is terribly narrow and that my only interests in life are sex and alcohol. In fact, I was merely priming you for an introduction to the official gay London lifestyle, as promoted every week in the pages of the gay free press. There are currently half a dozen gay publications freely available in London's gay bars and clubs. At least two of these claim to be national, meaning that they occasionally report on what's happening in other parts of the country and sometimes tailor their listings accordingly. One describes itself as 'international', meaning that in addition to being available throughout the whole of the Greater London area, it also has a website on the Internet. All of these publications are produced from offices in the capital and tend to concentrate on certain aspects of local gay life which are those normally associated with the gay pub and club scene – (i.e. sex, drink, drugs and disco music). In the past ten years, the gay press has grown in direct proportion to the expansion of the London scene, largely financed by the advertising revenue generated from the proliferation of commercial gay venues.

The relationship between the gay press and the gay scene is what you might call 'mutually beneficial'. These publications are free only in the sense that you don't pay for them. As for the freedom of the information contained inside, well that's a different matter, and one that depends as much on the advertisers as on any vague notion of editorial policy. It's no surprise, then, to find that the free gay press tends to be filled with gushing reports on the latest bar opening or clubnight, coupled with photographs of grinning gay men with their shirts off. Flick through *Boyz* or *QX* or *Thud* or *Scene Update* and you'll see much the same thing – page after page of 'news reports' on what's happening on the scene, together with adverts for bars, clubs, saunas and telephone sex lines, plus a detailed list, complete with 'genuine photographs', informing readers of which male escorts are currently available for business and what they look like in their underwear, or bent over a bed, stark bollock naked, with the words 'Spank Me, Fuck Me, Rim Me' written above their head.

The bottom line is, you can't turn a page in any of these publications without seeing a picture of a man's bare chest, arse or penis, or reading about the latest places to get drunk, take drugs and have sex. It seems to me that there are two ways of interpreting this. You could take the view that the gay press is simply reflecting the interests of its readers, that the people who pick up papers like *Boyz* want to be entertained, not educated, and there's no real harm in promoting hedonism as a design for life if that's what people really want. This is what I call the 'boyz just wanna have fun' approach. The other view is that the gay press has a responsibility to present gay life as it is actually lived by the majority of gay men, in as full and as honest a way as possible, and not simply focus on those aspects of it which happen to generate advertising. Indeed, you could argue that by constantly promoting a lifestyle that revolves around drugs, alcohol and the constant pursuit of sex as if it were the norm, the gay press actually does gay men a grave disservice. Judging by what you read in the gay press, you could be forgiven for thinking that gay men in London are a bunch of drug-crazed, sex-obsessed alcoholics with nothing better to do than sit around sipping cocktails and planning their outfits for the weekend, or debating whether to spend their last £60 on drugs or a visit from 'Dan the Donkey, 29, handsome footballer, 6ft, huge, throbbing 9″ uncut cock'. Of course, if anyone else dared to suggest that gay men were, shall we say, a little on the promiscuous side, the editors of those same gay publications would be the first to condemn them for it, crying 'homophobia!' before banking the latest cheque from the 'Hung and Horny' chatline, where 'hot gay studs are waiting to make you cum!' Proof, I feel, that we are all still in the gutter, but some of us are better at watching our own arses.

There are two things you can always rely on the British gay press to keep you informed about. The first is how dull and boring and nasty the straight world is. The second is how fabulous and exciting and wonderful the gay world is – especially that part of it they claim to represent. So it was that I recently read that London is the gay capital of Europe. What this really means, I suppose, is that London has more gay bars and clubs than any other city in Europe. Clearly, there are some advantages to this – though there would be a few more if the majority of the bars weren't all exactly the same and the majority of the clubs didn't play the exact same music. A friend of mine once remarked that London is a great place to be gay, with lots of places to go and lots of things to enjoy – if you happen to be a muscle Mary who likes house music. Still, we can't all be free-thinking individualists with interesting record collections and no desire to conform, or there would be nobody to keep gay businesses afloat and the mainstream media with a regular supply of photo opportunities featuring clean-cut young men sipping cappuccino on Old Compton Street. Whatever one's tastes in music, it is certainly true that the expansion of the London gay scene represents some kind of progress. Gay men are more visible now than at any point in history and in no place more so than in London. Still, whether this alone qualifies the city for the title 'gay capital of Europe' is open to question.

For one thing, the growth of the commercial scene has come at a cost to many of those small, non-profit-making gay organizations which used to exist in far greater numbers all over the capital, and which provided many gay men with a somewhat gentler introduction to the gay world, free from the fierce competitiveness and heavily sexualized atmosphere one finds in gay bars and clubs. Just as importantly, many of these organizations helped foster a basic understanding of gay politics and the need for people to pull together in a sense other than the purely sexual. One of the defining trends of the past decade is that while gay sex has become more and more public, gay politics has become increasingly privatized. Gay men wave their willies in public parks, backrooms and saunas, and send cheques to the Stonewall lesbian and gay lobbying group, entrusting them to be political on their behalf. Of course, there is nothing fundamentally wrong with supporting an organization like Stonewall (although I do think they have a tendency to let their self-importance get the better of them on occasion – especially when the occasion involves a brush with celebrity). What is really significant, though, is the way this 'chequebook activism' has contributed to the decline of gay activism in general, with the result that far fewer people seem inclined to get involved at a grass-roots level. Of course, not everyone can afford to express themselves politically by sending cheques through the post. And even if they could, there is a strong case for arguing that nothing raises awareness faster, or helps build a stronger sense of personal identity, than experiencing the bizarre world of gay politics first hand. Lying flat on your back on a busy road, with a placard across your chest and one fist in the air, may not sound like the most obvious path to enlightenment, but believe me, it doesn't half put things in perspective.

Part of the reason for this shift in the gay political landscape, of course, is AIDS and its impact on the lives of gay men in particular. AIDS has sapped our energies – both physically and emotionally. Since the early days of the epidemic, large numbers of gay men (and many lesbians) have been so wrapped up in the immediate fight to save lives that other, less urgent political concerns have been forced to take a back seat. What's more, AIDS has reinvested gay sex with its own sense of political purpose – and not always to the benefit of gay men. Faced with a disapproving world that equates gay sex with disease and death, it is easy to get carried away with the idea that all gay sex is, by its very nature, a proud expression of defiance and thus a cause for celebration. What this doesn't take account of is the fact that there are significant numbers of gay men out there who admit to having the kind of sex that is at best demoralizing, at worst self-destructive. Even today, there are gay men in London who are regularly putting their own and others' lives at risk by having unprotected sex – sometimes with complete strangers. In a recent survey conducted by the London-based group Gay Men Fighting AIDS, 34 per cent of gay men interviewed on Hampstead Heath admitted to having had unprotected anal sex over the past year.

The response of many AIDS activists seems to suggest that such men are simply acting out of ignorance and that the situation can somehow be resolved by mounting even more explicit safer-sex campaigns and handing out even more free condoms. The reality, I suspect, is rather more complicated. Gay men have unsafe sex for all kinds of reasons. Not knowing what condoms are for, or how to get hold of them, doesn't strike me as the most obvious. Far more important are questions of identity and self-esteem, and how they relate to the way we behave as sexual beings. For a lot of gay men, sex is the core of their identity. Sex is what marks them out as different and it is the thing they turn to in order to establish a sense of self-worth, to fulfil what are often non-sexual needs. Some gay psychologists have linked self-destructive patterns of behaviour in gay men to issues of low self-esteem which stem all the way back to childhood and which the sexually competitive gay scene does little to alleviate. Indeed, the nature of the gay scene may well be a contributing factor, creating as it does both the pressure to compete and the opportunity to indulge in a form of behaviour which, anywhere else, would be seen for what it is, but which the gay world insists on describing in terms of 'liberation'. Telling gay men to use a condom every time is all well and good. It would be even better if every other message they receive wasn't telling them to have as much sex as possible and to never feel bad about it. Gay men may not have the monopoly on sexual compulsion, but what is significant is that we have built a lifestyle around it. What's more, it's a lifestyle which everybody is expected to take part in. If you're a reasonably attractive gay man living in London and you're not out shagging several different men a week, some people start to look at you a bit funny.

Unfortunately, it is also a lifestyle which many gay men seem determined to defend – even to the point of denying that sexually compulsive behaviour exists on the gay scene, or that it has any bearing on the spread of HIV. Some years ago, a gay journalist friend of mine approached the editor of *Gay Times* with an idea for an article about a gay self-help group called Sexual Compulsives Anonymous. The editor replied that he would consider running the article, but only if the journalist agreed to end it by trashing the idea of 'sexual compulsives' altogether. More recently I read an article by a well-known AIDS activist who was so concerned about appearing 'sex positive', he actually ended up defending the kind of politically apathetic, sexually compulsive lifestyle promoted by some sections of the gay press, on the basis that being told to make yourself more attractive, have lots of sex, take drugs and drink yourself stupid was somehow 'empowering'. In a very direct way,

AIDS has made gay sex more public. In a less direct way, it has reinforced the notion that private pleasure turned into public spectacle is a substitute for political action – even when its effects are somewhat less than liberating.

Meanwhile, the same faith in emancipation through consumerism that kept the aspirational working class voting Tory throughout the 1980s seems to have persuaded the 1990s gay generation that the most important thing in life is to be here, queer, and always shopping, and that the only rights worth fighting for are the rights to look good and party. As Simon Gage, editor of *Boyz*, wrote not so very long ago, 'What's the point of concentrating on the down side of being gay (whatever that is), instead of gorgeous pop, handsome boyz and good times?' As I think this demonstrates, the days of gay consciousness-raising and self-empowerment are well and truly over. Or they would be, were it not for the likes of Peter Tatchell and his fellow activists in OutRage!, who soldier on in the unshakeable belief that pink politics matter more than pink pounds. Whatever one thinks of OutRage! and their often controversial style of campaigning, they do generate enormous amounts of publicity for gay causes and provide a regular forum for debate in which anyone with a commitment to fighting homophobia is encouraged to take part. Sadly, the numbers of people answering the call to get involved in such activities are a tiny minority. Gay men aren't the only people who appear to have lost interest in politics. But I can't think of any other group in society who are still deprived of so many basic human rights and who can ill afford to take what little freedom they have for granted. If the popularity of a publication like *Boyz* is anything to go by, there are rather a lot of gay men in London who seem to think that 'self-empowerment' means going to the gym and developing a firm pair of pectorals.

This wouldn't be quite so worrying were it not for the fact that, despite the many gains we have made over the past ten years, 'the down side of being gay' is still a reality for many people, as gay men and women continue to face prejudice on a daily basis – even in a city like London. A survey conducted by Stonewall in 1995 found that a third of all gay men living in the capital had been the victim of at least one violent homophobic attack in the past five years. One in five felt the need to conceal their homosexuality at work and almost half concealed it from one or more people. More recently, a survey sponsored by Southwark Council found that, between January 1996 and May 1997, sixty-eight cases of homo-phobic violence were reported to the police in the borough of Southwark alone. This is probably only the tip of the iceberg. As I discovered during my visits to Edinburgh and Somerset, suspicion of the police continues to run high among the lesbian and gay population, and many incidents go unreported. If London truly is the gay capital of Europe, then I dread to think what our European neighbours are forced to contend with.

But enough of this moaning. There are many advantages to living in London, and, as my mother always told me whenever I left some-thing on my plate at meal times, 'There are plenty of people in the world who are starving and would be grateful for that.' There are plenty of gay men in the world who would be grateful for a taste of what London has to offer, which probably explains why so many of them seem to end up here. The main advantage is the fact that London is so big. Size does matter, particularly when you're gay. (If you don't believe me, try comparing those dinky little dildos in Ann Summers to the humungous ones you'll find in your nearest gay sex shop.) The sheer size of London and the vast numbers of gay people who live here mean that there is always the possibility of running into someone you haven't actually met before or even had sex with yet. This is why, if you pop along to any of the larger gay clubs at the weekend, you will see hundreds of gay men running around like headless chickens, or constantly looking over the shoulder of the person they're talking to, frightened that they might be missing something.

Joking aside, the scale of gay life in London does have many serious benefits. Despite the pressure to conform to what the gay papers say a gay man should look like, or what music he should listen to, or how many people he should have sex with on a weekly basis, there is always the potential for thinking, 'Bugger that for a game of soldiers', and carving out a lifestyle of one's own. In fact, it is my guess that the number of gay men who regularly appear in the pages of the gay press, buffed of body and out of their minds at some club opening, probably amount to no more than two or three hundred. It just seems as though there are more of them, because they all look so alike. The reality is that the vast majority of gay Londoners don't care who is appearing at G.A.Y this week, or what the latest gay fashion craze is, or which bar everyone is being encouraged to prop up. They are far too busy pursuing their own interests, probably in the company of other like-minded individuals.

In any other part of Britain, this wouldn't be quite so easy. If you are gay and live in a small provincial town where there is only one gay bar, you don't have much of a choice about how you spend your evenings (at least if your main objective is to be surrounded by other gay people – which, for many gay men, seems to be the case). So you go along to that one gay bar, maybe play a game of pool and dance to disco whether you like it or not. Even in a city the size of

Manchester, the alternatives to the Gay Village way of life are limited. In London, this simply isn't so. For every gay man partying the night away in Soho, there are hundreds of others enjoying a very different gay experience in some other part of the city.

Historically, this diversity of gay male lifestyles has been expressed largely in terms of sexual practice. So, for example, you would find bars catering for men who enjoy dressing up in leather and having their bottoms spanked, or their testicles pulverized, or some other part of their anatomy taken beyond the limits of pleasure and pain. You would hear of clubs where men in rubber fisherman's waders and gas masks get off on urinating over one another, and others where they get their kicks by dressing as women and dancing around their handbags in celebration of all things feminine. You would find social groups catering to every known fetish (and a few more that remain something of a mystery), from the Gay Cigar and Pipe Smokers' Club to a group arranging intimate social gatherings for men aroused by the sight of other men in corduroy. Both completely genuine, I assure you. There have also been clubs and social groups tailored to people with specific body types, with names like Bulk and Chubbs 'n' Teddys. At one time, there was even a London-based support group for gay men with smaller than average penises. It was called Peanuts and so far as I can tell it ceased to exist a number of years ago. I'm not sure what happened to the men who used to attend. Perhaps they learned to live with what they were given and didn't need group therapy any more. Perhaps they joined a gym, developed enormous, bulky bodies and started blaming the size of their equipment on the steroids. Or perhaps they went along to a very different kind of club and discovered the benefits of penis stretching. In London, anything is possible.

Of course, the diversity of gay lifestyles in the capital hasn't been shaped only by what people do with their different-sized genitals or what they wear when they're doing it. Besides the question of sexual choice, there is also the issue of race. London is home to large numbers of black and Asian gay men and women, as well as many belonging to other ethnic groups. Confronted by the twin problems of homophobia and racism, and faced with a commercial gay scene which is owned, staffed and populated by predominantly white faces, many have felt the need to create a scene of their own. For years, this was limited to social and support groups, 'community disco'-style events and private house parties. David McAlmont, the flamboyant black gay singer, used to be a member of Fusion, a social group for 'black gay men and their friends'. Similar groups exist for men and women from other ethnic groups, and those wishing to make their acquaintance. One of the largest is the Long Yang Club, aimed at Oriental gay men and their admirers. They even have their own clubnight, held every Sunday at Heaven. Since the start of the 1990s, London's black gay scene in particular has truly come of age. Clubs like Time, Pressure Zone, Silk, Funky Feel, Nwangi and Lowdown helped bring black gay men and women out of the margins and into the mainstream of gay life in the capital, to a soundtrack of reggae, soul, ragga and jungle. Many of these clubs positively encouraged an interracial mix of punters, with some white men and women turning up to show their support, or simply enjoy a break from the usual gay club diet of happy-clappy house music and head-pounding techno.

It is only very recently, though, that a number of clubs emerged in London aimed at those gay men and women who feel alienated from the gay mainstream, not by virtue of the colour of their skin, or by the size of their genitals, or by the peculiarities of what they are into sexually, but simply by the fact that they detest everything that the commercial gay scene has come to represent. Some people have labelled it 'the gay indie scene' and certainly indie music has been a feature of it. But it has always seemed to me that it is about far more than simply people's tastes in music. It is about a different sensibility, a different attitude, a different way of thinking about what it means to be 'gay' and part of some so-called 'community'. Much in the way that punk gave the music industry a long-overdue enema, the arrival of gay clubs like Popstarz, Duckie, Club V, Viva Apathy! and Marvellous flushed some of the crap out of London's gay club scene. It wasn't just the music policy that was a shift away from the norm, though the combination of '90s indie, '80s trash, '70s disco and a sizeable helping of pop and rock classics did come as a breath of fresh air after ten years in gay clubland dancing to what often sounded like the same record on constant play. What's more, the cost of admission was usually around £3, compared to the £10 plus charged by larger commercial venues. Ecstasy was definitely passé. There was a far greater mix of men and women than you could find anywhere else in town, and barely a muscled torso in sight.

What really made the difference, though, was that the people responsible for this new wave of clubs didn't simply see themselves as offering an alternative to the gay mainstream; they were outspoken in their opposition to it. Some, like Popstarz promoter Simon Hobart and Duckie hostess Amy Lamé, even went so far as to describe themselves and their clubs as 'anti-gay'. In May 1995, when Simon Hobart started the ball rolling with Popstarz, he seemed to deliberately set out to offend as many people as possible. Aged thirty, and already an old hand at this game, Hobart had been involved in the club scene in London for ten years, working as a DJ at mainly straight clubs. In ten years, he had witnessed a variety of music and styles come and go on the straight club scene, and watched as the gay scene became more and more homogenized. By the time it came to promoting Popstarz, he was flipping out. Dispensing with the usual style of gay club flyer, featuring pretty lettering over pictures of half-naked hunks, Hobart took the opportunity to vent his spleen at the London gay scene with a series of flyers containing disparaging remarks about 'E-heads' and 'mindless techno'. Popstarz, he wrote, would be a club for 'people with hangovers, not hang-ups', a place where people 'don't have to take their shirts off to stay cool'.

The following year, in July 1996, on the same night that tens of thousands of lesbians and gay men were out celebrating Lesbian and Gay Pride in London, the theme at Duckie was 'Gay Shame and Lesbian Weakness'. A few months later it was 'Anti-Gay' night. As Mark Wood, one of the Duckie DJs known as 'The Readers Wifes' (sic) said at the time, 'Gay identity has become meaningless. It's become what I suppose straight people's idea of being gay is. So, there's a few drag queens and lots of very neat boys in very neat T-shirts, listening to music that doesn't say anything. You can't possibly ever be a threat to anything, or an agent of any kind of social change. You can't even get it together enough to make a decent pop record. Going to a gay club these days is like doing physical jerks for the army – music for keeping fit. What we do is anti-gay in the sense that if gay is everything the gay scene offers you, and everything the gay press tells you you're supposed to like, then everything we do is the complete opposite.' And just to make sure that everybody was clear about where they were coming from, the Duckie crew went on to host an evening dedicated to the memory of the Gay Liberation Front, the gay activists who first put

London on the gay map way back in the early 1970s and who seemed to have been all but forgotten by a generation too busy swallowing happy pills to spare a thought for their own history.

By the end of 1997, Popstarz and Duckie were both coming in for a fair amount of criticism. Popstarz had become too big to be a genuine alternative, people said. It had become a victim of its own success. Duckie was accused of being too élitist and sectarian, despite the fact that anybody was welcome. What really happened, I suspect, is that certain people started turning up at Popstarz and Duckie for the wrong reasons – not because they understood and respected what they were about, but because they saw them as trendy and therefore the places to be seen. This was most obvious at Duckie, where the live acts which had been a vital part of the club's unique appeal since the very beginning were often given a hard time by rowdy punters calling for the music to be turned back on. Perhaps this was only to be expected. The policy at Duckie had always been to provide a platform for up-and-coming gay performers who didn't stand there in drag, miming to old records, but who actually had something to say. Sometimes, the 'act' involved a prominent gay activist – Peter Tatchell, say, or Richard Kirker of the Lesbian and Gay Christian Movement – who was put 'In the Hot Seat' and asked to explain himself to the audience, and to answer any questions they might have. In other words, there was usually a political dimension to the evening, as people were asked to engage with something other than the next record, or the next pint. And politics, as I am sure we all know, doesn't always go down too well at parties.

I began this chapter by saying that London is a city of exiles. For many gay men living in the capital, the sense of being an exile is short-lived. They arrive in London as fugitives from the laws of provincial life and before you can say 'I Wanna be Free, Gay and Happy' they're running around in something extremely tight and outrageously expensive, screaming their massively inflated tits off and generally making the most of all that gay Soho has to offer. If not, then they're usually busy creating an alternative scene of their own – which, assuming it becomes big and financially lucrative enough, will eventually be embraced by the gay mainstream. Six or seven years ago, gay fetish clubs were all the rage. Clubs like Sadie Maisie proved that you could mix men and women, rubber vests and dance music, and suddenly promoters were falling over themselves to show their support for the new queer sex radicals and make a good old-fashioned gay profit into the bargain. More recently, gay indie nights have sprung up in the unlikeliest of places. Even G.A.Y, the last bastion of Kylie-pop, where pink balloons and suburban hairdressers are released at midnight, recently started its own gay indie/retro night. Whether the people who pack out Popstarz and Duckie each week will fall for it is another matter.

Some people, however, remain exiles long after they have made their homes in London and despite attempts to get out and about and make their presence known. It's shocking, considering the numbers of gay men in London who are thought to be HIV-positive, but gay men with HIV and AIDS are still not adequately catered for – least of all on the gay scene. A recent report published by the Health of Londoners Project, funded by the city's sixteen health authorities, found that HIV infection was the leading cause of death among men between the ages of fifteen and fifty-four in Inner London. Between 1981 and 1996, there were 4,750 AIDS-related deaths in the area, of which 3,780 were gay men. It is estimated that there are currently over ten thousand people with HIV living in Inner London. Responding to the findings of this survey, a spokesman for the group Gay Men Fighting AIDS pointed out that up to 40 per cent of all the people diagnosed with HIV in the UK are gay men in the Thames region. Other sources suggest that anything between 10 and 25 per cent of all the gay men in the capital have been exposed to the virus.

In some ways, gay men with HIV or AIDS have a far easier time in London than they do in some other parts of Britain. In terms of health care and other related services, London is still top of the league. There are drug treatments available here which aren't always available in other parts of the country. In Scotland, for example, a hospital recently withdrew the latest combination drug therapy for people with AIDS, blaming the cutback on escalating costs. In London, budgets aren't quite as tight. Furthermore, practically all of the major national AIDS charities are based in the capital, added to which there are dozens of smaller organizations offering advice, counselling, financial assistance and other forms of support to people with HIV or AIDS. Every Sunday, an organization called the Food Chain delivers a three-course, home-cooked meal free of charge to around five hundred house-bound people with HIV or AIDS across the capital. The fact that the Food Chain depends largely on donations and is staffed almost entirely by volunteers (almost two thousand in all, both gay and straight, drawn from all sections of the community) shows that there are people prepared to give time and money to make life a little more comfortable for those with HIV and AIDS. Yet commercial gay venues making proper provision for those with the virus remain practically non-existent. Try finding a gay bar in the West End which has a disabled toilet, for instance. Really, it's no wonder people get pissed off sometimes.

In July 1996, an article about gay men and AIDS appeared in the *Guardian* newspaper. Written by a gay journalist named Simon Edge, it explained why he and his lover, Tony Bird, were considering boycotting the forthcoming Gay Pride celebrations in London. Six months earlier, Tony had been rushed into hospital with a chest infection. The doctors diagnosed it as PCP or pneumocystis carinii pneumonia – one of the most common AIDS-related illnesses. Tony Bird hadn't even known that he was HIV-positive. By the time Pride came around, he was too sick to even consider marching. Simon Edge was sick too – sick of friends not knowing what to say when they discovered his lover had AIDS, sick of people always changing the subject. In his *Guardian* article, he explained why he probably wouldn't be marching at the weekend. 'Spending Pride with hundreds of thousands of lesbian and gay people ought to be supportive and comforting,' he wrote. 'But it's not that simple. This year I discovered something which is crashingly obvious to those for whom HIV infection is a fact of life, but news to everyone else: the gay community can deal with the disease, providing the diseased stay out of sight.'

A year later, Tony's health had improved enormously. Simon's mood had improved too, though he still stood by every word he wrote. He told me this when we met for lunch one day. An intense and articulate man in his early thirties, he had the look of someone who was tired of fighting. He seemed more weary than angry. 'People with AIDS are sidelined,' he said. 'Even within the AIDS industry there are people who masquerade as being compassionate, but who want nothing to do with people with HIV or AIDS themselves.' He referred to one well-known AIDS activist who sits on the board of several AIDS organizations and has a reputation for throwing men out of bed the moment they reveal that they are

HIV-positive. 'And he's not the only one. It's the contrast between a community which prides itself on the way it has dealt with AIDS and the reality of people not wanting to talk about it. I suppose a lot of the anger I felt came from the shock of realizing that, really, there was nothing special about the gay community. I suppose I'd always had this rather fanciful impression that we are this big wide community where everyone pulls together.'

The brutal truth is, we're not – least of all where HIV and AIDS are concerned. What we are, especially in a city the size of London, is a community divided. Despite the large numbers of gay men with HIV or AIDS in the capital, and the wealth of AIDS service organizations available for his use, it is still possible for a gay man diagnosed with HIV in London to feel extremely isolated. Of all the factors that distinguish the British experience of HIV from that in the US, this is the one most people tend to overlook. If you're a gay man with HIV or AIDS living in New York or San Francisco, the chances are that most of your friends will have some knowledge of what you're going through. In London, this isn't always the case. When Tony Bird revealed to two gay-activist friends in their forties that he had tested positive for AIDS, they didn't even know what a T-cell was. His experience isn't uncommon. While there are significant numbers of gay men in London whose lives have been utterly devastated by HIV, there are plenty of others who remain untouched. This, I believe, is why the AIDS activist group ACT-UP (of which I was a member) failed to take off here. Of course there were other mitigating factors. The nature of our public health-care system meant that the battle lines weren't so clearly drawn as they were in the US. And we didn't have the benefit of Larry Kramer screaming down our necks with talk of government conspiracies and genocide. But the main reason for the break-up of ACT-UP London was very simple. Even within the gay community, a lot of people just couldn't see what all the fuss was about.

Some still can't. Barely a month goes by without someone writing to one of the gay freesheets to complain about those bloody people with HIV, milking the benefits system for all it's worth and demanding sympathy into the bargain. I have a friend named Danny whose experience I believe to be fairly instructive in this regard. Diagnosed HIV-positive in 1984 and now in his early thirties, Danny doesn't want sympathy from anyone. He used to work as a stripper on the gay scene and still looks very much the part – six foot plus, with a body-builder's physique, close-cropped hair and a strong, chiselled face that belies his gentle manner. He claimed unemployment and disability benefits for a couple of years, to the tune of roughly £18,000 per annum. He wouldn't recommend it. Sat at home all day, depression soon got the better of him. He started volunteering for the Eddie Surman Trust – an organization which supports gay men who feel driven to suicide, often as the result of HIV. Lately, Danny has been trying to get back into full employment, driving a taxi for a gay cab firm. The biggest problem he faced was breaking out of the benefits trap. 'You get so much help that it becomes difficult to give it up,' he explained to me one day. 'It takes so long to get your benefits sorted out, it's a fucking big step to say, "Right, I don't want this any more." What happens if six months down the line you're flat on your back in a hospital bed? The social security will say, "Well, you wanted to come off benefits, so now you've got to wait six months to get back on them." And do you tell a potential employer that you're HIV+? Are they going to let you take a week off here and a week off there because you're ill? It's a real dilemma.' Shortly after Danny came out as HIV-positive, his career as a stripper took a nosedive. In a matter of months, the bookings dried up. Needless to say, he doesn't have any illusions about London's ever-expanding commercial gay scene. 'The gay scene does its bit, rattling collecting tins, but it doesn't do the most important thing, which is providing for people with HIV. It's as if they know we're there, but once you reach a certain level of illness, you don't fit in any more. Other people don't want to see it. They don't want to be reminded.'

Rejected by a gay scene willing to raise money but not consciousness, many men in Danny's position feel that they're faced with a simple choice – avoid gay bars and clubs altogether or create one of their own. In London, that's exactly what some people have been doing. One Sunday night in May 1997, I went along to Positive Zone, an early-evening club 'for HIV+ gay men and their friends'. The club was at a venue called Café Gaudi – a stylish, Spanish-tiled café-bar adjoining Turnmills, home of the legendary techno club Trade. At Positive Zone, the emphasis was on slightly softer sounds – classic hi energy, mixed with a bit of happy house. Later on, the music would gain speed and volume as Positive Zone made way for a club called Warriors, a full-on techno rave where people with HIV were positively in the majority and where the favoured form of dress was what you might describe as 'urban warrior' – shaven head, tattoos, piercings, military fatigues and heavy duty boots (no trainers allowed).

Arriving at Positive Zone a little after seven-thirty p.m., I was met by the organizers, Spike and Buffalo – self-proclaimed 'widows turned PCP warriors' with an 'in-your-face' attitude and a wardrobe to match. Buffalo was wearing fatigues, topped with a 'Warriors' T-shirt and a goatee. Spike had a tribal tattoo on one arm and a silver spike through his nose. Both long-term survivors, both tired of the way gay men with HIV were marginalized by the gay scene at large, they first opened Warriors in early 1996. It wasn't long before certain sections of the gay press started referring to it as 'the AIDS-fuckers' club'. Spike and Buffalo refused to let up. The advert for Warriors carried the slogan 'It's About Respect'. At Positive Zone, a neon sign above the DJ booth flashed the word 'Positive'. Sitting at the bar, sipping a Diet Coke, Spike explained the thinking behind the venture. 'A lot of people don't like the fact that we're very in-your-face about how the scene should take responsibility for HIV. But that's their problem. We've heard so many stories of gay men with HIV being given a hard time in gay venues, from people refusing to drink out of the same bottle as them, to a guy who turned up at a dress-code bar recently and was told to remove the Kaposi's sarcoma from his face. What we're creating here is a space where HIV-positive people can relax. We make ourselves available. If someone encounters prejudice, they know they're not alone. There are people here who will support them.'

So far as I could tell, this support went way beyond tea and sympathy. Despite Spike and Buffalo's insistence that Positive Zone was 'a club, not a drop-in centre', the distinction wasn't always that easy to make. Helping out with door duties that night was a drag queen dressed in a nurse's uniform – a joke at the expense of those who think people with HIV should limit their social activities to visits to the local clinic perhaps, but one which hinted at Spike and Buffalo's unofficial role as carers to the community. 'We've had several instances where people have come and told us they've just had a positive diagnosis,' Spike confirmed. Buffalo went on to say that it wasn't unheard of for people to come to the club seeking advice on combination therapy. 'People here aren't nearly so well informed as they are in the States,' he explained. 'Because HIV is covered under the national health, you go to the doctor and you walk out with thousands of pounds' worth of drugs. I think everyone should be entitled to free medical treatment, but it does encourage you to take things for granted. There isn't the same pressure to educate yourself.'

It's amazing really, the number of gay men you meet in London who don't see the need to educate themselves. And I'm not just talking about awareness of AIDS treatment options. I mean people who don't bother to educate themselves about anything. Take the question of age, for example. You'd think, wouldn't you, that an alleged 'community' of people drawn together by what they do with their genitals, with fewer opportunities for reproduction than the average heterosexual and without the rigid family structure that holds so many minority cultures together – you'd think that such a 'community' would value the experience of those people who have been around for just a little bit longer than the rest of us and see the potential to learn from it. But you'd be wrong. Sometimes it feels as if the loss of the best part of a generation to AIDS hasn't taught us very much. We still value youth and beauty over everything else. I once knew a gay man who came home from a night out on the town depressed because he felt too old. 'I was dancing away,' he said, 'and I suddenly realized that I had become the sort of dirty old man I used to laugh at when I was out clubbing. I was horrified.' I should point out that the man in question was barely forty when he said this – a sign, I think, of how neurotic many of us are about ageing and of the complete lack of respect we have for older gay men. I know it's hard to respect someone when they're running around acting like a teenager well into their fifties, but not every gay man over the age of forty is desperately trying to fit in with the *Boyz* crowd, or into a T-shirt several sizes too small.

It may sound hard to believe, but some people have got better things to do with their time than hang around trying to pick up someone half their age, popping Es and hoping nobody turns the lights on.

There are a few places on the London gay scene where older gay men are welcome. There are the leather bars, of course – though what this says about gay male sexuality and the process of ageing I'm not entirely sure. Do gay men actually become more pervy as they get older? Does the desire to truss another man up like a chicken and insert one's forearm quite a long way up his bottom become more pronounced the older one gets? Or is dressing up in leather and acting out the rituals of S&M simply a way of compensating for the fact that, by gay standards at least, you're no longer considered young enough to be sexually attractive in your natural, unadorned state? Beats me. What I can say for certain is that, in London, the sorts of venue frequented by older gay men tend to be rather short of punters in any other age category. This is especially true in the case of those quiet little pubs dotted around the capital, each with its own distinctive atmosphere and its own name, and each referred to as the Elephants' Graveyard. I think that choice of phrase says a lot about the way we as gay men regard our elders. I know that ageism is something we're all guilty of, no matter what our sexual preference. Still, referring to a place populated by people over the age of fifty as the Elephants' Graveyard doesn't suggest quite the same degree of affection as calling it, say, the Darby and Joan Club.

It's a reflection of the innate ageism of the gay scene that most gay men of a certain age tend to avoid the scene altogether and do their socializing in other, more convivial settings. This is why, in London, gay dining groups have a reputation for attracting men with rather high incomes and rather few years left before retirement. This reputation isn't entirely deserved. Lots of younger men also attend gay dining groups, for a wide variety of reasons, not least because they provide a welcome break from the pressures associated with the scene. The fact that such pressures tend to increase with age is also the reason why, at the other end of the London social scale, those gay social and support groups which don't cater to the specific needs of gay men looking for a taste of the Orient or gay teenagers on the verge of coming out seem to be full of gay men in their early forties and over. Most local area gay groups, for instance, tend to be run by and for gay men who are tired of being given the cold shoulder at bars and clubs and who have chosen to spend their evenings in the pursuit of something more attainable. The sense of community which many gay men say is missing in a city as big and as impersonal as London can often be found at the local area gay group, where everyone knows everyone else and that great divider known as gay sex rarely raises its ugly head. That's not to say that there isn't still an element of competitiveness. Put a bunch of middle-aged, often single gay men in a room together and invariably they will find some means of competing with one another. Like successful marriages, successful gay groups tend to rely on regular exposure to outside influences to keep things on an even keel. It is for this reason that many hold weekly or monthly meetings, where gay authors, activists and the like are invited to come and speak, and an argument usually erupts over whose turn it was to buy the biscuits.

A couple of summers ago, I was invited to attend a party in deepest Bromley, at the home of one of the members of the local area gay group. This particular group operates on the basis that each member takes it in turn to invite the other members to his house for a bite to eat or, as in this case, something a little more exciting. The host's name was Chris. I have known Chris for several years and like him very much, so I hope he won't mind me saying that he is one of those gay men who likes to retain an air of mystery about his age and who is generally assumed to be fifty-seven. I arrived at the party early, together with my lover, who, like me, was looking forward to the evening and apprehensive about it in roughly equal measures. In the kitchen, a mutual friend was preparing food. Chris himself was running up and down the stairs, trying on different outfits, before finally settling for a Hawaiian shirt and a pair of green army shorts – which, he explained, were exactly the same as those worn by German border guards. The theme for the party was beach wear, though, as I told 'mein host' at the time, under no circumstances was I parading around Bromley in my swimsuit.

As it turned out, I was in the minority. Shortly after we arrived, the doorbell rang. Chris opened the door and there on the doorstep was a tall, pale, bony man of about forty, dressed in nothing but a pair of flesh-coloured swimming trunks and yellow flip-flops, with a rainbow towel draped over his shoulders. Behind him, the evening sky was already dark and heavy with clouds. This was surreal, and as the night wore on it became even more so. More and more people arrived, gradually filling up the front room, where the buffet was spread out, and spilling over into the remainder of the house. Most were dressed in swimming trunks and little else. But the truly bizarre thing, the thing that threw me far more than their choice of beach wear, was their conversation. Obviously, they all knew one another. And they could be quite camp on occasion. But judging by their topics of conversation, they could easily have passed for a group of distantly related heterosexual men meeting at a wedding. For the first part of the evening at least, the conversation revolved around people asking questions of the 'What are you driving these days?' variety. People discussed the best route from Bromley to Brighton and debated the relative merits of petrol and diesel. Prior to this evening, the only time I had heard a gay man mention 'diesel', he was referring to a popular brand of clubwear. It was quite bewildering. Nobody actually came out and asked, 'How's the little lady?' but it wouldn't have seemed at all out of character if they had.

In the event, 'the little lady' was a surprise somebody had decided to keep until later. Two hours into the party, with the alcohol starting to run low, I was sitting in the garden, deep in conversation with a group of five men in their late forties, two of whom were making a play for a slightly younger chap in a pair of cut-off jeans with holes in the back. While these two were busy trying to poke their fingers through the back of the younger man's shorts, another member of the group, a rather quiet man whom I shall call Colin, suddenly leapt up from his chair and disappeared into the house. When he showed no sign of returning, I asked if anyone knew what had happened to him. 'Oh, Colin has had to leave the party for a couple of hours,' the man sitting next to me replied in a stage whisper. 'But his sister Colette will be joining us soon.' Sure enough, within a matter of minutes, Colin reappeared, dressed in a woman's swimming costume, with a big blonde wig, straw sunhat and enormous Sunny Mann-style sunglasses. 'Colette' sat in the seat vacated by Colin and proceeded to flirt outrageously with everyone in sight, soon driving away the man in the ripped shorts, who was understandably gutted by the fact that he had been successfully upstaged by an older man in a frock. Such is the power of drag. Everyone played along happily for the next hour or so, remarking on how attractive Colette looked in her swimsuit and making the odd sexist remark to ensure that she was kept in her place, and that their superiority as people with external genital organs was never called into question. Honestly, they could have all been straight. And just to complete the picture, the moment Colette grew tired of their advances and made her excuses and left, they all went back to discussing cars.

There are many advantages to being gay and living in London, and there are a few disadvantages too. On balance, I'd say that the biggest disadvantage of all is that you have less of an excuse not to attend Gay Pride. For the benefit of those readers who have no idea what I'm talking about, or those who think I'm mad, bad and dangerous even to consider suggesting such a thing, I should explain that the pressure to take part in this annual event, and to enjoy yourself, is so enormous that it can really put you off. Pride, you see, is the biggest event in the gay calendar.

It is also a natural way to end both this chapter and this book, since it is the one day in the year when lesbians and gay men from all across Britain and beyond gather together in London to demonstrate their size and diversity, to celebrate their ability to have fun in spite of all the injustices inflicted on them over the years and to parade down Park Lane in their underwear. The range of people attending and the inclusivity of the event have been a strong theme in recent years, marked by the decision to change the official name of the celebrations from Lesbian and Gay Pride to Lesbian, Gay, Bisexual and Transgender Pride. Short of calling it Lesbian, Gay, Bisexual, Transgender, Not Queer but Happy to Help Out When They're Busy Pride, it couldn't be any more inclusive – in name, anyway.

In reality, it's a rather different story. Every year the organizers of the event tell us that Pride is like Christmas for gay people and every year that becomes closer to the truth. In fact, the more I think about it, it seems to me that Pride in the late 1990s is exactly like Christmas for gay people. It's overcommercialized. You spend it with a few people you love and a lot more you barely know, and would probably like even less. And at the end of the day, you only do it for the youngsters – those baby dykes and fledgeling gay men (and bisexuals and transgendered individuals) who don't care what shape the event takes, so long as Gina G or Kylie is playing. Gay Pride is about gay youth and gay male youth in particular. Despite all protestations to the contrary, the way the event is organized and promoted is a clear indication that Pride, like practically everything else in the gay world, is primarily for the 'boyz'. And because Pride is for the 'boyz', it is taken for granted that politics should play an ever-diminishing part in the proceedings.

Pride is no longer simply about lesbian and gay rights. In fact, judging by the way things have gone in recent years, with sponsorship deals being struck with companies like United Airlines, who don't even operate a full equal-opportunities policy, Pride isn't really about lesbian and gay rights at all. This probably explains why the words 'lesbian and gay rights' tend to be missing from all the publicity related to the event. Instead, we are told that Pride is 'the biggest free music festival in Europe' – despite the fact that it isn't really free since everyone is encouraged to donate £3 on the day and it doesn't have any credibility as a music festival since the vast majority of acts appearing on the main stage are there only because nobody else will have them. I mean, would you pay good money to see a line-up that included Dannii Minogue, Peter Andre and some boy band that nobody has ever heard of? Of course you wouldn't. Not unless you were a thirteen-year-old girl anyway, and even then you might draw the line at Dannii Minogue.

Where this leaves us – or leaves me at any rate – is wondering whether there is still any point in celebrating Pride at all. I mean, what exactly are we so proud of? The fact that we are gay? Surely all we really need to demonstrate is that we aren't ashamed to be gay? And surely the best way of showing that you aren't ashamed to be gay is simply to be open about your sexuality and simply get on with your life, as plenty of gay people are doing all across the country? Throwing a big party in London every year to tell the world how proud you are only gets people's backs up. What's more, after a few years, proclaiming your pride from the rooftops begins to look a bit suspect, as though you aren't really proud at all and are simply acting in the misguided belief that if you say it loud enough and often enough, someone somewhere will eventually start believing you. So much of contemporary gay culture seems stuck in that moment of self-declaration we call 'coming out', endlessly repeating the same phrases and gestures until they become devoid of any real meaning but are no less comforting in spite of it. This, I am certain, is part of the reason why so many people attend Pride. Take away the girl singers and the boy bands and the possibility of getting a quick shag in a portaloo, and what Pride really offers is a form of group therapy. I'm not suggesting that there is necessarily anything wrong with group therapy. It's just that you can get bored of hanging out with the same group of people all of the time, and not everyone feels the need for therapy.

Perhaps my opinion of Pride would be slightly different had I never left Bridgend, or if I were a gay teenager stranded in Belfast or Edinburgh, a young scene queen partying the night away in Manchester's Gay Village, or a middle-aged gay man cut off from the benefits of urban gay life in some remote corner of Somerset, Derbyshire or Essex. I am prepared to entertain the possibility that my rather jaundiced view is in some way related to the fact that I live in London. The sense of freedom that many people say they experience at Pride is something I, like many others, take for granted. But I don't think it is simply a case of what some people call 'metropolitan world-weariness'. In the course of writing this book, I met gay men from some of the least 'gay-friendly' parts of Britain and from all walks of life, many of whom had never attended a Gay Pride event and felt absolutely no compulsion to do so. It wasn't that they were afraid of being publicly identified as gay. Most were completely open about their sexuality, often displaying far greater courage than those of us who enjoy the relative sanctuary offered by big cities like London and Manchester. The reason they had never been to Gay Pride was very simple – they just couldn't see what all the fuss was about.

One day, I suspect, we will look back and wonder why we made such a fuss about the fact that some people happen to prefer members of their own sex. No doubt we will think it rather strange that, in the late twentieth century, a group of people who described themselves as 'gay' managed to develop an entire lifestyle, complete with its own codes of conduct and measures of achievement, based purely on what they did with their genitals. We will certainly find the idea of gay loft conversions, gay saunas, gay villages, gay community centres and gay subdivisions of well-known terrorist organizations a little hard to swallow – if we don't already, that is. In the meantime, I think we each have a responsibility to be honest about the kinds of lives we lead, and the way we feel about them. Because at the end of the day it doesn't matter what part of this 'Queens' Country' you happen to live in. What is the point of building bigger and better gay ghettos, or bigger and better Gay Pride events, if we can't occasionally sit back and take stock of how far, and in what ways, they actually benefit us?

I suppose if I'm totally honest then I would have to say that I love and hate Gay Pride for much the same reasons that I love and hate gay London. Like gay London, Gay Pride is big, bold, brash, celebratory, heavily commercialized and generally rather noisy. And like gay London, there are times when it is too big, too bold, too brash, too celebratory, too heavily commercialized and far too noisy. Sometimes, I find myself secretly wishing that someone would just pull the plug on it all, or at least kill the music for a while and give us space to think.